LONDON'S

BEST KEPT

Secret

Books by Anabelle Bryant

London's Best Kept Secret

London's Wicked Affair

Published by Kensington Publishing Corporation

LONDON'S
BEST KEPT
Secret

ANABELLE BRYANT

ZEBRA BOOKS
KENSINGTON PUBLISHING CORP.
www.kensingtonbooks.com

ZEBRA BOOKS are published by

Kensington Publishing Corp.
119 West 40th Street
New York, NY 10018

All Kensington titles, imprints, and distributed lines are available at special quantity discounts for bulk purchases for sales promotion, premiums, fund-raising, educational, or institutional use.

Special book excerpts or customized printings can also be created to fit specific needs. For details, write or phone the office of the Kensington Sales Manager: Attn.: Sales Department. Kensington Publishing Corp., 119 West 40th Street, New York, NY 10018. Phone: 1-800-221-2647.

First Printing: April 2019
ISBN-13: 978-1-4201-4645-5
ISBN-10: 1-4201-4645-9

ISBN-13: 978-1-4201-4646-2 (eBook)
ISBN-10: 1-4201-4646-7 (eBook)

10 9 8 7 6 5 4 3 2 1

Printed in the United States of America

For my Aunt Mary Ann,
who has always encouraged me to reach higher,
dream bigger and take a risk in order to enjoy the reward.
And because she attempted every trick in the book
to arrange for me to hold a koala bear
without ever asking why.

For dedicated teachers everywhere.
In our changing world, your generous compassion
and truthful knowledge are needed now more than ever.

Most of all, for David and Nicholas.

ACKNOWLEDGMENTS

My sincerest gratitude and heartfelt thanks to Esi Sogah, my lovely and quite remarkable editor. I'm so fortunate to work with someone I truly admire.

Seeing my book reach readers evokes an abundance of feelings: excitement, pride, anticipation and, of course, extreme happiness. Thank you, Kensington Publishing and the many dedicated people who work their magic and enable me to share my stories with the world.

A special thank-you to my dear friend, Laurie Benson, who never complains about my squirrely conversation skills and always answers my random texts.

Lastly, if you're holding this book and reading these words, thank *you* for choosing to spend your time with Charlotte and Dearing. Happy reading.

Prologue

It was a devil's bargain to wager against a friend's future, especially when the outcome would ruin the man's life. Tonight, every dandy and windbag crowded White's, the infamous club with its avid gambling, adverse politics and plentiful liquor, a bachelor's paradise and a married man's asylum. One particular gentleman, clad in the finest squared-cut tailcoat and matched black wool breeches, approached the betting book with a gleam of mischief in his eyes.

"Who entered this wager?" He indicated a scrawl of ink on the third line of the left page. "I know the name mentioned here and find the proposition in poor taste."

A few dashers nearby eyed another member across the room and, with hardly a pause in the stream of conversation, the crowd parted.

"I did, and I stand by it." A second gentleman, also in black, though his cravat was a less expensive linen, tapped the line of writing with the tip of his glove. Nightly wagers of dizzying amounts allowed no middle ground between success or failure, and at times, terms were met by nothing more than a halfpenny. "I fancy a fortune can be gained on the outcome. Are you bold enough to accept the odds?"

"Still trying to stanch your bleeding pockets and recover

a shred of respectability? That's an interesting endeavor. The terms are rich. Ten thousand pounds is a staggering sum. But while I play at amusement, you wager your reputation. How will you possibly pay me when I win?"

"I haven't a doubt I'll emerge the victor." The second gentleman straightened the knot of his neckcloth, the bob of his Adam's apple the only sign he experienced a moment of hesitation. "I've already spent the winnings. Hypothetically, that is."

"A dangerous sport, one might say."

"The wager?"

"No." The first gentleman set down his ivory-tipped cane and picked up the quill and inkpot. "To squander monies, no matter how hypothetical in nature."

A few nearby patrons turned with interest as the book was signed, the daring gamble accepted.

"You're not going to win." A self-indulgent chuckle from the second gentleman followed this announcement. "And when you lose, you'll be back here after the last celebration of the Season to deliver a draft for ten thousand pounds, if it doesn't happen sooner."

A derisive cheer went up among the onlookers, and a few men reached for their purses, anxious to secure a bet of their own.

"I doubt it. You should get your affairs in order and dibs in tune. You haven't two farthings to spare." The first gentleman collected his walking stick and sent his opponent an expression of cynical amusement. "I'll be more than happy to take your money. Keep in mind, I'll not forgive the sum. It's all or nothing in our little transaction."

"As you say." The second gentleman made a show of matching the stare of those who'd witnessed the challenge. "And I plan to have it all."

Chapter One

"A kitten?" Charlotte Lockhart, Lady Dearing, withdrew until her shoulders brushed the embroidered tableau on the settee in her formal sitting room. "Whatever are you thinking, Amelia?" Her voice raised an octave and she forced out a calming breath as her friend reached into the basket on the rug and revealed a lively ball of black fur.

"There we are." Amelia Beckford, Duchess of Scarsdale, grinned with delight as she held the impatient feline. "Pandora produced a brilliant litter, and I'm determined to find each kitten a loving home. It's only natural I chose the sweetest of the lot for my dearest friend."

With reluctance, Charlotte accepted the tiny animal and settled the soft bundle in her skirt. Her posture immediately relaxed. "Lord Dearing will never allow—"

"I don't understand why not. Every woman wants for a little companionship when her husband is inaccessible." Amelia's eyes flared to punctuate her reply. "In your case, that matter can't be understated."

"But a kitten . . ." Charlotte found a secret smile, though she dashed it away just as quickly. "Lord Dearing and I have discussed this subject before and I—"

"I won't accept no for an answer. Besides, I've chosen

the most docile kit of the five." As if aware of their critical inspection, the kitten emitted a perfectly timed mew and blinked its pale blue eyes. "If the discussion with your husband progressed in the same fashion you've previously described, I suspect it was confined to one syllable. *No.*"

Impatient and adventurous, the kitten attempted a daring leap and became tangled in the folds of Charlotte's skirt, its claws snagging the fine woven muslin.

"She's climbing already."

"Well, of course she is. She's a cat, not a bootjack." Amelia tapped the toe of her slipper against the imported Aubusson carpet in dismissal of Charlotte's concern. "Now let's consider a proper name for her."

"Please." Charlotte gathered the kitten in her palms, although she stalled midway through the task when the feline licked her fingertips. The rough caress of the kitten's tongue tickled in the nicest way. "Just because Dearing and I have yet to find our way to marital bliss doesn't mean we won't. I wouldn't want to cause a disagreement. You don't understand."

"I understand more than you realize, and that's why I've decided upon this gift."

"I can't keep her." Charlotte gave a woeful shake of her head.

"I didn't travel all the way to London to have you refuse. Secret her away in your bedchambers. Dearing will never be the wiser." A brief excruciating silence ensued. "You're still retiring to separate rooms, aren't you? Good heavens, I can't imagine waking up anywhere than beside Lunden." A grin of delight danced around her mouth before she continued. "But never mind about that. My recent marriage and wedding trip temporarily derailed my efforts to see you happily settled, but I've returned now with renewed effort."

Accustomed to Amelia's enthusiastic conversational

skills, Charlotte sighed, and her exhalation whispered over the kitten's fur to elicit a soft purr of pleasure. The kitten was a pretty little thing. And how divine it would be to have a confidant who listened rather than strove to contribute or, worse, correct all the ills of her relationship.

True to Amelia's assessment, Charlotte had entered into marriage as a stranger to her husband and thereby encountered a unique set of circumstances. She'd returned home from a tea party one afternoon to be informed by her father she would be married within a fortnight. Lord Dearing had rescued her family from financial ruin and exemplified several times over he was the epitome of a respected gentleman. Still, ten months had proved too long to wait for a first kiss, a fond embrace or, dare she imagine, a passion-filled evening. Their expedient two-week courtship had overflowed with the planning and preparation most brides accomplished over months and therefore hadn't spared adequate time to become comfortable with each other.

"Every time I see that look of longing on your face, it pains me." Amelia reached across the oval occasional table and stroked the kitten between the ears. "Even if Dearing discovers your new companion, at least it will begin a discussion."

"Discussion?" Charlotte scoffed. "This rascal will cause an argument."

"All the better." Amelia bit her bottom lip as if fighting to hold another grin at bay.

"In what manner?" Charlotte knew her friend well.

"An argument is exactly what the two of you need! All your polite etiquette has gotten you nowhere. But a confrontation, composed of heated words and reckless sentiment, will lead to unrivaled passion. I daresay all that emotion needs to be funneled out somehow. Dearing is a hot-blooded male. He doesn't fool me for a moment. I see the way he looks at you when he believes no one is watching."

Charlotte narrowed her eyes skeptically. "It's not as if we've never kissed."

The weak assertion garnered a snort of disbelief from her friend. "Those chaste pecks on the cheek? That's no more a kiss than a caper is a banquet. I wonder if there's something we haven't noticed. Do you think he has an injury or other ailment preventing him from—"

"Amelia." It was Charlotte's turn to interrupt.

"I'm only considering the possibility."

"Yes, I know. I can hear you."

"It would explain quite a bit, wouldn't it? Perhaps I should speak to the gardener at Beckford Hall. He could prepare a healing powder if Dearing—"

"Amelia!" Charlotte all but shouted, and the kitten reacted, sinking her claws into Charlotte's thigh. Thank heavens the multitude of layers beneath her day gown protected her from the pain.

"You really shouldn't doubt me." Amelia stood with a firm shake of her skirts and prepared to leave.

"Perhaps he won't notice." Charlotte gathered the kitten closer to her heart. "Except for meals and the rare cordial exchange, Dearing is usually locked away in his study."

"Locked away? Find the key. Open the door." Each well-meant directive brought Amelia closer to the hall, her heels tapping out the words to underscore their intent. "And one last instruction—"

"Yes?" Charlotte carefully removed the wriggling bundle from her gown and hurried to follow.

"You must adore your new kitten as I do you." Amelia flashed a wide smile before she hurried across the threshold and into the foyer.

"Oh, no worry of that." Charlotte smiled and placed a gentle kiss on the kitten's nose. "I already do."

* * *

"Faxman."

"Yes, milord."

On alert, the wiry secretary rose from his chair, and Jeremy Lockhart, Viscount Dearing, silently commended the servant's attentiveness.

Faxman had served in the position for five years and proved a cheerful fellow who knew when to speak and when not. He also possessed a sharp mind and never complained when Dearing's rigorous schedule kept them both into late hours. Thus, Faxman was trusted with all financial transactions, shrewd fiscal contracts, investment maneuvers and monetary exchanges.

All except one.

Dearing settled his eyes on the corner of his desk, where a black leather box rested beside his silver letter opener. The locked box was a constant reminder of unfinished business. Some secrets were best hidden in full view. He returned his attention to his secretary. "Have you completed the documents for the Harrison stock and securities purchase?"

"I've just sanded the page, milord." Faxman angled his head to indicate the foolscap atop his work station. "Shall we continue our conversation from yesterday concerning the Tasinger and Oliver merger? Or would you prefer to examine the Benson proposal?"

The first notes of the pianoforte, faint and ephemeral, chased Faxman's inquiries, and Dearing looked at the elegant regulator clock above the hearth.

He'd worked straight through luncheon and beyond, the hour later than he'd realized. At the very least, Faxman deserved time to eat and rest. Otherwise, Dearing risked running the secretary into the ground and he couldn't have that.

"Never mind. Look at the time. You may go for now. Thank you." Dearing waited for Faxman to leave, but instead of gathering his belongings with haste as the servant was apt to do daily, the younger man stalled, his brows drawn low over inquisitive eyes.

"Mozart, isn't it?"

"Haydn's *Sonata No. 59* in E-flat major." Dearing drummed his fingertips against his thigh, all at once impatient for Faxman to be gone. This particular piece was his favorite and he didn't wish to spoil it with conversation.

"Lady Dearing's accomplished skill draws attention. My father preferred the instrument and oft said music has a way of expressing what otherwise can't be stated with words. At the risk of speaking beyond my position, when I hear Lady Dearing play, I recall my father's memory with fondness."

Dearing remained quiet for another beat. "That will be all, then, Faxman." The secretary's uncanny ability to voice provoking observations unnerved him.

"I'll return at half eight tomorrow morning." Faxman collected his satchel and coat from the hook near the door. "Good day, milord."

Dearing watched as Faxman exited, though his ears remained attuned to Charlotte's clever skill. How would she react were he to enter the music room and become her audience? Was she aware how deeply he favored her masterful ability?

With a deep sigh, he lamented that his wife remained a mystery. Ten months past, ten months wasted. They spoke little more than niceties and cordial conversation, and he accepted the blame for the stagnant, awkward tension that grew more pervasive each day. Meanwhile his body, in tune to his complicated emotions, yearned to breach the chasm between them.

He stepped backward in a feeble attempt to detach from the enchanting summons of her music, each note and chord a beckoning. His legs met the edge of the desk and his hand caught the corner of the leather box. With care, he laid his palm flat atop the surface and closed his eyes to the truth within.

How much easier it would be if he could pack away his emotions and keep them in a secure container. He shook his head. He'd adored Charlotte from the moment he saw her. And yet, he'd doubted he possessed the wherewithal to capture the beautiful and talented lady's attention. He was a reserved, quiet man, and while confident in his ability to master finances, his diffidence in matters of the heart left him the victim of lost opportunity. And so, he'd calculated the risk, measured the potential for success and chosen an alternate route to gain what he wanted. Yet despite the fact he'd executed the most ingenious business maneuver of a lifetime and acquired an ideal wife, the marriage left him desolate of satisfaction.

A cascade of precisely timed notes resonated through the hall to permeate his thoughtful reflection. As if they communicated on a level unmarred by indecision, the music echoed the sentiment within him.

All too soon, the tempo changed, and he fell in stride with each striking chord as it dominated the new rhythm and forced him forward. He arrived at the door of the music room and watched in silence, the pianoforte positioned near the large mullioned windows overlooking the gardens behind the house. Seated with her back to the door, Charlotte would never know the convenience he enjoyed due to the judicious placement of furniture. Her fingers caressed the keys; many a night he spent wondering how those slender fingers would feel lingering across his skin with the same scrupulous finesse.

The song came to a crescendo, and he angled his body forward, his heartbeat quickening. How absolutely fetching she appeared in the throes of concentration, cheeks flushed pink and delicate brows furrowed in attentiveness, though his view of her profile proved fleeting. The candlelit epergne atop the pianoforte lent a burnished glow to her silky brown hair, neatly arranged in a braided coronet. Would she object were he to remove the pins and thread his fingers through the lengths? Would she welcome a kiss placed to the graceful slope of her neck?

A sustained final note pierced through the haze of his admiration, and he turned into the hall and made his way abovestairs. Still his questions resonated. What if he'd charged into the room? What if he'd dared show, without words, how well and thoroughly he loved his wife? Guilt fueled his hesitation, the answer all too obvious. Were Charlotte to discover what he'd done to gain her hand in marriage, she would despise him and sever all ties with him forever.

Chapter Two

Charlotte greeted her mother with an enthusiastic embrace.

This home a mere six miles from Dearing House, she may as well have crossed to the other side of the globe, the households were so different. Her parents were a love match, an affectionate and demonstrative couple who raised their four daughters to practice the same. She'd grown from childhood to adulthood with the knowledge a true relationship offered more than a shared roof. Was it any wonder Charlotte found Dearing and his restrained attention disappointing and unnatural? Pushing the thought from her mind, she relished the comfort found in her mother's arms.

"You look lovely, dear." Francine Notley beamed as she held Charlotte at arm's length. "Your sisters will be delighted to discover you've arrived, but not nearly as much as your father. Why haven't we seen more of you? Your new husband isn't monopolizing all your time now, is he?"

The twinkle in her mother's eyes pierced Charlotte's heart. She was married less than a year and considered a newlywed. The assumption that certain intimacies were frequent and exciting was expected.

"Don't be ridiculous." She forced a laugh. "I've spent a good stretch of time organizing Dearing House and redecorating the rooms in want of a woman's touch." She didn't dare confess she'd struggled with the desire to rush to her parents' home too many times to tally and often practiced the pianoforte until fatigued. "Married life is an adjustment."

"You wouldn't deceive me, would you?" Francine's expression sobered, and a wrinkle of apprehension marred her forehead. "Your father and I struggled with the decision to arrange your betrothal and we worry still. We want every happiness for you, despite the haste."

"Of course. I know that without doubt." Charlotte had long ago accepted the circumstances that led to her marriage. Her father, a respected peer, had met with a devastating spiral of unforeseen loss, the likes of which no one at his club could explain. One investment after another had failed, to the point at which he no longer trusted his instincts, baffled by the lack of success where others profited. Eventually, facing unsurmountable debt amassed and his confidence obliterated, he'd retained a fiscal adviser who took control of the remaining monies. Regrettably, the sparse savings assumed by the adviser were lost in a matter of weeks and their fate sealed.

Charlotte never openly objected when she learned of the betrothal contract. Aside from her strong familial bond and sense of duty, she found Jeremy Lockhart, Viscount Dearing, as captivating and heroic as the characters in the gothic novels her sisters favored. Modest and at times insecure, she didn't possess Amelia's gregarious personality or unmatched beauty, so the appealing thought of a quick courtship with Dearing didn't upset her, confident their relationship would grow naturally into a lifelong friendship. The assumption Dearing had desired a promising marriage need not be debated. Despite her family not having made his acquaintance previously, the fact that Lord Dearing had sought her out signaled that he hoped for the same as she.

Furthermore, she welcomed the opportunity to help her parents. Her sisters would all need formal introductions to society, and then there were ceremonies and dowries to consider. Dearing had approached her father and proposed a solution to their imminent crisis at the most perilous moment. Charlotte had admired her new husband for extricating her family from ruin.

That was not to say she wasn't nervous and didn't question her ability to be the kind of wife such an admirable gentleman deserved. But in the larger picture, all things considered, she hadn't bemoaned her circumstances, certain that, once married, the natural course of things would prevail.

Unfortunately, from that point things hadn't proceeded as planned. Now, burdened with a distinct sense of disillusionment, she fought against growing fear and distress. Was it wrong for her to hope her husband found her comely? Acceptable at the least? She'd garnered attention from other suitors, and Dearing had initiated the marriage proposal independently.

She shook her head and dismissed those thoughts. Now was not the time for maudlin woolgathering. "How I've missed all of you. The quietude of marriage cannot compare to the lively chatter of Dinah, Louisa and Beatrice."

"Indeed." Her mother's smile returned. "You must stay through the midday meal. Father won't be home until noon, but your sisters will be downstairs any minute now."

As if carefully orchestrated, animated chatter filled the hall. The lively conversation paused as her sisters entered the room, and then transformed into a vociferous melee of questions and delighted squeals.

"Do tell us about married life." Dinah, the oldest of her

siblings, spoke above the others, impatience and laughter in her eyes. "We've missed you, and the letters you've sent are not as forthcoming as we'd requested. Have you set up house, or did Lord Dearing already have a reliable staff? What of the cook? Have you redecorated or does Dearing have an agreeable sense of style?"

All eyes turned in her direction. "You act as if you haven't seen me since the wedding."

"It's been *forever* since your last visit, as if you've fallen off the earth." Louisa, the mischievous middle sister, wiggled her brows. "We assumed you were blissfully ensconced in the nuances of wifely duty, swept away by the romantic pursuit of your husband and bound to midnight secrecy by the passion you share."

A burst of giggles followed Louisa's dramatic exclamation, though their mother shook her head and tutted her disapproval.

"You've read too many gothic novels," Charlotte reprimanded, all the while swallowing past the emotion her sister's comments evoked. If they knew the unfortunate circumstances of her situation, they would share her despair, yet she could never reveal how useless and unwanted she felt.

Dearing had left on a business excursion the day after their wedding ceremony, wherein the planned two weeks turned into four, then six. By the time he'd returned, her disappointment had hardened, resolve in place, buttressed behind walls of inadequacy and confusion. The following months were civil at best, until they now lived like cordial strangers.

"He's terribly handsome. You must agree." Beatrice, who went by the endearment Bunny, piped up next, her blue eyes glazed with a dreamy twinkle.

When Dinah and Charlotte first saw her, swaddled in

blankets, all pink skin and fuzzy hair about her head, they had immediately likened their newborn sister to a baby rabbit. Charlotte wondered how Bunny would feel once presented to society. Would she prefer the formal Beatrice or the tender image conjured by her endearing nickname?

"Yes, he is." Heat rushed to Charlotte's face, and she resisted the urge to place her hands on her cheeks. "Now, tell me what adventures have occupied the three of you since I've left." Determined to deflect another probing question, she resettled on the chair while conversation swarmed around her in alternating tales of lively chatter.

Dinah and Bunny produced fashion plates and elaborated on the gowns they hoped to wear during the next Season, though Louisa seemed less interested. Usually the most talkative, Charlotte wondered if Louisa had something else on her mind or merely had surrendered to her sisters and their enthusiastic descriptions of the latest designs and essential frippery.

Two hours later, when her siblings had scattered, Charlotte remained alone in the drawing room. Her father entered and, without a word, wrapped her in a secure embrace of welcome.

"Now isn't this the pleasantest surprise? Your sisters have badgered you to exhaustion, have they?" He led her to the overstuffed settee beside the hearth. "It's the only reason that would keep you here in the drawing room alone."

"I worried I would miss you. I'd be disappointed if we hadn't had the opportunity to visit." She tried but failed to keep her emotional state from coloring her words.

"Does something trouble you, Charlotte? Are you finding marriage agreeable?" The familiar strength of his hand settled over hers and his eyes softened. Both parents had asked the same question at first seeing her despite her bravest attempt to conceal her disappointment. She would need to do better.

At her silence, he continued. "Your betrothal was not decided easily. I know we've spoken of this before and you've never complained, but you must know your mother and I saw no other way to keep the family solvent. At the same time, we observed qualities in Dearing that convinced us he would make a fine husband. He expressed a great fondness for you. So much so, at first I doubted his sincerity."

"What do you mean, Father?" They'd spoken of the arrangement before, but her father never shared these revelations. "And why are we just discussing this now?"

"Considering the haste and circumstance of your marriage, there never seemed a *right* time. Although I see no harm in the explanation, most especially if it allays whatever has brought sorrow to the depths of your eyes."

"Please. Tell me everything." She wriggled her hand free and passed her fingers over her eyes. Yet it was her father's infallible composure that seemed to alter, a long-held breath released slowly before he spoke again.

"Good Lord, child. You behave as if I've shackled you to an ogre. Dearing didn't wander in from the street with a blank bank draft and an improper proposal, nor did I consider his offer lightly. After hearing him out, I made quick work of hiring an investigator. Never would I marry off one of my cherished daughters without full knowledge of my future son-in-law's history.

"As you are already aware, Dearing is a respected member of society. He assumed great debt to restore our financial standing and at the same time expressed sincere interest in you. Apparently, he'd heard you play the pianoforte at the Bellsums' garden party last summer and became decidedly smitten. He led me to believe you'd never left his thoughts."

Her father paused, and she knew her face had colored crimson. It all seemed rather odd, to have her father's reassurances of her husband's interest when Dearing made no effort to so much as touch her, kiss her or carry on meaningful conversation. Perhaps if her music affected him, she would insist he join her in the parlor each time she practiced. Or instead, she should rail at him and breech their silent civility, as Amelia suggested. *Something* needed to be done.

"Go on, Father. Please."

"There's not much more to tell. You're clever enough to know life is complicated. As I age, I pay closer attention to the passage of time. How could it be coincidence that Dearing would intercede and rescue our family, all the while proclaiming his affection for you from a chance viewing? Here stood a man of significant income, amiable, polite and well accepted, who arrived at a crucial moment. A greater power could only be at work." He cleared his throat. "Is there anything else, Charlotte? I doubt you wish to know the detailed marriage agreement and financial intricacies. Discussion of money is not meant for a lady's ears."

She wrinkled her brow and met her father's eyes. "I'm not sure." She couldn't help but sense there was something left unsaid. Something important. A sinking feeling of her own worth in Dearing's eyes stalled the question on her tongue. "No, nothing more."

She forced a smile, and the dull ache produced by the realization the situation was hers alone to resolve became stronger now than ever. "You and Mother were a love match."

"Yes, but not every couple begins with uncomplicated ease. An arranged marriage does not preclude a content existence. I'm confident your life will be equally as fulfilling given time, and I'm relieved you haven't more questions."

"You are?"

"Indeed." He nodded to confirm the point. "I wish for you to be pleased and settled. Besides, if I have limited time with you before you steal away, I want to spend it otherwise. Don't you agree?"

"Yes." She rose from the settee and smothered lingering doubt, unwilling to waste any more precious time during her visit. "Good heavens, you must be hungry. Mother mentioned a lovely luncheon upon your return. Let's find the others."

"Excellent idea."

He joined her with a reassuring glint of fatherly wisdom in his eyes. It fortified her determination to venture home and change things for the better.

"You should know our family finances are stable and secure once more. I honestly cannot explain the incongruity. The very same investments that crippled our resources less than a year ago are thriving and now earn three times the income."

Her father continued, though she scarcely heard the words, her mind awhirl, and all at once anxious to return to Dearing House.

Indeed it was time to take matters into her own hands.

"Will that be all, milord?"

Dearing raised his eyes from the document in front of him, though he hadn't comprehended a word. A glance of acknowledgment to his secretary was followed by an immediate shift to the clock. He'd accomplished little, preoccupied by the discovery that his lady wife remained out of the house while the hour approached three in the afternoon.

"Yes, you may go." The words were a murmur, yet they served their purpose, and he was left alone, ensconced in silence and muddled thinking soon after.

Earlier, the housekeeper was quick to relay that Charlotte had traveled to her parents' home. Unfortunately, Mrs. Hubbles proved slower to conceal the flicker of disapproval in her expression. What did the staff think of him, barely cognizant of his wife's whereabouts? Did they believe him disinterested? Self-absorbed? Certainly the servants gossiped about the separate bedrooms and formal relationship that hadn't lessened over time.

Another hour and Charlotte would practice the pianoforte. He'd come to long for the first notes of her melodies. No matter how deeply buried in business or entrenched in correspondence, it was as if his internal clock ticked off the minutes until he could breathe again. Breathe and imagine a different manner of living. One he'd planned meticulously but as of yet had failed to execute.

Voices echoed from the foyer as Hudson, the house butler, opened and closed the front door. Dearing at once recognized the high-pitched laughter of Charlotte's lady's maid chased by the dulcet tone of his wife's voice in response.

Why couldn't he accomplish the same carefree discussion filled with amusing anecdotes and charming rejoinders? He swallowed, his throat thick with conflicted emotions, feelings of desire, uncertainty and guilt.

He glanced across the room, his gaze settling on the black leather box positioned on the corner of his desk before he moved toward the hall. He paused a few strides from entering. Their town house was modest by societal measure, but the front of their property faced west, and with its large rectangular windows, the foyer became bathed in the late-day sun, setting every precious surface awash in a shimmering glow. His wife stood at the center of this light, captured in a golden caress, her profile limned, each loose tendril of hair kissed by gilded sunshine. His heart squeezed with her beauty.

The butler and maid had wandered off to attend to different tasks, though Charlotte waited beside the Chippendale console, an irritable frown on her face as she wrestled with one of her leather gloves, the button seemingly uncooperative.

"Allow me." He stepped forward, aware of her discomfit, evidenced by the jerk of her slim shoulders and whispered gasp of breath. Would that he caused her to feel at ease in his company, but nothing in their relationship had proceeded in a comfortable manner, and he held the blame. "I didn't mean to startle you." He'd all but reached her side, and her reaction compounded his ambivalence.

"I . . ." She paused. Her eyes scanned his face, as if she searched for something specific. "I didn't know you were there, that's all."

She'd abandoned the task at hand when he'd entered and now remained with one glove on, the other discarded beside her bonnet, and he recalled their wedding day and how soft her palm had felt within his, how fragile her grasp as he slipped the ring upon her finger. Yet those same hands commanded power, as if a sorceress, when she worked the ivory keys of the piano.

Sunlight colored her cheeks with a warm blush, her long lashes fanned above crystalline-blue eyes. His wife was stunning. What an utter fool he'd become. He'd lost his heart and subsequently lost his voice.

"Good afternoon, Lady Dearing."

"Milord."

"Shall I assist you?" It was a humbling offer, and one he gladly made. The opportunity to touch her could lead to a great many things if only he could push past the risk of rejection. His pulse beat hard in wait.

"Thank you."

He swallowed audibly when she extended her arm, turned over in graceful rotation to reveal the snag of threads and embroidery at her wrist, one mother-of-pearl button decisively tangled. His fingers were hardly as nimble as hers, but he wouldn't squander the opportunity now that he'd thrust himself into it.

When was the last time he'd touched his wife? A swift, unsatisfying peck on the cheek weeks ago? A chance graze of his forearm against hers as they left the dinner table? They'd never consummated the vows recited ten months' past. How long would Charlotte endure their arrangement without seeking an annulment, or worse, abandoning him altogether? Did she know of the many conditions he'd set into writing when the betrothal contract and debt quittance were signed? And when had he allowed guilt to consume him to such an extent he couldn't take what he so sorely wanted? Bloody hell, he'd become paralytic.

She cleared her throat, as if demanding attention, and he realized she stood with her arm extended, his hands motionless at his sides. Her eyes, impatient and rich with some other condition he could not label, provoked him into action.

Cradling her palm in his, he went to work at the task. The initial brush of his fingertips against the delicate skin of her wrist shot a visceral thrill, sharper than an arrow, to pierce his chest. She may have experienced the same, for he noticed she tensed, and again, that same unexpected gasp whispered between them. He inched closer, his head bowed over her arm, his touch exquisitely gentle, while hot blood pounded in his veins and myriad carnal demands intertwined with sensual suggestions to bombard his brain.

She exhaled, obviously enduring him more than anything else, but he noticed the light fragrance of gardenia, the prim cleanliness of starch and linen and the scent, begging him to breathe her in more. His fingers stalled on the button, unwilling to succeed and end what had only just begun. He'd waited so long. He tightened his hand on hers with subtle insistence and spoke, though he didn't look away from the task. "One minute more, please."

There it was again, the unbearable cordiality. It stifled every impulsive passionate desire barely contained within him. It was more than crippling shyness and the guilty knowledge of manipulative misdeeds.

Bloody hell, it was utter madness.

Chapter Three

Charlotte held her breath until her lungs objected, the ache of indecision and uncertainty commingled with the very air needed to sustain life. When she exhaled, she prayed it didn't sound as loud to her husband as it was perceived by her own ears. The foyer stood in ambient sunlight and absolute quiet, though she detected the imposing tick of the regulator clock in Dearing's study three rooms away. Or perhaps it was her heartbeat in her ears. There was no way for her to know. In truth, it was a wonder she could process any thought, shocked and more than a little nervous at Dearing's startling gesture.

When she'd offered her hand, desperate to conceal the tremble, she never expected him to draw so close. Yet here they stood with a scant six inches separating their persons, his body nearer than ever before. Her mind sped through the catalog of *intimacies*, though they couldn't be considered thus by definition. A chaste kiss at the altar upon the conclusion of their wedding ceremony, a few pecks on the forehead and cheek or the occasional rare brush against the shoulder when pulling out a chair or rising from the table at mealtime. These did little to slack the true interest her husband held for her.

As if drawn by a force she couldn't control, she swept her eyes over his tall, lean form. His head remained bent over her glove as if it needed complicated decoding, the same manner in which he concentrated on all things, whether a complex business agreement or a perplexing bit of the cartography he enjoyed as a challenge. Always impeccably dressed, his broad shoulders filled his jacket handsomely, yet there existed so much more than appearance to her husband, and she yearned to know it all. She admired his intense intelligence, his dedication to success, the personal sacrifice in saving her family by taking her to wife.

Now his lovely brown eyes were set to untangling a bit of loose string at her wrist in the most endearingly domestic and intimate gesture of their relationship yet. Did he feel the nervous flutter of her hand in his? Lord, her pulse hammered at such a pace, how could he not detect her ardent response?

The first stroke of his fingertip across her wrist nearly caused her heart to expire. Accidental, perhaps. Although the second stroke proved his curiosity survived. Or did she look for any excuse to believe he considered her attractive? Her father's assertion that her husband held her in high regard tempted her toward optimism.

Dearing's handsomeness was a feast for admiration. Thick wavy hair, the color of fresh-cut hay streaked with amber brown, begged to be touched. How she wished to pass her fingers over his jaw, feel the shadow of new whiskers, learn the angles and slant of his chin. His lips, so often held tight in rebuke or polite reply, were full and tempting, yet wasted on speech and other mundane tasks.

When he'd leaned forward to first examine the button snagged within the threads, it was all she could do not to sway into his embrace, learn his scent, absorb his warmth and force the issue. Why couldn't she take that final step?

Fear of his criticism? Rejection? Perhaps, in truth, he found her lacking. Best she admire him now in this isolated, cherished moment.

She angled her head the slightest bit and gained a better view. Surely he was not unaffected. His jaw tensed. A muscle on the side twitched with hard-pressed patience. She refused to believe the action was caused by the unruly buttonhole.

Every inch of her accelerated to high alert. Her heartbeat quickened. Her pulse rushed. All sensitivity seemed to gather and collect in that sensitized patch of skin where her husband focused his attention. Without effort, this profound awareness traveled to all parts of her body. Her knees lacked their usual integrity, and beneath several layers of linen and silk, her breasts grew heavy and tight. An ache began in her belly that had nothing to do with hunger or discomfort and everything to do with need and eager interest.

He made a sound of triumph then, a small grunt of approval, as if somehow, he'd divined her thinking and congratulated himself with masculine bravado, and the inane thought almost prompted her to laughter. But that in itself proved how ridiculous she'd become, to imagine her husband might desire her as she longed for him, just by the exposure of her wrist.

"That does it."

Did she hear a discordant note in his voice?

He stepped away before she could formulate an objection, and she watched as he combed his fingers through his hair much as she had wished to do only moments before. All the well-meant plans proposed during the six-mile ride to Dearing House abandoned her. She matched his eyes and waited as time stretched. He tapped his fingers against his thigh, and her attention lowered to study the habit. He cut a fine figure in his buckskin breeches, tightly fit over hard, muscular legs. Her gaze strayed a tad higher and she shot her attention to his face, alarmed at the wanton path of her exploration.

"Thank you." Was it wishful thinking, or had something changed in his demeanor, infinitesimal as it may be? More importantly, why would the successful, intelligent man before her offer marriage, proclaim to her father of a prolonged infatuation and then rightly disregard her after accomplishing the goal? Attempting to understand the quandary caused her head to ache as much as her heart.

While he remained silent, she forged ahead, desperate to end the awkward silence and retire to her room. Perhaps there she could sort her feelings and regain equilibrium. She would go abovestairs, change clothes and return to the music room. If luck held, she would invite her husband to join her. She dared an abrupt smile, satisfied with this new motivation as she moved past him to the stairs.

"Charlotte."

He couldn't see her face, so she allowed her lids to fall closed. He only addressed her as Lady Dearing or, at times, milady. Her Christian name on his tongue caused her soul to dance with immeasurable joy. She turned to face him, the pressure of her smile held back by sheer will. She didn't dare breathe.

"I plan to dine at the club this evening. I'll be leaving straightaway."

He didn't say more and brushed by her so quickly, her skirt hems ruffled in the air, stirred by his departure.

The clubs of St. James's were popular havens of male dominance; influential establishments of exclusivity and secrecy that served the wealthiest of London while providing sanctuary. Within their protected walls, the elite escaped the daily struggles of life, if their pampered existence could be described in such terms.

As a viscount with a quiet title, the irony was not lost on Dearing, who gladly paid the twelve guineas for each yearly subscription. The opportunity to converse with the crème of London's select echelon and perpetuate advantage afforded him through membership, outweighed the inflated initiation fee and subsequent renewals. Dearing belonged to three of the four most prestigious establishments: Boodle's, Brooks's and his preferred place of leisure, White's. It wasn't gambling or sport that demanded his frequent attendance but brilliant enterprise. Here one found capital and revenue commingled with cigar smoke and deceptive, sometimes astucious business, concealed by velvet drapery.

And it was within these clubs Dearing escaped his personal struggle of heart and intellect. The same that caused an unrelenting ache in his groin at the moment.

Tonight, behind the pale stone and ornamental wrought-iron fencing of White's, he ordered imported brandy, sank into a plush wing chair beside the hearth and executed shrewd transactions that would otherwise melt the constitution of the less stalwart. Undoubtedly, no one in London could manipulate, negotiate or devise a more advantageous business deal, and with that knowledge came reputation and a fair degree of quiet power.

Decidedly, it distracted from emotional distress.

He signaled to a lanky footman near the wall, who delivered his brandy two beats before Lindsey settled into the opposite chair. Jonathan Cromford, Earl of Lindsey, was the singular gentleman drawing air on the planet who knew of Dearing's clandestine indiscretion. Fortunately, Dearing considered the man a friend despite Lindsey enjoying the outrageous and somewhat foolish wagers of White's infamous betting book.

"Out for an evening of rabble-rousing, or is it business

as usual?" Lindsey quirked a lopsided grin and signaled for his standard libation. "I honestly don't know why I ask. Wishful thinking, perhaps."

Dearing nodded in greeting and waited for Lindsey to continue. The earl possessed the rare talent of one-sided conversationalist. As expected, Lindsey fulfilled the pre-conception.

"Nothing scandalous brewing at the club tonight for a bachelor such as I, but wouldn't you rather stay home this evening with your lady wife? Considering the obstacles you've cleared to achieve the arrangement, one would think you weren't pleased with the outcome." Lindsey accepted his drink and settled deeper into the upholstery, that same crooked smile traced across his mouth.

"I've no desire to discuss domestic affairs. I'd much rather pursue financial security." Like a rusty needle, Lindsey knew how to prick and infect with disconcerting persistence. "The stockbrokers at Capel Court are agog over the Caribbean tobacco industry. Imports from the islands rather than America seem a lucrative investment for the future."

"One must wonder what drives you, Dearing. You've more wealth than Croesus and are newly settled with a lovely bride. Why not leave a bit of profit for the rest of us?" Lindsey took a long swallow from his glass, but this time remained quiet.

"Wealth is a living, breathing animal, one that must be tended and fed or it will wither and die. Only a fool would neglect his coffers." Dearing settled his glass on the table near his elbow, comfortable with a subject more concrete than metaphysical.

Lindsey didn't remain silent for long. "Only a fool would near bankrupt himself to pay off another's debt."

This was said in an undertone, though Dearing tensed

nevertheless, his eyes fixed on his friend as Lindsey continued.

"Granted you've likely recouped your loss in the ten months passed, but was it worth it? Duplicitous subterfuge and deceptive machination are nasty endeavors. From the looks of your expression, I'd think not. It must be that competitive nature of yours."

"Perhaps." Of late, Dearing considered that same quality a blessing and a curse. Had he not possessed a double share of determination, he might have pursued Charlotte in a different manner. All he knew was that he wanted her, regardless of his tactics.

"By now, I would have hoped you'd enjoyed the plentiful spoils."

Whether cryptic meandering or bald accusation, Dearing wanted no part of Lindsey's provoking conversation. He'd come to the club for distraction, not further frustration, yet he found himself defending his position despite owing no one explanations. *Well, mayhap a few people.* "Things are complicated."

"I would think so." Lindsey threw back whatever remained in his glass. "If you ask me—"

"I haven't."

"It all came upon you too fast. Seeing the girl and deciding your future, while that subsequent endeavor posed a risky business at best. Never mind the fervent gossip afterward, I imagined it wouldn't go smoothly. You shouldn't have allowed Adams to provoke you. And you needn't deny his avid attention toward the lady in question didn't set the situation on fire. Once you learned Adams held an interest in Charlotte, your focus became singular in nature."

"Thank you for imparting your brilliant insight." Only a buffoon would misinterpret Dearing's sarcasm. The quick remembrance of the times he'd thought to approach Charlotte and then hesitated, backing away while others filled the space he'd left, that he ran the risk of destroying everything if he didn't overcome his insecurity. Fired by the thought, he snapped out an answer. "No one, not one man who walks this earth, would deny I accomplished one of the smartest and most profitable acquisitions in obtaining the majority share in Middleton Railway. The rack-and-pinion loco-motive will soon be the most efficient transport across England."

Yet it was more, so much more that drove him to his reck-less pursuit of Charlotte's hand. Society viewed his hasty proposal as just another of his judicious business deals, but it was decidedly more complicated than that, and at the center of it all lay his heart, an organ he depended on to pump blood and perpetuate life, nothing other than that until Charlotte, when his heart had turned over in his chest and, in an instant, he knew she was meant to be his. Adams's involvement might have set a flame beneath his boots, but it only hurried him along the path he'd intended regardless. How society interpreted the swift series of events helped conveniently bury a secret that should never be revealed.

"I concur, although marrying the chit to gain her father's single share was a most daring move, even for you. Granted, it did provide you the principal."

"I'm not ruthless. You misinterpreted the facts, as usual." His tone went sharp. Let Lindsey believe whatever he liked, whether that be an insightful investment or unspoken rivalry with Lord Adams. As long as no one discovered the truth, conjecture and idle gossip served his purpose.

"No need to clutter the room with objections and expla-nations," Lindsey replied, his mood unaffected.

"One has nothing to do with the other. I saw Charlotte Notley and wanted her. I always get what I want, unless it's peace and quiet when you're in the room." The security of their lasting friendship ensured no offense would be taken, and with a curl of the lips, Dearing enjoyed the gibe.

"I'll disregard the insult with the understanding you're unhappy from your lack of progress in the relationship area." Lindsey angled in as if disclosing a guarded secret. "What you need, my friend, is a courtship. Ladies prefer to be wooed, not bought and certainly not bartered."

Dearing took this under momentary consideration. At times, he despised Lindsey's forthright input, but in this, a valid suggestion was made. No one could disagree that last year Charlotte was one of the most sought-after women of the Season. Men vied for her attention, taken by her beauty and in awe of her skillful musical ability.

Who wouldn't seek a wife not just lovely of face and well-bred but talented and clever to boot? A man riddled with self-doubt and devoid of conversational skills around the fairer sex, that's who. The same assertive confidence that served at the club or led him through shrewd financial dealings evaporated when faced with meaningful affairs of the heart, and any notion of interaction with Charlotte fell in the latter category. Self-recrimination was a loathsome trait, so a more effective method proved necessary before another gentleman, Adams, claimed the prize. But the devious plan he'd employed to win her was another subject altogether. He answered Lindsey with noncommittal contrariness. "Possibly."

"Most definitely. Attempt to win her favor. Use the same merciless tactics you enacted to undercut Hurns in that venture with the copper mines. Solidify your relationship with similar fortitude as your bank account. It's rather elementary." Lindsey's voice adopted a droll tone. "Garner her esteemed affection in the clever manner you master those boring banking meetings over on Threadneedle Street. Accumulate wealth of the heart, not of the pocket." Satisfied with his bestowed advisement, Lindsey finally stopped speaking.

"That's ludicrous." Dearing looked to the earl's empty glass. "How much have you imbibed?" Then he took a long sip of his own brandy.

"Hear me out. It might work." Though Lindsey's words held a hint of amusement.

"You've oversimplified the matter." Dearing darted a sidelong glance to the room's interior to confirm no one stood close enough to overhear their conversation. "Matters of the heart are not so easily accomplished." He spoke in a stern tone, one that would dissuade most people from furthering the conversation.

"As you say." Lindsey signaled for more liquor. "I must wonder what has brought about this perpetual state of vacillation and doubt. I've known you to be quite the Lothario over the years. Shall I remind you of that actress you snuck into the dorms at Eton? We all carried on with her, though you seemed the most taken. In the end, she threw you over for Adams, didn't she? Not that anything could come of it. Still, I haven't found another female who can—"

"I need no detailing of my history. Are you striving toward some convoluted discussion point, or do you aim solely to annoy me?" Patience thin, Dearing's question came out with a growl. Reference to meaningless tomfoolery from years gone by did nothing but irritate at the moment. He experienced no difficulties with women when nothing was at stake, but the opposite held true concerning his wife.

He kept to business because it was quiet, unobtrusive and didn't force him to examine heartfelt emotion. And that was exactly what he'd experienced when he first saw Charlotte. His chest tightened, his breathing stalled. A reaction strong and tangible rushed through him and left him forever changed. In that instant, he knew he had to have her at any cost.

"True, who gives a tuppence about the past? Especially with the distasteful ending that episode entails. You're no fun at all these days, though I've regaled half of society with that story." Lindsey accepted a second glass from the footman and sobered. "All I'm saying is, this entire situation has changed you, and not for the better. I assume you find your wife attractive." He waggled his brows, as if the insinuation wasn't crystal clear.

Dearing leveled a stare that could not be misconstrued. "This is different. My wife isn't some nameless actress at Eton. She's important." *The lady owns my heart.*

"And so, you prove my point. Every business dealing is equally as rich and significant. Handle this venture in the same manner."

Nothing was said for a minute or two.

"And how do you propose I accomplish this? We both know what's at stake." *Nothing so fundamental as a share in a railroad company.* Dearing shook his head in dismissal. Had he really voiced that question and encouraged Lindsey's counsel?

"Negotiate. Persuade. Invest, and then leverage that same collateral with an ultimatum." Lindsey settled back against the cushions. "This could prove great fun."

"It's not meant to be. You have no idea—"

"Oh, I beg to differ. I wouldn't look into the betting ledger if I wore your boots. Take my advice and capitalize on it. It pains me to see you so morose." Lindsey hardly looked pained. "What's the first rule when exploring a new investment venture?"

"Know your opponent," Dearing answered with a grumble of tolerance, reluctant to add fuel to his friend's persuasion.

"Exactly." Lindsey paused to take another swallow of brandy. "Learn everything there is to know about your lady. It's as simple as that." He snapped his fingers, much to

Dearing's annoyance. "Do it soon, before today becomes yesterday and desire becomes regret."

"Are you suggesting I investigate my wife?"

"In a strictly personal capacity only." Lindsey smiled that crooked grin, warmed to the subject. "Learn her habits, her likes and dislikes. Does she prefer tea, coffee or chocolate in the morning? Blancmange or plum tarts after dinner?"

"I couldn't say." Dearing grimaced. His lack of knowledge concerning Charlotte proved abominable.

"Which flower does she fancy? Which scent? Is she an early bird or a night owl?" Lindsey's glib questions peppered the air between them.

"I don't know." Derisive contempt cooled Dearing's tone. "Enough."

"Truth is, you're rubbish at romance." Lindsey raised his brows as he lounged in his chair, at ease with the predicament. "You have your work detailed for you, so rely on the facts of daily living. I'm certain you must have observed something."

"Charlotte is dedicated to her music." Dearing's expression eased. "Every afternoon she plays the pianoforte."

"Then buy her a new one." Lindsey spoke the words slowly, as if explaining the dangers of fire to a young child. A young, daft child.

"What?" Dearing almost laughed. "There's nothing wrong with the instrument we have now."

"That's not the point." Lindsey chuckled. "How you've reached the age of twenty and eight without the most rudimentary understanding of the female species baffles me. Women enjoy gifts. Little, delicate tokens and big, heavy pianofortes. Mark my words."

"Thank you." Dearing didn't say more. Any compliment would further inflate Lindsey's robust self-importance, and the earl already carried a bit of the dandy in him, impeccably dressed with a gold pocket watch and chain to match his exclusive Mayfair address. Regardless, he raised several points worthy of consideration.

In truth, Dearing's experience with women was limited to casual, inconsequential dalliances, as if he'd unknowingly reserved his heart for Charlotte. But now, when he must overcome his infuriating shyness, when his very future lay at stake, he needed to act. No more time could fall prey to ambivalence.

If only Dearing's tongue didn't knot itself whenever he stood near Charlotte's person. Her light floral scent and delicate blush were his utter undoing. From the first moment he'd seen her, he'd known without a doubt he had to have her. Somehow, when he'd viewed her across the room, she'd reached inside him and claimed his heart, though they hadn't been introduced, never conversed, not one word. There was no explaining it, and he hadn't wasted time trying to unriddle the happenstance. From that point on, he'd thrust himself into a rash series of events he refused to consider this evening. More importantly, what had he accomplished since?

Lindsey stood, off to create more mischief, no doubt. He threw Dearing a careless grin with a few parting words. "Get on with it, Dearing."

And that was the wisest advice the earl had offered all evening.

Chapter Four

Charlotte untangled the kitten's claws from the tattered hem of the bed's counterpane. At one time, the lace formed a delicate scallop pattern, but the last two days had brought with them irreversible change. She hadn't named her pet as of yet, but *Tragedy*, *Disaster* and *Calamity* were under deliberation. Thankfully, her maid had taken an immediate liking to the kitten and kept its existence a secret, supplying food, milk and repair as needed. Despite Jill's greatest effort and supervision, with remarkable speed, the kitten had shredded two embroidered reticules and chewed several holes through the toes of Charlotte's silk slippers.

"You're an adorable bit of trouble, aren't you?" She lifted the warm bundle into her arms and leaned into the pillows strewn across the headboard. Disappointment at spending another evening alone overrode her desire to practice the pianoforte, so after a quiet dinner, she'd come upstairs earlier than usual.

Now, the silent stillness of the house mocked her. How could one find utter elation—*the way Dearing had stroked her wrist, not once as required to loosen the button but twice, bespoke desire*—only to fall straight to bottomless despair. *He fled the foyer as if his boots were afire.*

Was it so very wrong to want happiness? To believe were they to know each other beyond formality, friendship would form and affection might grow? Didn't their relationship warrant a fighting chance? He'd sought her out. She believed it proved his dedication. But had she blinded herself with hope and wishful thinking? Her parents were a love match and her father had reassured her not all successful loving relationships began with eloquence.

If she didn't believe, if she didn't encourage optimism and pray and seek more, then what of her future? Would her life be composed of endless nights of intolerable silence and regret-filled conversations with cats? She sucked in a frightful gasp. Perhaps Amelia already foresaw the future. Perhaps this little annoyance covered in black fur and whiskers was the beginning of a depressing collection of feline companions meant to occupy hours of marital loneliness, and Amelia, with well-meant intentions, sought to prepare her for that fate.

No. Charlotte shook her head to rid the ghastly conclusion from her brain. Amelia would never perpetuate such an outcome.

Amelia had met the Duke of Scarsdale and, despite enormous obstacles and scathing odds, conquered his reluctance and won his heart. It was a veritable love story complete with a happily-ever-after conclusion.

Charlotte wrapped an arm around her stomach and closed her eyes. If only she could lie with Dearing and conceive a child. As desperate as the wish, a babe would at least ease the pain in her heart. A child would cement their marriage, secure his companionship and offer a chance at happiness, if nothing more than a life with their son or daughter were Dearing to leave again. She recognized these ideas as distressing and lonely, the hope of a woman who'd surrendered, but some part of her yearned for the connection a baby would bring. Unconditional love and a relationship free of judgment were gifts a child could offer.

Breathing deeply, she expelled the negativity anxiously waiting to flood her soul. She wouldn't allow it. The kitten wriggled free from her hold and bounded across the mattress in a series of frenetic hops.

"Perhaps I should write to Amelia." Somehow voicing it aloud strengthened the idea. "And you . . ." She shook her finger in the kitten's direction with the reprimand. "Were you not so clever and adorable, it would be easier to give you back or set you free." She collected her pet and brought it nose forward for further conversation. "What would Amelia do in a situation like this? If only to have her abundance of spunk and fortitude. With certainty, she would not lock herself away in her bedroom, isn't that true?"

Dearing seemed determined to keep their relationship formal and conversation sparse. That needed to change. He must want more from a wife. He'd incurred financial loss and rescued her family. It had to mean something. The man couldn't be as cold as he'd like her to believe. And she knew that to be true because when her button had snagged, she'd noticed otherwise. She saw the same emotion she'd glimpsed when they'd recited their vows at the altar. That one fleeting moment when his eyes held her in complete adoration.

A smile broke loose of its own volition and tiny sparks of anticipation fired within. His nearness did strange things to her. The scent of his hair and shaving soap, the broad expanse of his shoulders, even the masculine angle of his chin, caused a swirling of excitement and unexpected hope deep within her belly. How wonderful it must feel to be held in his embrace.

And when he'd said her name . . . His deep tenor rang across the foyer like music set free. It reached for her, tugged at her heart and demanded she listen. Unfortunately, it was followed by the harshest dismissal.

Setting the kitten atop the counterpane, she closed her eyes and attempted to bring the moment back to life, but the image proved elusive, overcome by the too-much emotion abloom in her chest. A series of different scenes materialized. Scenes she cherished as a voyeur rather than a participant. Images she gleaned from the inside out, collected while her husband was unaware she watched, sometimes through a nearby window or door left open a mere few fingers' width.

There was early-morning Dearing, his hair damp from his valet's attention, chin clean shaven, impeccably dressed in calfskin breeches and waistcoat. And midday Dearing, poring over his business correspondence, embroiled in fervent argument with Faxman or, sometimes, at intense study of an unrolled map atop his enormous desk. Or evening Dearing, the shadow of fresh whiskers dusting the slant of his jaw, the creases of work and related concerns at the corners of his eyes. She wished she could feel the stubble on his skin as he kissed her, or learn the worries that kept him tense and withdrawn, but instead she had only a disjointed collection of images and wishful actions, devoid of experience. A picture book, not a love story. How she yearned for something different. A life full of affection and laughter, similar to childhood dreams and womanly ambition.

The kitten meowed loudly and brought her sorrowful thoughts to an end, yet one question persisted. What would Amelia do? With certainty, her friend would not lock herself in the bedroom and accept a dissatisfying future.

No, Amelia would devise a plan.

It was late the following afternoon when Dearing breeched the connecting door that led to his wife's bedchambers. Charlotte practiced her music belowstairs, and despite hours in his study reviewing contracts and correspondence with Faxman, he'd found not one shred of concentration, intent on stealing into his wife's rooms to gain a new understanding of her in ammunition of furthering his cause. To this date, their marriage was an abysmal failure. Without consummation, any pastor or judge could annul their vows and wipe clean the slate, setting her free.

The thought of Charlotte as anyone else's wife kicked up his temper another notch, anger at himself and the clumsy handling of their relationship already a constant fuel. Why had he allowed it to become so complicated, weighted by the realization that once Charlotte learned the truth she would abhor him? Inevitably, someday he would be exposed despite how hard he worked to bury the past, both recent and distant.

Yet Lindsey's sharp questions and logical assertions prevailed. Why not attempt to enjoy the spoils while they existed within reach? Perhaps when the dreaded day of his exposure arrived, and Charlotte refused to speak to him, he could look back and grasp hold of the experiences collected beforehand.

Bloody hell, she hardly spoke to him now.

Or what if a stranger fate awaited? What if his lovely wife forgave his calculated deception? Surely the narrow possibility existed. Could he convince her somehow to trust him, or dare he consider a deeper emotion? Either path led to unanswered questions and further annoyance.

No matter. It was time for a change.

Assured his wife's lady's maid remained in the kitchen, he twisted the knob and opened the panel of Charlotte's bedchambers. Motionless within the doorframe, he paused for a deep breath and entered, careful to step over the pale area rug and leave no trace of his trespass. This was Charlotte's personal domain and he'd never seen it. Never smelled her perfume as it lingered in the air or traced his fingers over her belongings. Didn't know which flowers she preferred on the bureau or how she arranged her wardrobe, by color or article.

Lindsey was correct. How dismal and unacceptable these beginning months of his marriage. But all was about to transform.

He noticed first the tidy manner in which his wife kept her room. Everything seemed to have its place, with not a pillow angled or hairpin discarded wrongly. Much like her person, the room was neat and orderly. It was the reason he felt driven to assist with her gloves, her expression troubled and her hair slightly mussed from the effort.

He strode toward the vanity and breathed deeply, rewarded with the light resonance of gardenia and other florals. His groin tightened in reaction. She was lovely, his lady wife, in appearance, fragrance and musicality. She perfumed her hair. At least he assumed so from the few times he'd stood close enough to notice. He'd much prefer to smell the scent upon her skin, mixed with the musky evidence of desire and lovemaking. His body concurred.

Like an unexpected visitor with the devil on his shoulder, Lindsey's words resounded in his head. *Get on with it already.*

From there on, Dearing needed no encouragement. He stroked his fingers over her bed linens, peeked into her wardrobe and noted the items on her bedside table. Charlotte read poetry; several volumes filled her bookshelf. She favored pink with accents of celery green and white eyelet, the bedlinens a testament to that preference. Her toilette appeared simple: scented soap, lemon sachet and a light perfume that seemed as ephemeral as the curve of her smile or the light in her eyes. Additionally, he noted the silver hand mirror had a small chip in the lower left corner and her hairpins were terribly mismatched.

Women enjoy gifts. Little, delicate tokens and big, heavy pianofortes.

Refusing to overstay his visit and be caught—or worse, have *strange voyeur* added to the oddities his wife likely listed after his name—he turned toward the adjoining door in preparation to take his leave. It was there he noticed a dodgy furred shadow peeping from beneath the counterpane.

A kitten. *A kitten?* Charlotte kept a kitten? Hadn't she asked his permission at one time and he'd dismissed the idea without thorough consideration, his personal concerns in a quagmire? He paused, the surprising realization enough to evoke laughter. Perhaps his wife was not as silent and obedient as he perceived. She'd secretly defied him, and for some strange, unexplainable reason, the notion delighted him most of all. Especially as he now saw the absurdity of the walls he'd constructed between them.

With a quick bend of his knee, he collected the kitten and brought it to his chest. "Aren't you the unexpected revelation, spying from the shadows and no bigger than a cricket?" His words were met with a mewl that could have signaled agreement, hunger or distress. "I wonder what Charlotte has named you?" He rubbed between the kitten's ears, much to the animal's delight, or so he presumed until the kitten twisted in his grasp and sank two sharp fangs into the pad of his thumb. With slapdash reflexes, he abandoned the ferocious kit to the mattress and gingerly thrust a finger into his waistcoat pocket in search of a handkerchief. It would serve no one to leave a drop of blood on the ivory carpet in evidence of his intrusion. Most especially as the area rug remained in front of the adjoining door to his bedchambers.

Quick to blot his wound and wrap the cloth around his thumb, he narrowed his eyes at the kitten, sprawled lazily atop the bed. Then he strode toward the door, his mind pensive with all the information he'd gained.

* * *

Charlotte ended the complicated operatic composition midway through, too distracted to concentrate on chords and progressions. Practicing her music had always proven an escape. A chance to lose herself in melody when other circumstances disappointed. The last few months, she'd all but worn her fingers to the bone, yet the same restlessness and helplessness lived within.

Now strengthened by her recent vow to orchestrate a plan to win Dearing's affection, she riffled through the sheet music selections on the rack and with a faint huff of impatience gathered them together to place them aside. Setting her fingers to the keys, she closed her eyes and began a Mozart concerto, a favored arrangement that spoke to her heart as much as her skill.

Blinking away distraction, she watched her hands command the music, striking notes with determined confidence while maintaining exacting control. If she could fill her mind with music this evening and funnel troubled emotions into every scale and crescendo, she would be able to think clearly. Tonight, at dinner—

The hair across her nape prickled to attention. A scuffed sound, the shift of a chair as it accepted a person's weight, caused her fingers to stall upon the keys.

"Please continue."

The stark request echoed within the room and stricken, she jerked her gaze over her right shoulder, aware and at the same time incredibly startled to discover Dearing had chosen to enter. Hadn't she hoped, wished, prayed he'd do so days, weeks, months before?

"Good afternoon, milord." She offered a tremulous smile. Was he angry? His expression remained inscrutable despite the ample lantern light. What was it he wanted of her this evening to discern it from so many others?

"It wasn't my intention to interrupt."

He offered some semblance of a smile that neither

proved genuine nor reached his eyes. She couldn't be sure considering the distance, though she did notice how handsome he appeared. His attire was flawless as always, broad shoulders defined in strong angles by the precise cut of his jacket. The taut stretch of fabric magnified his physique by his masculine pose, his arms crossed upon his chest, his legs stretched before him from pressed trousers to polished ankle boots.

"Please continue." His voice rang out with aristocratic control.

She returned her attention to the pianoforte, though her heart pounded with such fierce tempo, she'd hardly be able to command the keys. Before she played one note, vanity intruded. Good heavens, what did she look like? She couldn't very well smooth her hair to assure it was not in disarray. Without a doubt, he'd note the tremble in her fingers. By force of exertion, her coif usually suffered while she played. Hairpins were often lost, used to hold her sheet music when they'd tumbled free.

And then there was her position. Back to the door and seated, Dearing would be staring at her spine. Was her posture natural or forced? Did her bottom look all the larger for her skirts spread outward on the bench? She took a shuddered breath, all at once unable to begin.

Yet he waited.

And this was what she wanted.

An opportunity, no matter how small and insignificant. She would impress him with her skill, if nothing else. Her musical aptitude far outshone her beauty or clever mind.

She placed her fingers on the keys, aware he'd come into the music room by his own volition. She hadn't needed to offer a pathetic invitation and wouldn't waste this advantageous occasion. Her husband had entered the room to hear her play.

Her husband.

As much as she cherished the role of *wife*, she longed to regard *her husband* by his given name. Jeremy. Such a fine name. Strong and rhythmic on the tongue. She'd never uttered it in his presence. Not even on their wedding day. Oh, she said it often enough to herself, whispered it in the darkness of her bedchambers before she surrendered to sleep, but never face-to-face. It all seemed odd and unacceptable, and yet his request for formality persisted, permeating their relationship daily.

He cleared his throat and jarred her back to the present.

The first notes startled her more than they should, and her nerves hammered against her ribs in a disconcerting mixture of trepidation and cautious optimism. She'd intended to play Mozart's *Idomeneo* but instead found herself producing Haydn's *Sonata No. 59* in E-flat major. She hardly knew why, the pieces so vastly different, but as always, she gave herself to the music, each precise note and chord an extension of pent-up emotion.

She wanted, no, *she needed* to perform the piece perfectly. He wouldn't detect an error, most especially at the sonata's fast pace, yet deep down where her heart ached with the affection she so truly wished to offer him, she yearned to produce this perfect gift. A token of sorts. The same as his attendance within the room. Perhaps at last they would begin to communicate on some level other than cordialities. Music held power. The right melody could evoke enough emotion to change the world. At least, she so believed.

She finished with pride, the arrangement pristine, but she did not turn immediately. For the smallest sign, a comment or sound of approval, would go a long way to soothe her thrumming nerves.

In that agonizing wait for his reaction, she recalled the first time she laid eyes on Jeremy Lockhart, Viscount Dearing, and the precious fragility of hope, anticipation and expectation she'd entrapped within her heart, akin to rare gems. She'd made her offering, become his betrothed with the promise to share her life in exchange for his, but things had gone terribly awry.

"You're quite accomplished."

She heard a note of pride in the compliment, though it was voiced haltingly, as if it stuck in his throat and he wasn't sure whether to allow it freedom. She stood from the bench and turned. The lingering ache in her chest, which accompanied the memory of what might have been expanded with suffocating insistence. "Thank you, milord." *Jeremy.* "Would you like to hear another arrangement?"

"Not this evening." He stood, his shadow climbing the wall behind him, looming and overpowering, like so many unspoken words and unsettled emotions.

His eyes searched her face, but she wondered what he sought. Could he read her mind, divine her secrets and look into her heart? Surely he saw the longing there.

"Will you dine at home this evening?" An innocuous question. One she felt abashed to ask.

"Yes."

His eyes swept over her, from top to bottom, and she questioned her appearance a second time. She would need to take greater effort in dressing. She wished to please him.

"I visited my family recently. Mother and my sisters are well. Father arrived, and we strolled in the gardens together." She babbled, attempting to fill the soundless air between them, struggling to keep her husband in the room where conversation seemed more difficult than the complicated chords and intervals on her sheet music.

His expression changed markedly at the mention of her father. Nothing drastic, but she noted his jaw tightened and one dark brow twitched. She couldn't imagine why. Her father thought highly of Dearing. Indeed he was their heroic rescuer.

"I will see you at dinner, then."

He spoke at last, pivoted with enviable exactitude and left before she puzzled her way through his reaction. Yet to delay in the music room long would be a foolish mistake. She needed to decide on the quintessential dress for dinner.

Entering the hall, she nearly collided with her husband's secretary as he took his leave for the day.

"Pardon me, Mr. Faxman. I was lost in thought." She shook her head at her own foolishness.

"No apology necessary. I experience the same condition daily." His matter-of-fact tone assured.

"Are you leaving now?" She glanced toward the windows, assessing the sun's position.

"It would appear Lord Dearing is finished for the day. There's no work to be done once your music begins."

The secretary offered a congenial smile, though his words brought her distraught surprise. She believed Dearing enjoyed her music, but if it prevented him from accomplishing his work, it presented a different problem altogether. Was that why he'd entered the room today? She'd broken his concentration beyond repair? What was he doing locked away in his study for all those hours anyway?

"I should be off." Faxman moved toward the door, and Hudson emerged from the shadows.

"Good afternoon." She hardly managed the words as she made her way to the stairs.

Chapter Five

Dearing muttered a string of black epithets as he paced the floorboards of the library. Bloody fool. Why hadn't he acted on opportunity? He cursed himself a thousand times as he recalled the subtle willingness in Charlotte's eyes. He'd accomplished the overture, entered the room and complimented her skill, and yet when he could most benefit from a romantic gesture, he'd shut down, backed away and left.

When he'd perpetrated his plan, he was blinded by the solitary goal of winning Charlotte before another swooped in, whether Adams or some unbeknownst preferred suitor. He never anticipated the backlash of guilt for the heinous deeds he'd enacted, nor the complicated emotions that spread through his blood like fever. As much as he embraced the victory of winning, he'd stolen Charlotte's control of the situation, forced her father's hand and created a dichotomy of sorts. He might woo Charlotte into loving him, but were his secret revealed, she would despise him thereafter.

Yet he must push forward.

He strode to one of the large gateleg tables near the windows and stared down at the map unrolled atop the surface. Cartography was an avid interest. He enjoyed the precise measurement required to combine science and aesthetics, often drawing intricate depictions as if somehow through his control of latitude and longitude, he could find the balance needed in his own life. He spared a glance to the room's interior, littered with the evidence of his gravitation, then returned his attention to the parchment on the table. His eyes fell to the compass rose, and he traced a finger over the orientation arrows. Why couldn't marriage include such distinct directions?

North, to Charlotte's mind. He would dazzle her with clever conversation and amusing anecdotes. East and west, their alignment extended as if arms in which to enfold her. And south. He chuckled a low acknowledgment as his finger skimmed the parchment downward. Yes, he knew what pleasure awaited there.

Despite Lindsey's jests, Dearing was a hot-blooded, passionate man whose hard body begged to be buried within Charlotte's softness. Late at night, when the house lay silent, he knew that condition too well. But he desired more than a relief from physical attraction. His desire to know every aspect of his wife's intelligence ran deep, despite their marriage remaining at the shallowest level. He'd created the complex interwoven reality of the situation and now he must find his way forward.

Resolved to accomplish further success on the pathway to his wife's heart, he held on to a shred of hope, unwilling to dredge up the insecurity and concern that plagued his good intentions. Too often, irrational suspicions forced themselves to his head and took control of the doubt within his soul.

There was simply no way Charlotte could discover his past. He'd taken every precaution. He patted his waistcoat pocket, where beneath his handkerchief he kept the invaluable key that opened the leather box on his desk in his study. Thankfully, his secrets were secured, just as they needed to be.

* * *

Charlotte lay back on her bed in an attempt to calm the arrhythmic complaint of her heart. Why hadn't she gone to Dearing directly? Breached the distance between them and smiled at his attention to her performance? How would she ever convince her husband to care for her if she couldn't seize the smallest opportunities Fate haplessly threw in her direction? First her glove, and now this.

She'd give a lock of hair to know what he considered in his quiet watchfulness of her piano playing. Faxman implied it disrupted her husband's concentration. Hopefully, the secretary misconstrued the circumstance. Still, Dearing's silence provoked her as if he seamlessly deciphered her thoughts when she had no idea to his pensive attentiveness. If only she possessed a bolder constitution, like Amelia.

Amelia indeed.

What would Amelia do?

Charlotte recalled the retelling of Amelia and Scarsdale's first kiss. Her friend could barely sleep from the thrilling impact. Charlotte desired that same insomniac affliction. Tonight, she must look her best, be poised, witty and attractive, and with the fortification of wine, venture into the world of flirtation. Hopefully, the combination would thaw Dearing's heart; otherwise their marriage would remain isolated, all for naught. She had no other weapons at her disposal.

She stared at the embroidered white canopy atop her lonely, chaste four-poster bed, a symbolic mockery of her virginity. She exhaled thoroughly despite the thread of dismal failure that wove its way into her chest like a tourniquet around her heart.

Not a moment later, her secret pet sprung atop the counterpane in pursuit of a dust mote. Seeking the warm comfort of friendship, she gathered the kitten into her palms and brought it close for an affectionate cuddle. "You need a name, don't you?"

The kitten mewed in objection and wriggled free, pouncing away to larger conquests and the tempting ribbons on the silk box pillows. Charlotte closed her eyes, blinking hard to clear the threat of tears. Attempting to focus on the kitten as distraction, she twisted her head to the left, where her eyes settled on the adjoining door to her husband's chambers, a silent sentry to all she wanted on the other side, an opening into his world. If only the panel were a window.

With a sigh of resolution, she sat up and swung her legs over the side of the mattress. Her feet brushed the chilled floorboards, and in much the same manner as her kitten, she hopped to the thick wool rug in search of warmth. Her right heel settled atop something sharp and unyielding. After a grumbled complaint, she moved aside to reveal a key. What was it doing on her rug? She hadn't lost it, and she doubted Jill had cause to carry a key about her rooms.

She examined the nondescript bronze as it lay flat in her palm, turning it over twice before she eyed the doorknob of the panel directly in front of her. *Dearing's rooms.* The doorknob didn't have a keyhole on her side, and she knew it to be locked from previous disappointing endeavors. Dare she try again? Which emotion would surface if she discovered the lock held as usual? Her pulse tripped at the suggestion the door could be unlocked, and so she laid her hand upon the brass and twisted, but it held securely.

Perplexed, she folded her fingers around her newfound treasure and settled on the edge of the mattress once again. Had Dearing entered her room when she was otherwise occupied? Why? The notion struck her as oddly encouraging, and with the key held tight within her palm, she sent a hurried prayer upward. Perhaps things were changing for the better. Tonight at dinner, she would offer conversation as titillating as her musical ability and then—then she would flirt.

Dearing accepted his dinner jacket from his valet and dismissed the servant with a polite nod. Tonight, he intended to change the status of his marriage from cordial to personal and, soon after, intimate. The natural progression of things—courtship, affection, betrothal and wedding trip—had been cast aside for the sake of perception and appearance. Society might surmise the obvious terms, but Charlotte would be spared the whispers and critical eye of those who perpetuated gossip. He'd stepped in at the penultimate moment to rescue Elias Notley, Charlotte's father, simultaneously sacrificing the subsequent advantage of knowing his wife beyond a congenial introduction. That was not to say he wasn't besotted, but everything warranted urgent reconciliation. There existed no other way to secure her hand, salvage the Notleys' financial security and remove Charlotte from the marriage mart before another gentleman learned of the crisis and charmed his way into the family. Now Dearing found himself in a struggle to gain ground due to his negligence.

He wasn't one to allow passion to eradicate logic and prided himself on his business acumen, controlled and concise, with the skill of razor-sharp negotiation. He possessed the visceral satisfaction of claiming Charlotte as his wife, though he hadn't truly *claimed* her as of yet, and any thoughts of an intimate relationship were secondary to making amends within their marriage first.

He tilted the cheval glass and combed his hair quickly, noting he needed to have it cut, the length overlapping his collar. Deep within his waistcoat pocket, the key to all misery lie hidden, and he refused to think of it this evening. He drew a deep breath and headed for the stairs, toward a new beginning. He had no plans to waste opportunity any longer.

He found his wife in the drawing room near the hearth, and his breath caught at first sight of her silhouette, much like that evening all those months ago. Perhaps she too realized they stood at a dangerous precipice, a beginning or end, for her gown was more formal than he'd seen her wear. A beat of blame reminded him he could not boast of knowing her wardrobe, having squandered so many evenings away from home.

"Good evening, milady." He strode into the room, quickly closing the distance between them. "You look lovely." And she did. He clenched his jaw with the realization of all the time he'd wasted. Could it be this simple? To compliment and converse, to ignore the past in hope of building a better future? A world of possibility tempted, slightly beyond reach. His fingers curled at his side. He itched to take her hand, but he didn't want to misstep.

"Thank you, milord." She offered a slight smile and her eyes sparkled at his attention, luminous and brilliant in the firelight.

"Sherry before dinner?" Reluctant to look away, he nodded toward the sideboard, where several crystal decanters stood in wait.

"Yes."

Her answer sounded tentative. He could only guess she wondered at his unexpected attention. He spent a minute pouring her glass and a brandy for himself. With his back turned, he took a hearty swallow and refilled two fingers of liquor before he brought their glasses forward.

"You play the pianoforte with masterful skill, Charlotte." To hell with titles and formality. He'd originally intended to offer her time to adjust rather than be thrust into the organic intimacy shared between lovers, the luxury sacrificed when he'd swooped in and proposed the marriage contract with shrewd efficiency. But where had etiquette led? Down a narrow path with impenetrable, self-imposed walls erected in defense and fear. Walls that needed to be plundered and conquered. His grip tightened on his glass. Tonight, he would begin the siege.

Charlotte could hardly form words for the effervescent nervousness alive within her. Dearing had entered the room, a commanding presence, his eyes only on her as his strides ate up the carpet between them. Thank heavens she'd chosen the aubergine silk with cutaway lace sleeves. The elegant neckline and exposed shoulder design complemented her décolletage, with just enough skin to tempt and tease. She'd never worn the gown, convinced Dearing remained uninterested, but things were seemingly altered, and she didn't care why.

A wicked thrill whirled through her as she accepted the glass of sherry and his fingertips brushing against hers with unexpected contact. Heat bloomed across her nape. What if he found her wanting? Deficient of the charm and beauty he'd expected when he bought her hand in marriage?

She wouldn't allow those misguided ideas to take root and instead took a second sip of sherry. If only she could decipher her husband, one minute staid and reserved, the next utterly charming, always with feelings opaque and concealed.

Now candlelight glistened off each strand of his thick hair, the color of ancient gold, his eyes the warmest brown. Desire unfurled, new and eager, and she welcomed the sensation.

"I'm pleased you're home this evening." She hoped she didn't sound forward or foolish for all the agony she'd spent choosing the words.

"As am I."

His eyes moved over her, stalling for several breaths at her neckline, and she hoped the simmering heat of excitement didn't pinken her skin. "We haven't shared as much time together as I'd hoped." There, she'd said it aloud. Would he withdraw or admit he'd handled their new marriage with clumsy disregard?

"Yes, and I accept fault for all that kept me out of the house." He glanced away and back again, his expression softening.

"I . . . I share that fault."

"Let's put it behind us, then."

His gaze searched her face before he reached forward and tucked a wayward lock of hair behind her ear. His fingers lingered, just as they had the other day, and she saw bold desire in his eyes. Her husband wanted her. How gloriously delightful. Her exhalation came out in a series of shallow breaths, each a whisper of hope and anticipation.

How could it be that this strong, handsome man, successful and well respected, had chosen her for a wife? At times, she grew perplexed in seeking a reason. While she believed herself amiable and kind, attractive in the classical sense, Dearing hadn't known her beforehand and yet had offered to bind them together for life. In doing so, he'd saved her family from utter despair.

"I've never thanked you properly." It was the truth. Despite several attempts during their brief engagement, she'd never managed to voice how grateful she and her family were for his magnanimous rescue, the moment never appropriate. "You went away on business for so long after the ceremony, and I likewise suffered a fair amount of sulking."

His expression altered. Did he interpret her comment as disappointment in their union? She hadn't meant to imply it. Her brooding stemmed from a long list of confusions and the sudden loss of her perceived future. Desperation replaced anticipation. She needed to salvage the conversation before she ruined the evening.

"My family will always be indebted to you." Her mouth twisted in a wry smile at the poor choice of words. "I mean to say, Father was at the brink of depression. He tried every way imaginable to recover our security but met with failure repeatedly. Mother could hardly sleep or eat. Even my sisters, who are often the instigators of mayhem and megrims, were solemn and downtrodden, aware our reputation would be ruined, our family with an uncertain future. We were snared in an impossible position. Status and dignity prevented my father from revealing our penurious fate, and yet there were no funds to provide the ample dowry any suitor would expect." Unbidden tears welled in her eyes as she recalled the hopelessness they'd all experienced. She'd worried heartily over her father's health, the strain and distress etched into his face for what seemed like endless days and nights. "Until you stepped in and rescued us." Her words were spoken with gentle awe, for she would never be able to express her full gratitude.

"Charlotte . . ."

Was he uncomfortable with her praise? It didn't matter if his objection was meant to deter; she adored the sound of her name in his voice.

"Please allow me to continue." She offered him a genuine smile. "I realize our courtship was nonexistent and our union is unconventional, but whatever the terms and your reasons for it, I consider your gesture benevolent and heroic."

"Charlotte . . ."

His brow wrinkled with what looked like irritation. She spoke the truth. Did it somehow ring false? Uncertainty, bold and insistent, consumed her, but when he didn't say more, she rushed on, afraid she'd never have the courage or opportunity to reveal her innermost respect. This could be their new beginning, a forging of fragile, tenuous compatibility, and she refused to flounder or fail.

"I may not be the ideal wife, but I will strive to be amenable in all ways."

He looked away, toward the windows at the front of the room, and his mouth flattened in the same way he seemed to press down emotion with control and restraint. She waited for him to return his attention, and several long minutes stretched between them. He exhaled thoroughly, as if shedding whatever resistance had taken hold. Though it was his next movement that had the hairs on the back of her neck raised.

He thrust two fingers into his waistcoat, as if searching for a handkerchief or pocket watch, though there was no chain to indicate he carried a timepiece, and with that ordinary and otherwise meaningless effort, his entire countenance was transformed.

Something like alarm lit his eyes. She watched him clench his teeth, his jaw all at once hard set and angry. And then, with nothing more than a curt glance, he excused himself and left the room.

Chapter Six

Dearing took the stairs by twos. He'd made a hash of things. Something had changed this evening. Happiness seemed within reach. Until Charlotte mentioned his *rescue*. Because it was not a rescue. It was not a noble, self-sacrificing dispensation. He'd seen her, fallen love-struck, and selfishly pursued his desire in disregard of a gentleman's code of conduct or etiquette's stricture. He'd eschewed a proper courtship and created circumstances evidenced by secrets that could never be told. Nothing courteous or benevolent existed in his action. He wouldn't forgive the deed by polishing history. Worse yet, he'd assumed a controlling share of stock that enabled a pathway to a fortune.

How long until Charlotte created her own truth from his deception?

Tonight, the evening had gone to hell. Just when he'd begun to believe they could get on together and he'd prepared to bare his soul, Fate kicked him in the ballocks and he discovered the key was missing from his waistcoat pocket.

Thereafter, no logic could be formed. His heart clenched with fear and apprehension.

He carried the key with him always, moved diligently from waistcoat to waistcoat with each clothing change.

Now he hurried to his bedchambers to check the contents of the coat he'd worn earlier, an outcry of condemnation loud in his ears. Throwing wide the door, he strode to the wardrobe and abused each garment in an attempt to inspect each pocket, the search in vain.

Bloody hell.

He removed the handkerchief and thrust his fingers in the pocket to strain against the stitching in hopes of finding the elusive key, but it proved another failure. Where had it gotten to, and how would he find it? With a breath of exasperation, he refolded the cloth and belatedly noted the smear of dried blood, a red alarm against the crisp white linen.

Wait.

The kitten.

The bite.

The handkerchief.

He must have dropped the key in Charlotte's bedchambers. But why hadn't he heard it jangle against the floorboards to announce its fall? *The thick wool rug before the bedchamber door.*

He'd become distracted. Lost a little in the idea of rightfully loving his wife in her far-too-pure four-poster bed.

Damnation.

He needed to return to her rooms at once or he'd find no peace. He shot his eyes to the door between their chambers. Where was Charlotte now? Still belowstairs in the dining room, or had she retreated to her rooms after his abrupt departure?

He exhaled deeply. It could very well be she'd had no opportunity to find the key, for that part of the room led to only one place, and his lady wife had never come knocking. No doubt it still lay upon the rug, nestled within the woolen nap, awaiting his return. He would open the door, retrieve the key and exit undetected.

Shifting his attention to the hall, he listened outside his bedchambers, annoyed with his own breathing for the loudness in his ears. The house stood quiet. Now seemed the opportune time, the staff likely attending to dinner or taking a meal in the kitchen.

He crossed the room and twisted the knob to crack the door a hairbreadth. Jill, his wife's maid, hummed a faint tune within the interior. He opened the door a little wider. Her back was turned to him, her arms filled with clothing as she flitted around the room in completion of her tasks.

He closed the panel and waited, counting to twenty, then thirty, before repeating the attempt. At last, he watched the maid depart and returned to his task. Perspiration dotted his upper lip and he wiped a palm over his face as he entered his wife's rooms.

How would he explain his actions if he were caught?

No time existed for that unsettling predicament, and he crouched low to examine the rug at his feet. Flattening his palm and skimming the wool, once, twice, as he muttered a curse. The key wasn't there. Had Charlotte recovered it? Or mayhap the maid in her routine cleaning? It could be any female servant, housekeeper to chambermaid, who maintained the house and carried a jaunty chatelaine of keys about on her duties.

He stood, and for lack of direction scanned the room, relieved when the cursed kitten who'd caused his anguish didn't materialize to provoke him further. The bedchambers were prepared for the evening hours. Fresh water filled the ewer beside the basin on the nightstand and a vase of pink roses graced the bureau. A fresh towel hung on a hook near the full-length mirror. Atop the vanity, an open jar of pins and a silver hairbrush waited alongside two thick white ribbons. He'd never seen his wife's hair unplaited. That realization cut to the bone.

Everything about their relationship was restricted, bound or otherwise out of reach. His chest tightened. It was all his doing. He swallowed with the unpalatable truth. He shifted his eyes to the left and settled his focus on the mattress where, across the bedlinens, a gauzy white night rail lay silently in wait. He ran his fingertips over the cloth, barely touching it and at the same time wanting to wind the fabric around his fists to bring it to his face to inhale its fragrant perfume. He stepped back, his jaw tight with regret and desire. He should leave. Every moment spent within Charlotte's chambers caused his heart to ache further, his temperament to spike, and yet he remained a breath longer.

Another poor decision.

A pair of fancy pantalets were set upon the foot of the mattress. His wife must favor delicate underthings, the white silk edged with fine lace trim, the shimmer of tightly spun gossamer a tinder to his banked lust. He swallowed, his mouth inordinately dry, and wiped at the sweat across his brow. His heart endured a heavy beat.

A soft sound across the room at last tore his attention from the frilly scrap of temptation. A blur of black near the windowsill served to return his wits. He exited the room, more determined than ever to win his wife.

"I think Dearing was in my rooms." Charlotte strove for a casual mention as she and Amelia wended their way through the crowd on Bond Street, a footman trailing behind. In truth, the suspicion her husband snuck into her bedchambers when she was otherwise occupied had pestered her through the night. Most especially after his odd behavior before dinner.

"You're not sure?" Amelia smiled, her head canted to match their eyes beyond the brim of her velvet lace bonnet. "Whatever do you mean?"

They'd come to Bond Street for a morning of shopping, and as Amelia was now a duchess, a footman followed them at three strides no matter where they went. Charlotte understood the purpose, but she missed the privacy once shared with her dearest friend.

"I wasn't there when he entered—if he entered," she explained. "I'm not certain."

"You're confusing me." Amelia nodded toward the milliner's window, and they wove their way across the walkway and entered the shop, the footman abandoned near the inside doorframe. "By the by, what did you name your kitten?"

Charlotte took a deep breath, gladdened to be away from the crowd and within the quiet interior of the popular hat shop. "I haven't decided. Anyway, I believe Dearing entered my room because I found a key."

"A key to what?" With a brisk wave, Amelia shoed away the shopkeeper, who approached with alacrity, the gleam of prospective sales an immediate lure. She then removed her bonnet, looped the ribbons over her wrist and began to inspect the newest fashions on display.

"I don't know." Charlotte continued the thread of their conversation as they browsed. "But I found it lying in front of the adjoining door that leads to his bedchambers."

Amelia turned, her eyes wide. "Finally, this becomes interesting. What else did you discover?"

"I inquired with the servants and no one had any idea where the key belongs or what lock it opens. The household keys are all silver plate and this one is bronze." She touched her bodice, where the item in question remained pinned inside her corset for safekeeping. "I don't believe it opens the adjoining door as it wouldn't make sense that Dearing needed a key. The lock is on his side only."

"This design is absolutely stunning." Amelia reached for a cobalt-blue headpiece trimmed in champagne silk ribbons.

She examined it carefully but didn't try it on. "What else happened? I can tell by the anxious look on your face, you are near bursting to share details."

"We had a moment." Charlotte beamed. Perhaps the evening hadn't progressed as she'd anticipated, but there was no denying something had happened when Dearing touched her cheek. If only she hadn't babbled on about gratitude and heroics. Maybe he perceived her as bird-witted. She would strive to become a clever conversationalist.

"Do tell," Amelia insisted before she replaced the hat on its stand and moved farther down the store aisle. Charlotte followed, anxious to gain her dearest friend's perspective.

"We were having a drink with conversation before dinner and he was different. I could see it in every way, from the look in his eyes to his manner and words. He appeared relaxed and at ease in my company instead of rigid and restrained." Her voice tapered to a low, awestruck whisper that captured Amelia's direct interest, her friend focused with rapt attention.

"What happened?" Amelia clasped Charlotte's hands in hers.

"Things proceeded well. He appeared sincere, his conversation heartfelt, but then I mentioned his valiant rescue and all emotion shut away in an instant. He was suddenly the staid aristocrat who cared very little for his wife." The threat of tears pricked her eyes, and she looked away, the array of mobcaps and scarves strewn across the counter to her left an instant blur of color.

"I'm sorry." Amelia gave Charlotte's hands a squeeze before releasing them. "But his indecision doesn't fool me. Something is holding him back, and the only way you can discover it is to continue to seek him out. If you believe he was in your rooms, then you must find a way to get him back there. Surely we can think of some ruse—"

"I won't employ trickery and deceit. Honesty is the one

trait I respect above all others, and I'm certain it's a quality Dearing reveres. He expressed genuine interest in having me as his bride and I couldn't bear the thought of stooping to some dishonest ploy to win his affection. Deception is an unbecoming business, and I'm not comfortable with the idea." She toyed with a pair of kidskin gloves on a nearby counter, unable to look Amelia in the eye and reveal the piercing turmoil in her heart.

"Are you comfortable sleeping alone each evening? With one-sided conversations and lonely meals? He caused this chasm of awkwardness by leaving without explanation directly after your wedding only to return with a continuation of the same odd behavior." Amelia placed a hand on Charlotte's shoulder. "Of late, he's led you to believe hope exists. We can't ignore the opportunity."

"I'm guilty of a fair amount of avoidance," Charlotte mumbled, quick to defend Dearing, or at the least share in the responsibility of their failed relationship.

"If that's true, it was a result of his choices." Amelia tugged Charlotte forward and placed a frivolous bonnet in her hands. The hat was fashioned in ladybug red and trimmed with artificial apricots, grapes and cherries. The garish design produced the effect desired. The mood shifted, and Charlotte relaxed a little. "Time to exact a drastic change."

"Yes," Charlotte agreed, huffing a forced breath of fortification. "I know I could come to love him if he'd only allow me the privilege." Indeed, she was already in love with the idea of loving her husband.

"I believe he cares for you." Amelia placed the fruit-laden bonnet on her head and tied the ribbons under her chin. Then she screwed her face into a ridiculous grin. They broke into laughter so loud, it drew the unwanted attention of nearby shoppers. The moment passed and left them with the more serious subject unfinished. "What is it you want from marriage, Charlotte? Are you interested in children only, or do you wish for the other half of your heart? To spend time with the one person who completes your soul?"

"As you have with Scarsdale." Charlotte exhaled deeply. "Yes. I want true love. To understand Dearing's hopes and goals and to share a precious intimacy." She smiled, more for the hopeful future she painted than from amusement. "To know each other so well, we can finish each other's sentences without thought."

"You should make a list." Amelia matched her grin. "I find lists can be quite helpful."

"Perhaps, although I don't believe that's necessary. I have my most precious desires memorized by heart." Charlotte flicked a wayward cherry on the hat's brim as Amelia replaced it on the table. "Thank you, though. You're the dearest friend and I treasure you."

"Thank me after you've succeeded. When you're thoroughly loved, sated and exhausted from lovemaking." Amelia winked, aware her words would evoke an audacious reaction.

"Amelia, please. Someone will hear you." More likely, any passerby would notice Charlotte's vehement objection.

"Oh, posh. You worry about the silliest things. Now, let's talk of another important subject, your darling kitten. What shall we name her and how is the little imp getting along? I'm sure she's not nearly as much trouble as you'd anticipated."

Chapter Seven

Dearing reread the investment contract on the desk in front of him, though he comprehended not a word, his attention divided. One portion of consideration awaited the melodic notes of the pianoforte. It neared Charlotte's regular practice schedule, and despite the correspondence he had to accomplish and the papers from his solicitor to attend to, he kept a watchful eye on the clock. In a daring move, he'd affected a change in the music room, and he wondered how it would be received. An amused grin begged freedom whenever he considered it, but he tamped down anticipation and refocused on his work.

In truth, all was for naught.

While the larger portion of his mental capacity strained to hear a sonata or waltz, a more-demanding physical part of his body recalled the lacy white pantalets he'd seen atop the mattress in Charlotte's bedchambers.

He'd been reduced to the basest level of depravity, panting after his wife's undergarments, but he couldn't stop the inevitable. He already craved her nearness, her affection and admiration. That dainty silk scrap proved an incendiary flame to his lust.

"Excuse me, milord." Faxman came around the writing

table and approached as he cut a diagonal across the room. "I've discovered an unexplainable ambiguity within the ledger's third-quarter calculations and need a word of clarification."

Dearing snapped to alertness, discarded his romantic musings and forced himself to rights with a strong throat clearing. He stood and offered his attention. "Let's have a look."

"At the end of last year, you purchased controlling interest in several companies at a swift pace. I recall drafting the contracts as quickly as possible, sometimes three in a day." Faxman indicated a page in the ledger as he angled nearer with a clear view of the figures.

"I recall." Indeed, he did. "To your point, Faxman." This was not a subject Dearing wished to explore.

"Soon after, you consolidated the companies and sold them off without profit in what seems an exercise in maximum effort and little return. For what reason would anyone undertake the endeavor when clearly there were other means to obtain the companies without significant loss or expenditure of time? It seems an odd series of transactions, with sparse margin for gain, and I wonder if something is amiss. The numbers don't quite sum to equivalence."

"Not every transaction is perpetrated for monetary advantage." Even as he spoke the words, Dearing knew his astute secretary would not be deterred. Had anyone offered Dearing the nonchalant and nonsensical explanation, he would have rebuffed it in no uncertain terms. Now he drummed his fingers against his leg with impatience, pondering just how far Faxman would pursue the subject.

"Of course, milord. Excuse my inquiry. I only meant to affirm my calculations were correct. I fall victim to eager curiosity at times, though Father often said one must embrace any opportunity to learn. With your superior insight, I'd despise squandering such an ideal moment."

"I see." Dearing watched Faxman closely and hedged

further. "A commendable trait. I can list several reasons why transactions occur other than for profit. Influence, status or an invigorated interest could prompt me to acquire a new holding." Surely an affliction as debilitating as love should be on the list, but Dearing ignored that revelation. "Mark the page and leave the register atop my desk. I'll review your findings later this evening."

Faxman retrieved his pencil, made a few notations in the margin of the ledger and set it on the corner, in the same place Dearing once kept a black leather box to which he'd lost the key.

Thankfully, the conversation proceeded no further, and Faxman returned to work. Stalled only momentarily, Dearing did the same, although it was nary a few breaths later that the initial chords of music broke through the silence. He resisted the temptation to abandon responsibility and seek Charlotte straightaway. Instead, he forced himself to continue staring at the papers in front of him, all the while wondering how she had perceived his gift. Would she be delighted or dismayed?

After what seemed an interminably long stretch of nothingness, Faxman gathered his things and with a brief word departed for the day, leaving Dearing alone at last.

Charlotte walked into the music room, her mind busy with contemplations gained from her morning shopping excursion. Amelia may be an unconventional duchess, but she was a most cherished friend. Charlotte valued her opinion and suggestions and, with few people to take into confidence, considered each shared conversation a dozen times over.

Lost in thought, she approached the bench and drew back in surprise. Atop the pianoforte, basking in late-day sunlight, a crystal vase filled with lavender roses glistened in welcome. Vibrant and extravagant, the roses evoked an immediate smile. Mrs. Hubbles, the housekeeper, must have arranged for this thoughtful addition. Charlotte turned to seek the woman out in gratitude, her slipper heels tapping a cadence across the tiles.

She found Mrs. Hubbles near the linen closet above-stairs, instructing the lower maids in a reorganization of fresh-pressed sheets and folded towels. The interior of the large closet smelled of starch, and Charlotte noted the ring of keys in the older woman's hand, none of which were bronze.

"Excuse me, Mrs. Hubbles."

"Yes, milady." The housekeeper stepped away from her task. She was a pleasant woman, well rounded over the years, who ran the household with efficient authority, and though Charlotte had not interfered in the routine of domestic keeping, she found Mrs. Hubbles open to suggestion and agreeable to change whenever a small request was made.

"Thank you for the lovely flower arrangement atop the pianoforte. It's quite unexpected and brightens the room considerably. How very thoughtful." Charlotte enjoyed fresh flowers in her bedchambers, and a modest arrangement adorned the foyer's chiffonier, but other than that, she hadn't assigned flora and ornamental plants through the house. She wasn't certain whether Dearing enjoyed nature or considered the cost a wasteful indulgence. The financial impact of his reconstitution of her family's solvency was never far from her mind.

Sadly, there was too much she didn't know about her husband. Now armed with Amelia's instructions and confidence, Charlotte was bent on change.

"I'm glad the roses please you, milady, but 'twas not my doing. Lord Dearing sent one of the footman to the hothouse in Covent Garden to fetch that particular shade. He was quite emphatic, and I daresay all of us in the servants' quarters were hopeful the roses were available, as his lordship doesn't

often instruct us to specifics concerning personal matters."
Mrs. Hubbles's kind eyes twinkled with what could only be
delighted approval.

"I see." An unexpected tremor of hope skittered down
her spine upon hearing Mrs. Hubbles's explanation. Dearing
had chosen the flowers for her? He'd sent a footman out
specifically? This was no random errand or slapdash decision?

Dinah, Charlotte's sister, favored horticulture and rou-
tinely educated the family with an assortment of botanical
facts, including the language of roses. Lavender roses represented enchantment and fascination. Had she perceived
the color correctly? Charlotte hurriedly returned to the
music room to admire the flowers more closely. They were
lovely, their pale blooms fragrant and lush. A heady rush of
anticipation caused her pulse to race in such a fashion, she
almost couldn't stand still.

Her husband's gesture touched her heart. They hadn't
exchanged wedding presents, and he'd only given her an
obligatory gold band for her finger, and yet this quiet, unforeseen gift, personal and romantic, meant the world to her.

Could it be Dearing suffered from anxiety or shyness?
Painfully unable to express his feelings? Did he worry, as
she did, that by not having a normal courtship, she would
find him lacking? She wondered at this theory. She knew
from her father and other tales overheard that Dearing was
a fierce, if not vicious, negotiator in all business dealings.
For a viscount with minor recognition in aristocratic circles,
he'd made his mark through shrewd insight and the ability
to capitalize on opportunity. In the same manner, he'd accu-
mulated sizable wealth and the respect of his peers, but that
was in the business world. Could a powerful and progressive
man be victim to inhibition and insecurity in his personal
affairs? This brought with it a sense of understanding,
though it still didn't explain his changeable nature whenever

she mentioned his timely fiscal rescue. She mourned the lack of knowledge she possessed concerning her husband in any other situation than their sparse interactions.

And perhaps it didn't matter. As of late, their relationship had changed. She touched her fingers to her chest, where beneath several layers of silk and cotton, the key remained pinned to her corset. She needed to lure her husband back into her bedchambers. Indeed, the suggestion instigated a plan. She had no idea how all these separate parts would add up to a whole, but the possibility her husband cared for her, enough to wish to please and gift her with roses, invigorated her music as she set her fingers to the ivories moments later.

She chose a selection from Beethoven, a piece entitled "Appassionata," filled with complicated chords and intense mounting emotion, an outlet to the burgeoning hope and sensual wishes of her soul. When she finished, she sat quietly and huffed a breath of satisfaction, the complicated arrangement newly mastered. Before she calmed her sprinting heartbeat, though, a solitary round of applause entered the room.

Excitement spiked through her, red hot and piercing. She knew it was Dearing before he neared the piano, and her lips trembled, her mind in a flurry to arrange words in a coherent sequence. She twisted on the bench to glance over her shoulder, and there her husband stood, not less than three strides away, his expression unreadable, though something seemed different. Her breath caught, a confident expression of desire and command aligned with dark possessiveness in his eyes.

"Have I interrupted you?" Faxman's suggestion that her music disrupted Dearing's concentration had stayed with her, though she knew better to dismiss it.

"Not at all. Have I?"

He watched her, his penetrating gaze warming her from the inside out.

She stood and moved aside from the bench. "Of course not." She reached up and traced a finger over one of the flowers. The petals were soft and velvety, the color unmatched. "Thank you. How did you know I adore roses?"

"I didn't. I merely thought them fitting." He paused the briefest moment, a wary look in his eyes, though a trace of a smile curled his lips. "You like them, then?" He spoke as if the words were being pulled from within him, one by one.

"Very much so." How fragile their conversation, as if both were aware they walked on ice, the smallest misstep able to crack the delicate attenuation of their newfound words.

"I hope to learn your likes and dislikes." He'd moved closer, his shadow cast across the ivory keys. "I want to know you, Charlotte."

"You do?" She swallowed past a dozen questions and tilted her face toward his. What had brought about this change? After weeks and months of nothing more than con-geniality, their communication limited and stilted. How could he doubt she wanted anything less than a loving rela-tionship? Any minuscule indication he desired more from their marriage than cohabitation and strained amiability would be received with accolades, but this—this, expressed a far more potent sentiment. Within her soul, a wild, mad-dening joy bubbled to life. "I wish to know you as well."

His eyes darted away and back again. Had she not watched him so closely, she might have missed it. He half-smiled, as if unsure whether to reveal a secret, and for a moment, she felt caught, uncertainty once again taunting.

"Milord—"

"Jeremy." He closed the distance between them with a single stride. "You should only call me Jeremy."

His voice dropped low, perhaps meant for himself more than her, and she remembered a moment during their vows when he'd looked at her with unabashed adoration, when there was no mistaking the emotion in his eyes or voice. She hadn't seen anything remotely similar until now. How sad their relationship had undergone such change.

She'd been granted permission to use his Christian name, and yet the occasion slipped away with unremarkable passing.

He paused for less than an exhalation and time seemed to slow.

"Come closer, Charlotte."

The warmth of his words moved over her like a caress. Was that desire thrumming through his voice? She didn't know. Her pulse pounded in her ears. Emotions clanged like cymbals. The air in the room became thick, heated, over-filled with every nuance and notice of *him*.

It was what she wanted, longed for, but now, with the moment upon her, she could hardly hold a thought long enough to answer. He moved nearer, his tempting mouth only inches from hers, while puzzling conjecture prodded her mind. She forced all questions into the past, where they belonged, and with a whispered gasp leaned into him.

He'd never kissed her on the lips. Never shown an inclination to do so. But if the agonizing torture of all those days and months resulted in the divine pressure of his kiss at this moment, she'd never complain. To want and wait for something for so very long, and then to achieve it, was a miracle of sorts.

Dearing groaned into the kiss, some low, primal sound, barely able to keep a leash on desire, and at the same time desperate not to bring ruin to an opportunity so finespun and late in coming, it could only be a figment of his imagination.

But no, her soft, sweet mouth was warm and responsive beneath his, and he wondered for a fleeting moment if his heart beat so hard, it might break from his chest. He breathed her name, and a fragrant perfume drenched his senses, already fraught with constrained passion. How he yearned, the feeling deep within, beneath pride and fear, behind his heart hidden in shadow. He wouldn't waste this precious moment.

She'd never been kissed.

He knew as soon as he brought his mouth down on hers. The tentative pressure of her mouth against his was definitive confirmation. Her lips trembled, and the subtle innocent resonance reverberated in his soul before a swell of masculine satisfaction and possessiveness, some antiquated sense of cupidity, gained control. He slid his hands from her upper arms to her cheeks to frame her face and hold her as he deepened the kiss. She gasped, and he plundered her mouth in answer, licking into her, sweet and delectable, hot and wet. Much to his pleasure, she held her ground, and when her tongue caught with his, inexperienced and at the same time curious, the kiss turned lazy, lush and indulgent.

Her hands clasped his forearms. Her fingers pressed through the linen of his shirt to sear her touch upon his soul, until by degree her grip lightened, her body relaxed against him, soft and delicate.

Oh, but she proved a quick study. The same intensity and finesse she applied to the mastery of a demanding orchestral concerti, she now dedicated to the lesson at hand. How easily he could unleash his long-restrained ardor. With nary an effort. Still wisdom willed out, and he ended the kiss lest he ravish her, *frighten her*, so he raised his head though he barely withdrew.

Her eyes fluttered open and she watched him, lips dark pink and kiss-swollen, a hint of wonder alive in her expression.

"We've never kissed like that." The confession whispered over his lips. "It was pleasant."

"Pleasant?" He suffered a slight clearing of the throat before he canted his head and spoke directly into her ear. "Then I haven't done it correctly."

He didn't wait for her reply and captured her mouth with precise control this time. Previous apprehension dissipated in a heartbeat. He brought her tight into the circle of his arms and threaded his fingers through her neatly coifed hair. Finding the laced braids, he tugged a little, just hard enough to hint at forbidden sensations, as his baser needs overrode all other considerations. He'd like nothing more than to unravel the lengths here in the music room beneath the buffered candlelight, lower her to the thick Aubusson carpet and explore every inch of her body. His mind sped with erotic images as his tongue slid against hers, their breathing caught in perfect rhythm. She moaned into his mouth, a soft, entrancing sound, and he broke away to list kisses across her cheek, higher, against the delicate whorl of her ear.

"Charlotte."

"Yes."

Her voice sounded breathless, though she tensed within his hold. Why did she brace herself? Whatever the reason, it was his doing.

"You tempt me in a hundred ways." Her face smoothed against his as she turned, but he would not relinquish the moment and so brushed kisses across her throat, below her ear, his own voice a rumble against her petal-soft skin, pale, tender and lovely. "A thousand, actually."

Chapter Eight

Charlotte bit her lower lip while her husband, *her husband*, nipped a path along the slope of her neck, his words an unexpected incantation. What had brought about this drastic change? This intense acknowledgment that was so unlike all the weeks and months of nothingness? And dare she believe the alteration permanent, or would hope be cleaved in two tomorrow when once again Dearing abandoned her at breakfast or locked himself away for the majority of the day?

She didn't wish to break the spell, but the threat of disappointment surfaced despite all effort, and she voiced her fear, willing to take the risk to spare her heart. "Jeremy." Her voice broke on the last syllable. She took an abrupt breath as he lifted his head to match her eyes. "You're different. Unguarded and attentive. Is this the real you?"

Her question seemed to evoke a series of emotions, though his answer was fast in coming.

"Would it suffice to say, it's the part I like best?"

Truly, his answer was no answer at all, and she couldn't help but wonder over her husband's contrary behavior. Perhaps no guarantee existed, no surety to be found in their unlikely union, but she possessed enough wherewithal to encourage conversation and with any luck secure common ground on which to build a stronger relationship.

"Tell me about your interests. At times you spend hours in your study with your secretary. If we're to become better acquainted, we should share what might have come naturally if we'd a formal courtship." Had she truly suggested they stop kissing and talk? Foolish. Beyond foolish, really. Yet this opportunity was a gift not to be wasted. He dropped his hands, stepped away and eyed her with a wary gleam.

"You're interested?" He seemed skeptical of her curiosity, though his hesitation was slight. "Monetary matters and business negotiations are unsuitable subjects for a lady and terribly boring at that, although I hone my mind's acuity with cartography. Studying maps and at times drawing them is an exercise of meticulous precision and exactitude."

"I wondered about all those maps." She dared a slight giggle and relaxed by degree. "I suppose treasure hunting was a leap of imagination on my part."

He chuckled at her response, and the rich, velvety sound rippled through her. It was the first time she'd ever heard him laugh. If only she could capture the sound in a jar and listen to it later, alone in her bedchambers.

"Ah, treasure hunting is a fanciful idea. But no, I'm afraid cartography is a staid and rather quiet preoccupation. Although sometimes a man finds treasure where he least expects it." Half his mouth quirked in an attractive grin, and his piercing attention caused her skin to heat. "What is it you truly wish to know?"

She swallowed, a plethora of questions jumping to the fore. *Did he care for her? Why had he chosen to marry her? What explanation existed for his peculiar behavior nearly every day since they'd wed?* "Have you any extended family?" She bit her lower lip again, this time in punishment for cowardice. "Your secretary and few others attended our expeditious ceremony."

"Considering the short notice, Lindsey and Faxman were sufficient witnesses. Besides, I have little family to share. My mother passed when I was away at Eton, and my father followed not three years later. I've managed, independent and self-sufficient, for most of my adult life." He paused, but for no longer than an exhale. "Please don't pity the fact. I know you come from a large family. My background and modest title have allowed me to do what I enjoy best, negotiate business, and at the same time enjoy the spoils of better society."

His voice dropped low with the last of it, and she realized he meant *her* as one of the aforementioned spoils more than the predicament of his status.

"Is there anything you'd like to know about me?" Her meek question composed a dare no matter it soft-spoken.

"Myriad things, Charlotte." His expression transformed, and his gaze fell upon her with direct intensity. "How did you become so accomplished on the pianoforte?" His question seemed to contradict the emotion in his eyes.

"I owe my love of music to my mother. She sang to me each night before bed, and as I grew older, I expressed the desire to make music to accompany her lovely voice. My father indulged all his daughters and promptly purchased a pianoforte. I became immediately enchanted. The sleek keys and strong melodies charmed me into relentless practice and I fell hopelessly in love with the instrument."

"One can tell by listening to you play."

His expression grew pensive again. Would that she could read his mind. She rushed on, her stomach aflutter from his compliment and at the same time perplexed, unable to decipher the meaning.

"You know my father, of course, but I'd like you to become acquainted with my mother and sisters in a less formal manner. Perhaps we can invite them to dinner soon." It was an adventurous suggestion, one she would never have been able to give voice if it weren't for his bold kisses and charming conversation. Somehow, their embrace had crumbled the first impervious wall, and she forged ahead, heartened and encouraged.

"If it pleases you." His tone suggested he was less than.

"My sisters will be thrilled. You have no idea the amount of questioning I endure when I visit home. A dinner gathering will diffuse their collective meddling for a long while." She persisted, amused by her sisters' inquisitive interest and hopeful she'd draw Jeremy's good humor and agreement.

"As long as we strive to keep the conversation informal, with no discussion of business, past or present."

It seemed an odd request and a small concession. She recalled how his mood had changed when she'd mentioned her family's shared gratitude for the financial rescue. Answering with a vigorous nod, she reached out to touch his arm, and he caught her hand instead, pulled her forward until she stood before him, the space between their mouths rapidly decreased.

"Thank you." The words accompanied a gasp, and her pulse leaped. Did he think she thanked him for tugging her closer? Indeed, she was thankful for that too.

"What else do you wish to know, wife?"

The words were an affectionate tease and her heart beat heavy in her chest. Neatly captured in his arms now, his breath warmed her cheek, and were she to move the slightest, another kiss would be had. Her husband was indeed a charmer. No wonder he'd accomplished so much with so little early on in life.

"Do you know how long I've wanted to hold you close?" He tugged her tight against his chest and did not pause enough for her answer. His words shocked and thrilled at the same time. "Since the first moment I saw you perched on that proper piano bench like a china figurine. It was your beauty that snagged my attention, and your skillful playing that entranced me. I became transfixed and couldn't bear to look away."

"I don't understand." And she didn't. She met his eyes, brown though nearly black, long lashed and so intense at the moment that words tripped off her tongue. "We'd never met. We had no introduction that evening. You'd never spoken to me and—"

But he didn't allow her to finish, effectively silencing her with a hard kiss.

And what a kiss.

His mouth found hers half-open and he took advantage, the delicious heat of his tongue a sensual rub that erased any haunting inconsistency or unruly prevarication.

Little made sense beyond the moment, and it didn't matter. She gave herself over to him and melted into his embrace.

He was a man of control. He planned. He pursued. He achieved. Ten months ago, he'd plotted a deceitful intention and by use of his sharpest weapon, his intelligence, he'd succeeded. By that same control, he kept emotion on a short leash. Still, it hadn't protected him from falling in love. Love was a complex matter that knew no control.

Tonight, he'd pushed past the risk of failure. Tonight, though no easy task, he'd silenced the voices that warned him away and, with that, overcame hesitation. Now the reward of his efforts stood within his embrace. He skimmed his fingers across her cheek, felt her quiver beneath his fingertips, the gentle reaction so visceral it stirred his soul.

How she would loathe him when she learned the truth.

He forced the intrusive reality from his brain. He would make her love him. It was the only course of action.

He captured her mouth in a kiss meant to obliterate any wayward hesitation she might have, but it accomplished much more. He'd waited and wanted for so long, the tether on restraint had frayed dangerously thin. He needed to stop kissing her or he would never stop kissing her.

Reason led him to an end. "Until dinner, then." He murmured the words against her lips and moved away.

"Yes."

She sounded breathless but didn't say more. She straightened her skirts and stepping back a pace in kind, as if they could think more clearly and examine the interaction if only they decreased proximity.

She was finely made, his wife, of graceful figure and uncommon beauty, and if he did not overwhelm her or cause her to think him false, then perhaps somehow they could see themselves to happiness. He wanted nothing more than that.

Much later in the evening, when dinner was finished, the glow of a pleasant evening spent in the company of her husband was reviewed in the privacy of her bedchambers. With a grin of fascination, Charlotte playfully danced a length of ribbon in front of the kitten's nose as she retold the whimsical musings and otherwise besotted flirtations shared through the meal.

"Jeremy is quite appealing when he puts his mind to the task. I was entranced through all four courses, so much so, I haven't a fig what I ate for dinner tonight." She untangled the ribbon beneath the kitten's claws and shimmied it across the counterpane. "We shared more conversation in this one evening than the ten months of our marriage."

There hadn't been any more kisses, but that didn't matter. She had yet to recover from their intimacy in the music room. Her body tingled still, the remembrance alive and treasured. She trailed her fingertips across her collarbone, relishing the sensation, and as she dropped her hand, it skimmed over the key pinned in her bodice. She shot her eyes to the adjoining door to their bedchambers and then rose from the mattress with a smile.

"We don't need to wonder about this key anymore, do we, little one?" She spoke over her shoulder with a glance to the kitten atop the bed, paws at work shredding the scrap of ribbon. She unfastened the key so it lay flat in her palm. Without another thought, she opened the porcelain hairpin jar on her vanity and dropped it inside.

Atop her bed, the kitten jerked into the air, a series of playful hops that caused Charlotte an immediate grin. "Look at you. You're as elusive as a flash of light. I've decided your name. I'll call you Shadow." She pivoted with impish glee and scooped up the kitten to cuddle it close. "Now, let's discuss my husband's kisses. I refuse to believe anything more divine exists."

Dearing settled into his usual chair at White's and signaled a footman for brandy. He'd purposely removed himself from home this evening as an act of preservation. Dinner had proceeded smoothly. His wife proved a wit, her animated conversation almost a distraction from his lust, but not quite.

Damn him if he couldn't solve that problem soon.

He'd known he'd wanted her after one evening in what seemed like years ago instead of ten months. Independent from a young age, he was a man who knew his own mind, satisfied with life until he saw Charlotte, and his world shifted. He resolved in that moment he'd never regain balance until he learned more about her, discovered why she affected him so. From that point, he'd made discreet inquiries, from which all answers led him to believe his chances at capturing her attention were slim. He was a viscount with a quiet title surrounded by gentlemen with far more to encourage their appeal. Yet there was no time to gain ground. He saw his rivals, most particularly Adams, watch Charlotte with admiration in their eyes and attractive marriage offers on the tip of their tongues. He needed an edge, a unique and private crisis; otherwise, any gentleman would win her before he made the slightest progress.

Her family, well-known and respected, socialized with the upper crème of society. He lived on the outer fray, mostly by choice. Yet with the same decisive intuition employed to negotiate impossible business transactions, he'd chosen not to live with remorse, but rather to use his intelligence to gain what he wanted.

And he'd managed it, hadn't he?

Until now.

What he hadn't anticipated was the torturous wait between the betrothal and the establishment of a contented union. Self-inflicted through his own poor actions, he'd created injured feelings and now, at last on solid footing, believed happiness was within reach. It wasn't lust that drove him, though as a healthy male he yearned for the intimate relationship consummation offered. No, a bond far more precious needed to be established for their marriage to survive the possible exposure of his misdeeds. He longed to confess his admiration and know in his heart Charlotte held the same esteem for him.

Thereby, tonight he'd removed himself and likewise prevented temptation from a prodding knock on Charlotte's bedchamber door, inviting himself in. He would offer her more time.

Damn her lacy pantalets.

Confident she was also aware of the inevitable, evidenced by her genuine, enthusiastic reaction earlier, he measured his time, investing interest so as to avoid regret. Had he any hope she would forgive him if his treachery came to light, they would need the surest marriage, one based on trust and affection, a strong, resilient relationship to endure a betrayal of great proportion. Not a single night of consuming passion.

He accepted a brandy from the silver tray and swore into his glass with the first swallow.

"Isn't this an unexpected pleasure?" Lindsey materialized from a dark corner and leaned against the mahogany buttress aligned with the bookcase-lined wall. "How goes things at home? Have you taken my advice? You look more at ease, although an appearance here when you should be acting the attentive husband doesn't bode well."

"Good evening, Lindsey." He slanted a glance in his friend's direction.

"What are you about? I thought you were making an effort, garnering favor, gaining ground and whatnot."

"Mind your words." Why was it Lindsey made it sound a game when nothing could be more serious?

"I see. A delicate subject, at best." Lindsey settled in the overstuffed wingback chair on the diagonal, his back to the hearth and his face in shadow. "You must relish the challenge."

"Unlike your lineage, I came to London penniless and there I inherited a title, the coat of arms as tattered and worn as the shirt on my back. Still, I overcame adversity and made a tidy fortune." No emotion colored his tone.

"Indeed you did, though you might have accomplished the same with a few mindful wagers in the betting books." Lindsey's careless grin made a fleeting appearance.

"Then I suppose you're right, I relish the challenge." Dearing forced himself to relax. In this, all was different.

He'd fallen mindlessly in love.

It sounded foolish, and he would never admit to such folly, but the truth knows the heart and vice versa. He had no other way to explain his immediate need to claim Charlotte.

It was that shift in balance, a feeling his life would never be right without her in it.

"I'll never forget the look on Tomlin's face when you fleeced him."

"I didn't—"

"When the poor fool realized you owned his estate and stable." Lindsey placed his empty glass on the table between them as swift as the change of subject. "You shocked the old earl and added another enemy to the list."

"You portray me as ruthless when you know better." His voice held a strong note of warning, and while he considered Lindsey a friend, the man often provoked him in the worst manner. They'd known each other for years, through all kinds of hardship, and Dearing trusted Lindsey without hesitation, yet lately, it was as if the earl possessed a hidden agenda that included irritation of the finest degree.

"All I'm saying is that you've collected an assortment of adversaries, all who would delight in ruining your happiness were your secret ever to be known."

At the mention of exposure, a chill settled in Dearing's stomach. What malevolence provoked Lindsey's rash comment? "Then it would serve all involved that the matter stayed locked in a box where it belongs." He forced an expression of ease, though his innards jerked tight. He'd lost the key, and while he tried to believe it was of no consequence, because whoever found it wouldn't be able to match it to the lock, another power within him, some unnatural shadow of fear, reminded him he needed to keep his past hidden at all costs.

He blew a long breath and turned the tables. "Why aren't you out gambling or whoring? Isn't that how indecently wealthy bachelors waste their evenings?" His amiable tone had evaporated.

"I've heard rumors to that effect." Lindsey donned the grin of a sinner. "But none for me. At least not of late."

A few beats of silence stretched between them until a raucous uproar across the room drew Lindsey's attention, and he was off to nose around without the vaguest acknowledgment.

Dearing watched his friend depart and wondered further at the strange and unexplained happenings lately. He drained his glass and stood. Life had grown complicated, but one thing remained simple: He would continue to court Charlotte, surprise her with gifts and compliments, and strengthen their bond. From that point, their relationship would mature and her love would be had. Sooner rather than later, he remained sure.

Chapter Nine

Sooner presented itself the following day, and anxious to perpetuate his plan, Dearing found Charlotte in the music room studying an assortment of sheet music. Best he get the words out.

"I have a surprise for you," he greeted her with a smile.

"Do you?" She blushed becomingly and offered him her attention.

He'd discovered how easy it was to please his wife, and that in turn pleased him beyond measure. Reluctant to give credit where due, he acknowledged Lindsey had provided good advice. Without a doubt, Charlotte and he were getting on nicely.

"A ride through Hyde Park." He watched her delighted surprise, and the tightness in his chest eased considerably. "I've already had the phaeton readied. If you'd like to fetch your pelisse, we can leave straightaway."

"Oh." Surprise shone in her eyes. "I'll only need a few minutes." She hurried from the room with a quick glance over her shoulder, as if she doubted his sincerity or worried he might change his mind.

In wait, he scanned the sheet music on the rack beside

a carbon pencil poised halfway through a notation. He appreciated how she made sense and melody from the dancing symbols, his relationship with numbers a less fanciful pursuit. He lowered the cover over the pianoforte keys and strode to the paired windows overlooking the sparse gardens behind the house. He'd never given thought to the land's development. Business dealings were confined to the club or within the offices involved by the transactions. He rarely entertained, and were he to have a guest, it was never someone who would take the time to admire a flower garden. It would all need to change with a wife and extended family. This week he would consult a variety of grounds-keepers to hear proposed plans for the area directly behind the house, as well as the narrow path that led beyond the property. Faxman could confirm the appointments. He mentally listed the tasks to be accomplished and, lost in these arrangements, was surprised when Charlotte found him in the same place, her bonnet, gloves and pelisse donned for their excursion.

"This is unexpected." Her wide blue eyes sparkled as she again viewed him in question.

"I'd say it's about time we got on with this courtship." He almost chuckled.

"Courtship?" She shook her head, and the ribbons on her bonnet mimicked the movement. "We're married already."

He did chuckle this time, her expression that endearing. "I doubt we're the first to rearrange the natural order of things." He extended his elbow for her to slip her hand through. He hadn't touched her since they'd kissed and wondered if contact would pacify his randy longing or further ignite it.

The latter proved true.

With that unsettling thought, he escorted her through the foyer, passed Hudson, who crimped an eyebrow in approval, and out the wrought-iron gate to his phaeton, in wait at the curb. His team nickered as he handed Charlotte into the carriage. Apparently, they agreed with his plan as well.

Dearing House was situated in close proximity to the square, and Charlotte often walked the few blocks with her friend Amelia, now Lady Scarsdale. He'd learned from Hudson, a few days earlier, Amelia had visited recently, and that the duchess remained in London for a limited time. Perhaps he would suggest they plan a social call or other pleasing diversion. His mind spun with ways to light Charlotte's face with additional smiles. Had he believed it so simple, he might have approached their marriage with improved finesse instead of overthinking the diabolical consequences of his underhanded manipulation.

He climbed in and left all condemnation at the curb.

Much as expected, the park was abustle with those who wished to be seen, the gravel drive crowded with buggies and gigs jockeying for prime position. He'd purposely had the phaeton outfitted so they might do the same. With a slap of the reins, he sent the team into the fray, maneuvering with eloquence until the horses cantered along the path, and the steady pace afforded them the opportunity to converse.

"It's a lovely day, isn't it?" Charlotte darted a glance around the brim of her bonnet before she looked to the roadway. Several passersby nodded as they proceeded in the opposite direction.

"Indeed the weather is favorable." He paused, his mind at work to produce some type of conversation beyond the mundane. "I glanced at your music arrangements and marvel at how you make heads or tails of the notes." They stalled for a moment, stuck in a bit of congestion.

"I'm sure I'd think the same of your documents, although

I'd enjoy learning more about your maps. I find that subject intriguing."

"I will make a point of sharing a discussion, then." The phaeton jolted forward and he instinctively clutched Charlotte's hand, anchoring her to his side until the carriage wheeled forward smoothly. "Look there." He transferred the reins to one fist and indicated a barouche parked along the cobblestone curb. "We're too far to gain notice or I'd introduce you, but there's the carriage of a business associate and his wife I admire."

"Are they friends of yours?" She shifted on the seat, her head canted to the side, interest palpable.

"Only acquaintances, though the man and his work are popular throughout London. The gentleman operates a lucrative investment business well-known for intuitive profit. He foresaw the invaluable use of the mousetrap long before other London financiers had put on their suspenders."

"Oh." Her eyes flared, the thick fan of lashes aflutter as she blinked and turned to face him. "Do you wear suspenders?" Her voice came out whisper-soft, and he angled closer to hear the words.

For a brief moment, he considered kissing her. Damn, her mouth was tempting. "Not unless you want me to," he answered, and convinced himself to refocus on the roadway. It would present the biggest scandal to be seen kissing in Hyde Park, no matter the lady at his side was his wife. Still, he stole another peek.

She appeared equally as distracted, though she continued their conversation while he adjusted his position in an effort to break his body's command otherwise.

"What a fine man. I admire him already." She twisted to catch a last glimpse backward.

Dearing straightened his shoulders. He'd like to hear his wife say the same of his person.

"Perhaps I'll have the chance to meet the two of them another time."

"I imagine you will, once we begin to accept invitations about town." He didn't need to turn to know Charlotte wore a smile.

Yet that ever-present awkwardness soon became a third person on their outing. They rode along in silence a long moment, and concerned the perpetual plague of inelegance would intrude on their progress, he scoured his mind for a suitable topic, surprised when he produced the ideal tease.

"I've been thinking." His voice danced with the words, though he did his best not to look in her direction. "I should like us to have a dog." He caught his tongue between his molars to keep a grin contained. "A strong, protective animal."

"For the stable?" She pulled in a tight breath, as if she feared his answer.

"No, not at all. A hound cannot provide security if it's not in the house." Unable to resist, he darted a glance to her profile, partially obscured by her bonnet, though he noted the jaunty tilt of her chin. "Wouldn't it be pleasant to have a spaniel asleep at your feet by the fire or keeping you company under your piano while you practice? A friend as well as a protector. So many breeds are loyal and vigilant. A large foxhound or heeler would be a smart choice. They'd chase down any mouse or wayward nuisance on the property." He might have heard her gasp, her cheeks pinkened and eyes on the sky. Damn if she wasn't fetching when she was nervous. He only wished he could spend more time looking at her instead of the road.

"I'm fonder of cats," she managed in a whisper.

"Are you, now?" The bays accomplished a narrow turn and he leaned into the sway, his upper arm unintentionally brushing against her shoulder. "I'm not sure I knew that."

His comment seemed to fortify her reply.

"There are a great many things you don't know about me." She turned, the soft curve of her lips an invitation no doubt.

"And I look forward to discovering them, each and every one." His voice dropped low, as if he shared something confidential, and she flushed deeper when she realized his gaze had settled on her mouth. The clip-clop of hooves on cobbles peppered the air, the ambient noise of the park seemingly apart from the little world they'd created.

"No secrets." She exhaled deeply and touched his forearm with her glove. "We should have no secrets from each other."

"No secrets, then, my lady, on my honor."

The intensity in her eyes spoke more forcefully than her words, and he flicked the reins harder than necessary, making a promise he knew to be a lie. If he could win her heart, perhaps he could—

Too soon, the moment was lost. A cloud drifted over the sun.

"Dearing." Two majestic stallions, raven black and fancifully adorned with braided manes and expensive leather harnesses, aligned with the phaeton. "I cannot believe my eyes, and I haven't a sip of brandy yet today."

"Lindsey." Dearing greeted the earl, his brows lowered in warning. "Mallory." He was again reminded of why he seldom took his carriage through Hyde Park, where one might be forced into conversation with the likes of Mallory, Adams or another unsavory lord. He immediately rued the loss of the unexpected intimacy he'd shared with Charlotte. "Lady Dearing, may I introduce Lord Mallory, a business acquaintance." As an afterthought, he added, "You've already met Lindsey."

Charlotte greeted the two men on horseback, though her mind lingered on the pleasant ride she shared with her husband. They'd flirted and teased, or at least she believed they had, until his sobering mention of acquiring a dog. Then she'd inwardly panicked. A dog wouldn't do. Her kitten remained hidden, and while Shadow was somewhat easier to contain in her youth, eventually the cat would have the run of the house. Adding a dog to the mix would be disastrous. Other than that prickly subject, their conversation had proved effortless.

What had transpired within the boundaries of their relationship to bring about this change? She couldn't reason a cause but was not foolish enough to overthink it. Perhaps they were finally growing comfortable in each other's company.

When he'd captured her attention and agreed to no more secrets, his eyes had glimmered with something intimate and forbidden, as if he promised things she could hardly imagine. It was a wonder her brain functioned at all. Every glance he lent in her direction made her stomach knot tighter. But oh, it was a good sensation.

She assessed his profile as he engaged in lively conversation with Lords Lindsey and Mallory. Her husband's face was cast partially in shadow by an interloping cloud, but there was no mistaking his handsomeness by the very definition of the word. He possessed strong bone structure, a proud angular jaw and dark brows that seemed to make his eyes that much more piercing. No wonder he commanded control within all business negotiations. His masculinity caused her to melt. What would an adversary see?

What a fine stroke of luck Dearing and her father had met with unusual circumstance and not gone nose to nose in a competitive financial transaction. Father was a softhearted, convivial man who would have lost. Somehow, she knew that to be true. Not to suggest her husband was ruthless or underhanded. The opposite seemed evidential. His powerful presence was alluring instead of overbearing. She felt safe, protected, and she wouldn't trade that feeling for all the world. Now if she could only convince him to love her . . .

With unexpected urgency, the bays lurched to the right, unseating her for the briefest moment as a sleek gig whipped past on the outer lane, a high-pitched feminine squeal dislodged in its brisk wake, the laughter strangely reminiscent of her sister Dinah's. Whoever the driver, he had little regard for others, maneuvering his vehicle at breakneck speed along the crowded path. This sudden interruption broke apart Dearing's conversation, and the men said farewell shortly after. The remainder of the ride was less eventful, though when she returned home, her husband proved he had decidedly different intentions.

Hudson had barely stepped away from the foyer when Dearing hauled her against his chest and dragged her toward a recessed alcove. She giggled, much from the surprise of his actions and the thrill of his arm wrapped like an iron belt around her waist. So she hadn't imagined the reverberant tension between them as they sat properly atop the phaeton's bench.

"You wicked temptress." He nuzzled a few kisses against her cheek before he withdrew far enough for her to focus.

"Milord?" The word was mostly question. Out of habit or befuddlement, she'd forgotten his recently imposed rule.

"Jeremy," he corrected before he captured her mouth, her sigh lost to his kiss. But he wasn't finished speaking as he angled across her lips, his words a silken murmur trailed down the sensitive skin of her neck. "Endearing as hell. That's what you are."

"Mmm." Stringing words together seemed beyond her capability at the moment and she willed her tongue to cooperate, to say something, anything, to acknowledge how much she enjoyed his affection. Too late. Her husband demanded her mouth's attention, distracting her tongue with a more pleasant endeavor.

The kiss turned wildly heated in the span of a gasp. Somehow, all the pent-up frustration and anticipation of the past weeks, months, culminated in a profound force beyond her comprehension. It was as though they couldn't draw close enough, kiss deep enough. She was giddy, excited and somewhat dizzy all at once, and the persistence of myriad questions beleaguered her still.

"Charlotte?"

She shivered when he said her name, still unaccustomed to the sound of it. And too his voice had gone rough, a husky, intimate tone, which caused her body to react as if the word stroked over her skin.

"How long is your hair?"

Perhaps he'd experienced the same condition. He managed the question, though she never felt the kiss break. With a desperate vestige of restraint, she answered in a murmur, "To my waist."

This time it was he who groaned.

"I must see it." His fingers slid up her neck, leaving a trail of gooseflesh in their wake. Pins began to fall, and she pulled away to regain her wits, far too aware they remained in the front foyer.

"Here?" She managed just the one word of objection. Perhaps she hadn't reclaimed her balance, or worse, sought his permission to behave scandalously.

"Come abovestairs with me."

He appeared overcome. Delightfully so. A condition she'd never witnessed in her husband and likely unfamiliar to him as well. Still, his low tenor did strange things to her insides, the thrumming resonance unlike any music she'd created, and she fought mightily against the temptation to capitulate.

But why shouldn't she?

He was her husband. She was his wife. This was the way of things.

Still, so much remained unsaid.

And undone.

Yes. Too much remained undone. And she yearned to get to the *doing* part.

She smiled, and the bright spark in his gaze acknowledged her agreement to his intimate suggestion.

"Will you come to my chambers?" She sounded a seductress and the forbidden idea caused her pulse to race harder.

"As my lady wishes." He paused then too, before he reached forward and placed his palm to her face. He cupped her cheek and tilted her chin for a slow, penetrating kiss that seemed to promise every carnal fantasy imaginable. Her knees threatened abandonment and she leaned into his strong support, much to his approval.

A sense of urgency ignited the air and they clasped hands, silently moving to the stairs, where their hurried steps created a symphony of thud and scuffle against the treads. Charlotte didn't look backward or forward, trailing behind Jeremy's lead, their arms extended as if he tugged her along despite she went willingly.

They reached the door to her bedchambers and she paused, slightly out of breath from their rush, or perhaps the invigorated cadence of her heartbeat and the impending promise of what was to come. He paused as well and gently released her grasp before he turned, hand on the doorknob, a half smile on his lips as he opened the door.

"Shall we?"

"Oh, yes." She nodded and stepped over the threshold.

Chapter Ten

Dearing closed the door and threw the latch. He wasn't some green lad fresh out of school with youthful lust and exaggerated fantasies, but damn if his heart beat hard enough to bruise the wall of his chest. The amusing thought that Charlotte had forgotten about the kitten provoked another layer to his enjoyment. When would she realize?

Not a second later, she stepped back and whirled to face him. Apparently, she'd just remembered.

"What's the matter?" He fought to keep a grin contained. "Is something wrong? You're as jumpy as a cricket."

"I . . ." She sucked in a breath, her expression conflicted, "thought I saw a shadow."

"No one's here but the two of us." He glanced toward the connecting door. "But if you'd prefer, we can move to my rooms."

She needed no other encouragement, and in a swish of skirts she stood before the door, waiting for him to lead them forward. The extra moment seemed to provide time enough for her to regather her bearings.

"Peculiar how this door hardly gets use."

Her remark pricked his curiosity. Did the minx realize he'd

visited her rooms? Good thing he'd left the knob unlocked. "Indeed."

His bedchambers held a comfortable warmth that aligned with the heat within his veins. Several lanterns lit the interior as the heavy draperies were closed, and the maid had left an adequate fire burning.

Somehow, through the simple course of paying close attention and initiating agreeable conversation, he'd lost the reins of control. A ride through the park had become a race with patience. By the time Lindsey and Mallory had approached, he could barely keep a thought in his head aside from the desire to return home and strip Charlotte bare.

Damn the vivid remembrance of her silky delicates and what was beneath.

Now, at last, they'd come upon their moment. One that should have occurred ten months before, on their wedding night.

An assertive knock reverberated within the room and he was startled, lost in the prospect of bedding his wife. He should ignore it altogether. Or dismiss Hudson or whatever servant dared to execute inexcusably poor timing.

"Will you answer the door?" Charlotte watched him closely, and he heaved a long breath of patience despite a frisson of irresistible energy humming through every cell of his body.

"One moment." He glanced in the direction of the bed, and Charlotte's eyes strayed in the same fashion. They were of one mind despite that she walked toward the large four-poster as he turned to the door.

He kept his conversation with Hudson brief and waved away Charlotte's immediate inquiry before he gathered her in his arms, flush against his body, too tired from waiting to answer any more questions. That situation, the visitor downstairs in the drawing room, would resolve itself when he decided, disinclined to tolerate another interruption, having stood in his own way long enough.

He lowered his mouth to hers and lost himself in their kiss. She tasted fresh, his lovely wife, and just as he imagined all those many times he'd wished to sweep her off the piano bench and into his arms.

And willing. Charlotte, who he'd assumed would shun him a dozen times over, melted gracefully into his arms. He'd forced himself to overcome hurdle after hurdle—shyness, guilt, self-recrimination—and now, though those same feelings lurked at the ready to remind him of past misdeeds, he ignored their threat and embraced his deepest desire.

The room fell silent, as if she divined his thoughts. The slow crackle of the dissolving fire the only noise aside from their breathing. He broke the kiss and rested his forehead against the top of her head, a few soft strands of hair caught to remind him of an unfinished task.

With gentle persistence, he removed the remaining pins and unwove her braids until her hair spilled about her shoulders. Long ribbons of golden brown fell to her tiny waist, just as she'd suggested. He threaded his fingers through twice, awed and at the same time anxious, his eyes searching her face for any sign of objection.

Her cheeks were flushed, but her eyes sparkled, alert and clear, and he caught her mouth again, his tongue licking into her heat as his hands worked the buttons down the line of her back. Much to his pleasure, she arched against him, impatient and eager. Bloody hell, the constrained passion would cause his heart to stop before he barely began if he did not temper himself.

With a swift fold of fabric, he lowered her bodice to bare one creamy shoulder and smoothed his palm across her breast, hidden beneath layers of silk, though he swore her heat singed him. The tight peak of her nipple scored his palm, traced a line to pulse directly to his groin, where his erection, hard and hot against the falls of his trousers, demanded he move faster.

He exhaled, his breath encouraging gooseflesh against the pale delicacy of her skin before he chased it away with a series of kisses. She wrapped her arms around his shoulders and he nuzzled her neck, trailing affection across the length, aglow from the refracted lantern light.

Lord, he'd waited so long. They both knew what they wanted and precisely where it led, and he was assured by that conclusion whenever his wife nestled closer. Lowering a strap, he untied two ribbons and removed yet another barrier. He wanted to taste her skin, feel the heated satin of her breast against his tongue. Damn if it wasn't the same underclothes he'd yearned to see that he now hurriedly cast aside. All the while they stood in a locked embrace, kissing and not kissing as the situation offered opportunity, the bed a mere two strides away.

How foolish not to take her there.

He turned within their embrace, a waltz step modified by his own devise, and brought them aside the mattress. Her nervous flutter of realization urged him to smile, but he didn't waste the time, his mouth otherwise employed.

At last they sat, in a less-than-decorous movement that evoked her sudden gasp, the mattress buffeting them with softness as he carried her backward. From there he lost his train of thought completely.

His wife lay atop his bed, her hair unraveled in waves of bronze and umber, stark in contrast to her ivory-smooth skin. One half of her bodice lie undone, her breasts pressed high and tight within her corset, as tempting and succulent as forbidden fruit. On the right side, where he'd fumbled his way through layers of silk and cotton, the dusky shadow of one areole was exposed. His prim and proper wife looked incredibly mussed, a temptress in his bed, and never more beautiful. He groaned with pleasure. His cock throbbed with want.

Reclining beside her, he angled her chin and continued their kiss. Her eyes were closed, though the lashes fluttered, and she returned his attention by encircling his neck and pulling him over her. He skimmed his palm up her waist, over soft curves and linen, until he held the weight of her breast in his palm. He brushed his thumb over the tip, felt her shudder and surrender, before he released her mouth to taste her breast instead.

She smelled like gardenias with a hint of lemon, an addictive scent, and he inhaled to keep her deep inside. Every stroke of his tongue over her breast caused a delicious tremor to ripple through her, and his mind sped away at how exquisite it would feel to finally bury himself in her delicious—

A sturdy knock pounded on the door, and she froze beneath him. He carefully withdrew and grunted a curse as the sound came again.

Christ.

Didn't Hudson value his position? His life, for that matter?

"One moment," he muttered by way of apology, though he seethed inside, passion quickly transformed into its counterpart, anger. Still he had to answer. The butler must have an imperative reason for disturbing him twice, didn't he?

"What is it?" Dearing's hushed whisper was anything but quiet.

"My apologies again, milord," Hudson answered.

"Yes, well, explain quickly." He'd cracked the door a mere six inches, blocking the servant's line of vision with his body, though Charlotte would likely have reassembled herself by now, attentive to what occurred at the door. He knew this much about his wife.

"The lady belowstairs is distressed to a point of hysteria." Hudson's grave expression worsened. "Mrs. Hubbles offered tea and refreshments, but it met with refusal. I'm afraid the visitor will not leave until she speaks with Lady Dearing."

"Have you informed the visitor Lady Dearing and I are indisposed? It may be afternoon and calling hours, but that does not mean we're receiving. She will need to call upon her sister another day."

"My sister?"

The hair on the back of Dearing's neck prickled with dread. He hadn't heard Charlotte's approach. She moved as silently as her hidden kitten. Yet one glance over his shoulder revealed she'd listened to the entire conversation. His blunder would not be easily explained.

"Inform the lady we'll be belowstairs shortly." He closed the door and turned, all traces of their intimacy vanished. Charlotte's hair was now gathered and secured in a knot at her neck, her dress refastened aside from a few flagging buttons that likely declared mutiny from the grievous look upon her face.

"You knew my sister waited for me downstairs and you didn't tell me?" Her tone inflected hurt and disbelief, her lovely blue eyes stricken with emotion.

"I didn't see any reason why she couldn't wait a bit."

Voicing his inconsiderate lapse of judgment caused her lids to flare. "So then, this seduction was to be quickly done?" There was no mistaking what emotion held her now. "How selfish and thoughtless. I didn't believe you so."

"Charlotte." He stepped toward her, but she promptly moved beyond his reach. "You misunderstand."

"I couldn't think otherwise."

"If I behaved selfishly it was because I wanted you in my arms. I've waited ten months—"

"By your own admission, that was your doing." She took two steps in an attempt to reach the door to the hall, but he blocked her passage.

"I realize I should have told you straightaway, but I wasn't thinking clearly. Charlotte, all I can think about is you. You consume my brain and chase away coherent logic. Now to have you in my bedchambers, in my bed, after kissing you senseless, I can offer no other excuse."

His sincerity had *some* effect on her, though he wasn't sure to what extent. Her expression softened the tiniest bit, though her eyes still flashed sparks of anger.

"We agreed in the park only a few hours ago that we would harbor no secrets." Her words were spoken harshly, with a confused quality of hurt and anger that made his lie all the more unbearable.

"Let's agree to discuss this later, after your sister leaves," he offered, in hope she would be mollified. "And I wasn't keeping this a secret. Your sister only just arrived."

This met with a sharp glare that might have communicated a number of things, until she spoke. "I have nothing to say to you."

"You will." A lick of frustration made his words a challenge. This was ludicrous. A few moments ago, they were atop the bed in each other's arms.

"I doubt that." She shook her head, and with a breath of disappointment or some other equally dissatisfied emotion, pivoted on her heel and made good use of the adjoining door, slamming it as she left him alone.

Chapter Eleven

Charlotte hurried downstairs toward Hudson, who stood sentry at the entrance of the drawing room. "You have a caller, milady."

Hudson was a tall, likable servant well in to his sixtieth year. His eyes were kind, his appearance pristine, his demeanor beyond efficient, though Charlotte had the distinct impression he wondered at the odd circumstances surrounding her sudden marriage to the master of the house. It wouldn't do to question a member of the staff concerning Dearing's history, and yet Charlotte remained more tempted than she'd ever admit. Hudson undoubtedly knew everything there was to know about her husband or, at least, more than she'd yet garnered.

"Has my sister waited long?" An unexpected tremble revealed the emotion in her question.

Concern marred Hudson's face in a mask of unease. "More than an hour, milady."

Alarm spurred Charlotte's feet into motion. If one of her sisters had arrived unexpectedly at Dearing House, it could only signal trouble of the worst kind, and she'd distinctly heard Hudson tell Jeremy the visitor appeared overset.

Anger toward Dearing's blithe dismissal was renewed in a heartbeat.

Charlotte found her sister in the front drawing room. She'd hardly stepped over the threshold when Louisa whirled to face her, cheeks reddened from crying and hands tightly clasped. Her sister's gray cloak appeared stark against the cream and violet interior, and a foreboding tremor of dread seeped into Charlotte's bones.

"What is it?" She closed the door and rushed to Louisa's side. "Is everyone well? What's brought you here?" She'd only visited the family a few days' before, and planned to write to Mother now that Dearing had agreed a small dinner party was due. Instead, her sister stood before her with red-rimmed eyes and puffy lids in evidence of emotional distress.

"Everyone is fine. Everyone but me. Promise me you won't tell a soul." Louisa shook her head vigorously, her curls swaying with the movement as her tears overflowed. "I don't know what to do or where to go, but I'll need your promise first, Charlotte."

"Of course." She grasped her sister's elbow and gently steered her to a chaise, where nearby a brazier of red coals burned in the hearth. Before Charlotte entered, she'd mentioned to Hudson that a tea tray and refreshments were needed. Hopefully, it wouldn't be long before it arrived. Louisa appeared pale and deeply troubled, but warmth would not solve her problem, nor would tea. Once they settled, Charlotte waited. Her sister was already beside herself with turmoil; rushing her into an explanation would only worsen her condition.

"I don't know what to do." Louisa twisted on the cushion, tears barely withheld. "I'm in trouble of the worst kind. I can't tell Dinah or Bunny. Mother and Father will send me away. I'll be alone through the worst experience of my life.

All because I believed myself in love. I trusted him. I still do. But I don't know anymore."

"Slowly. Everything will turn out right. Tell me what happened." Charlotte sought to console her sister, though a strong wave of apprehension clogged her throat. It wasn't difficult to unriddle what might cause a parent to send a daughter away from home.

"Promise me first."

"Of course I promise." Perhaps not the wisest of decisions. What if her initial assumption proved wrong and Louisa confessed something truly unfixable? Well, then, Charlotte would ask Dearing for his assistance. Once she remedied the circumstance within her own relationship, naturally. The thought brought with it a feeling of firm reassurance despite their quarrel abovestairs.

"I'm—" Louisa's face displayed horror, as if the words were unthinkable. "I'm with child."

Charlotte wasn't prepared for the blunt admission, although some part of her had suspected Louisa's carefree attitude would someday lead her astray. Her sister lived in the moment, unmindful of consequences or repercussions. In truth, Charlotte had already leaped to the same conclusion, but hearing the words spoken in the fraught quiet rattled her soul. She swallowed thoughtfully and digested the news. "Are you certain?" She struggled to maintain an even tone.

How ironic her younger sister should explore physical relations when Charlotte's own body remained chaste. And how would she ever assist Louisa? This transcended the bounds of requesting her husband's help. This trespassed into a singular confidence, and a complicated one at that, when she'd only just demanded no secrets be kept. Still, she'd do anything to relieve the turmoil and doubt in Louisa's eyes. Insecurity wouldn't serve her sister well, no matter how the situation was resolved.

"I've missed my flux the past two months." These words

came out infused with broken sobs and tears. "I've sacrificed my virtue and future for a man who no longer wishes to speak to me. He's all but vanished from London. I haven't seen or heard from him, no matter I've tried."

A knock at the door preceded Mrs. Hubbles, who entered with a maid trailing behind her. The tea tray was set on the table near the corner, and both servants reserved the propriety to silently set about their task and leave just as efficiently.

"Shall I fetch your tea?" Charlotte grimaced at her foolish question. She drew Louisa into her embrace and offered the support needed while Louisa cried out her despair. She moved her sister's hair aside to lightly stroke her back until the emotion abated.

"Do you love him?" Charlotte asked the question, though she couldn't imagine sharing one's self without the emotional bond. It was why she needed desperately to breech the emotional chasm Dearing had created at the beginning of their marriage. Her heart and mind were too closely knit together.

"He's terribly dashing. I couldn't believe he paid me the slightest mind." Louisa sniffled and forced a weak smile as she withdrew from the embrace. "I'm not the sister who usually draws attention."

Her sister's answer wasn't exactly what it needed to be, but Charlotte didn't press. Their situation was bitterly ironic: one sister in love and lacking the physical intimacy, while the other upset for having the opposite.

"Why would you say such a thing?" Charlotte shook her head in the negative and squeezed her sister's hands. "Any gentleman would be lucky to pay you mind."

"Well, he won't even see me now."

Charlotte was surprised but, upon comprehension, reconsidered. Most rakehells denied their indiscretions when women were altered beyond repair. A soiled dove had no place in society. Unwed mothers were often sent to visit a relative, where the child could be born without social disgrace. And then, there was the shame. Her parents had feared the discovery of their impending fiscal ruin, aghast that anyone realized their finances were no longer secure. The family had hardly recovered from the threat of penury. Yet this humiliation was much worse. If Charlotte's marriage had salvaged their reputation and ensured a future for her three sisters, Louisa's actions had condemned the family with a scandal of worse proportion.

"Does anyone else know about this?" Surely Dinah and Bunny would notice if Louisa behaved oddly.

Louisa gave a confident nod. "No. I've kept my meetings private. No one knows anything beyond a few mornings when I've claimed of a megrim or unexpected malaise."

"Are you sure?" Charlotte found it difficult to imagine her sister behaving so secretively. Maids talked, even if it didn't extend beyond household chatter. "How did you manage to meet with this disreputable scoundrel?"

"Please don't judge him. He's a good man. I must believe that true. He's perhaps just as scared and panicked as I." Fresh tears threatened, and Louisa wiped them away. "He probably needs time to think, although I would feel so much better if I could speak to him."

"So he's aware his relations with you have resulted in this situation? A child?" She whispered the unspeakable words, somehow afraid to voice them aloud.

"Yes. At least, I tried to tell him the last time we were together, but he left abruptly. I haven't heard from him since, and I'm not sure if he understands what I attempted to say." Louisa wiped her nose with a crumpled handkerchief and exhaled a sigh of forlorn sadness. "Aside from you, no one else knows, which makes it most difficult. But I had to tell someone. I feel wretched and frightened. I feel—" She broke off on another sob.

"Sometimes love isn't all it seems or what we believe it

to be." Louisa caught her eye, but Charlotte looked away and rushed on, the battle to maintain a calm note in her voice difficult. "I'm sorry you've found yourself in this situation, but we'll solve your problem together." She squeezed her sister's hands in reassurance despite that Louisa's partial answers were hardly helpful. "You can't be sure there will be a child."

"I will soon enough." A tense silence followed Louisa's admittance. "What will I do? Thomas hasn't spoken to me or sent a message. Everything has to be done so carefully, and yet I'm utterly alone in this. I need your help, Charlotte."

"And you have it. I give you my word." Charlotte drew a deep breath. What could she do? How would she help? She couldn't undo the clandestine tryst, but mayhap she could convince the gentleman to accept responsibility. Surely he must care for Louisa to have pursued her. A niggling voice inside her head reminded her that rogues cared little for anyone aside themselves, and so far this person had proved to be no gentleman. Yet Louisa objected when Charlotte labeled him as such. A marriage of necessity was not uncommon and, in a strange parallel, echoed her situation with Dearing. While not forced to salvage her family's security, it followed that the act proved necessary to save their reputation.

"I've written a letter." Louisa rose from the settee with inspired energy and set to work on the strings of her reticule. "I need only to confess my feelings to him and I'm convinced this will all turn around. When last we were together, I was too nervous to speak my heart. I blurted out my fears and hardly made known my thoughts for the future. If I explain to Thomas how much I care for him, it will open his eyes. I'm certain." She thrust a folded piece of foolscap forward. "I've no way to deliver this note otherwise. Previously we depended upon his coy planning to communicate, but with Thomas's sudden silence, I have no

choice but to ask for your help. Will you do this for me?"
Louisa pushed the paper into Charlotte's hands. "Will you
take this letter to him?"

Charlotte stared down at the paper in her hands. It was
unseemly and unacceptable for a woman to call on a bachelor's apartments. The same constraints that restricted
Louisa from visiting her estranged lover applied to most any
female. Charlotte would not invite scandal, not when her
marriage had finally established a course to happiness.

Her mind spun with ideas, formed and rejected at equal
speed. She could hire a messenger to see the note placed
into the gentleman's hands, couldn't she? In that way, no
harm would come to her reputation.

"Please"—Louisa gripped Charlotte's hands meaning-
fully—"don't task a footman or messenger. Most of all,
don't tell your husband, who will interfere in the worst way.
No one else can know in case . . ." She stopped for another
sniffle and then continued, abandoning her previous comment. "By my heart, I must know Thomas has received this
message. The only true way of knowing is if you deliver it
yourself and convey my sincerity. Tell him we must speak.
Please, Charlotte." She indicated a scrawl of pencil on the
folded note. "I've written his address in the corner. I trust
you to gauge his reaction and plead my case if he decides to
ignore my request. A simple exchange of words is all I ask.
Just long enough to explain my feelings."

Charlotte bit hard into her lower lip. She'd stated in no
uncertain terms that she wouldn't tolerate secrets between
herself and her husband, throwing that very thing into their
argument upstairs, and now she contemplated being the one
to break her rule. One look at Louisa's stricken face, though,
and Charlotte knew she had no choice in the matter. Her
sister had sought help and she couldn't fail her.

In truth, this secret had nothing to do with her husband.
Her dedication to Louisa—to all her sisters, for that matter—

superseded any agreement and sense of loyalty she had with Jeremy. This rationalization quieted the little voice in her head that labeled her a hypocrite.

"I'll see this delivered." Charlotte forced a strained smile. "Now, how is it you've come here without alerting Mother and Father?"

"I claimed I was fatigued and needed to rest. Then I snuck out and hailed a hackney. Thomas suggested the ploy, and it worked whenever we planned a meeting." Louisa stood up and retrieved her abandoned reticule, though she didn't turn, her eyes downcast. "You needn't lecture me on propriety or danger. Believe me, I know the boundaries I've ignored, and the risks attached to my actions. I've learned my lesson, but until this matter is resolved I can think of nothing else." She started toward the door.

"Wait." Charlotte followed. "I'll have one of Dearing's carriages take you home. He's already aware you're here, so it makes little sense for us to pretend otherwise."

Her sister gave a stilted nod of acceptance.

"Very good." Charlotte expelled a breath of relief. "This situation is difficult enough without additional risk to your safety. Let me inform Hudson and we'll get you back home. I'll send a note as soon as I see your message delivered. Try not to worry." She folded Louisa into a tight hug, hoping to reassure and at the same time affirm her commitment. "It will all come to rights, I promise." She released Louisa, and with a quick glance over her shoulder, went out into the foyer to find the butler.

They avoided each other. Not a word passed between Charlotte and Dearing for the next two days, and while she attempted to convince herself it was not so different from before they'd kissed, these soundless days, when she'd stare at her sheet music and her husband remained locked in his study, served to amplify loss more than underscore rightness in the matter.

Before, she'd managed by clinging to her music, the latter portion of the day the most unbearable, when sunlight fled and servants vanished into their rooms at night, the weight of the house's silence at its intangible climax. Gone was the echo of a maid's steps in the hall or the clink of dishes cleared from the dining room. Almost as succinctly as clockwork, her husband would disappear into his study and their fragile coexistence would continue.

She didn't question it then. Why hadn't she? He hadn't barred her from the room. Though he kept the door locked, there were times when she might enter, explore, discover. Upon examination, she wondered why she'd never crossed the threshold of his privacy. Was it fear of rebuke, some careful courtesy turned admonishment that kept her paralyzed on the opposite side of the hall? An inconvenient rise of sentiment caused her to swallow hard, her eyes held shut in a long blink. But she forced her lids open. This was now. And now she had no head for the pianoforte, distracted by awakened emotions and barbed remembrances. *Passion. Temptation.* A glimpse of what might lie within reach. All too aware she and Dearing had begun to walk toward happiness, only to discover their path forked again.

Worse, she hadn't acted upon her sister's plea as of yet, conflicted by fidelity toward Louisa and fear of destroying the newfound trust she'd forged with her husband. It kept her awake through the night, her appetite likewise affected, so she took a tray in her room, unaware whether Dearing knew of her absence from the dining table or whether he also avoided the meal.

Now, in the light of a new day and determined to assuage her sister's concerns no matter how confused, Charlotte donned her hooded cloak and said goodbye to Hudson in the foyer. She left Dearing House on foot and walked to the corner to hail a hackney in much the same way Louisa had conducted her clandestine meetings. With any hope, by evening this predicament as well as several other troubling misgivings would be laid to rest.

The address led her to the best part of Mayfair. Louisa had expensive taste in lace trim and fanciful bonnets. Apparently, her discerning interest extended to lovers as well. How many times had she helped Louisa salvage a situation gone awry? Too many to count during their childhood. Carelessly broken china figurines or torn, grass-stained skirts seemed harmless by comparison, yet this was unlike any girlish dare or impulsive decision. This time, the outcome of Louisa's actions would irrevocably change her life.

Charlotte exited the hack. She pulled up her hood, paid the driver quickly and hurried up the stone steps of the front stoop. A brass knocker in the shape of a lion's head gleamed in the filtered sunlight. She forced herself to drop the heavy brass, unwilling to allow indecision or, worse, speculation, to mar her commitment to the task.

An elderly butler answered the door and showed no hospitable kindness. She craned her neck to look down her nose. Tall and starchy, the servant's expression appeared as pinched as if someone had placed their palm upon his face and gathered his features to the center. Uncontrollable laughter, nervous and inappropriate, bubbled up with the thought and tried to force its way out. She managed, just barely, to press her lips tight enough to keep it at bay.

"I've a message for Lord Gordon." She didn't present a card or give her name. Every moment she remained on the stoop was a damaging threat to her reputation.

"The master is not at home. May I take your card?"

A tick of despair, for lost opportunity and dashed hope, contributed to her silence.

The butler, seemingly unwilling to wait a moment

longer, prodded her hesitation. "Would you care to leave your calling card?"

She barely offered her regrets before she pivoted, hurried down the stairs and further to the pavement in search of a hackney for rent. She'd gathered her courage, ridden across town and called at the door with risk of ruination and yet Lord Gordon was not at home. She'd need to repeat the process or, worse, find another way to speak to him on Louisa's behalf. Alas, things would not be reconciled so easily.

Chapter Twelve

"How is it every time I see you of late I'm reminded of a staggering loss in funds?" Lindsey pressed a hand to his coat pocket, the symbolic gesture an exaggeration meant to imply his purse lie at risk.

The deeper meaning was not lost on Dearing. "Have you invested unwisely, then?" He held no doubt his friend wagered heavily on most everything, but how unscrupulous and imprudent the bet posed another question altogether. Their friendship thrived from an ambiguous respect of one's habits, ignoring otherwise surreptitious behavior. For that very reason, Dearing kept his nose out of White's wager book.

"And here I believed everything progressed seamlessly." Lindsey turned a lopsided grin that women too often found charming.

"Only fools believe what they haven't witnessed with their own eyes." Abashed by his retort, which sounded unerringly like Faxman, Dearing returned a speculative stare.

"Noose around your neck too tight?" Lindsey settled in his usual chair.

"I'd rather not discuss it." Yet for no reason he could fathom, he continued to speak. "I'm at a crossroads, undecided whether to throttle my lady wife or kiss her senseless."

"I've found kissing far more pleasant and persuasive by half." Lindsey's waggish outlook was his strongest trait. Another long beat of silence ensued. "No matter the disagreement, you'd best remember one thing."

"And what would that be?" He should have cut out his tongue before asking the question.

"If we're cataloging admirable character traits, you've married far above your rank. Don't give the lady reason to notice." Lindsey enjoyed a low chuckle.

"It's a wonder you don't find yourself at fisticuffs more often." Dearing motioned to a footman. He found no humor in Lindsey's words because, in truth, Dearing worried about the same thing. The house had stood unusually quiet the past two days. And no matter weeks and months had stretched before when neither he nor Charlotte uttered a word, somehow, having caused her to laugh, having tasted her lips and come so close to at last exploring her body, the silence permeated not just every corner of their home but every inch of his soul.

It brought with it an ominous shadow that warned circumstances might forever be altered. When lately he'd believed it possible, he wondered now if she'd ever come to love him. Everything seemed misplaced. Charlotte hadn't practiced the pianoforte either, and he found that one aspect most disturbing as she'd regularly sought refuge in the lovely notes of her music.

"What's taken hold of your brainbox now? You've gone as motionless as stone."

The footman arrived with their liquor, and Dearing used the additional moment to reclaim his façade of comfortability.

"Why were you out riding with Mallory? He's a Mayfair prig with too many opinions, too much time and not enough eloquence. The man interferes where he shouldn't. I've warned you he's not to be trusted." Dearing took a sip from his glass. Expensive brandy had a wondrous way of smoothing over jagged emotions and numbing them into mute abdication.

"I'd rather Mallory believe I consider him a friend. It's wiser to keep the man at arm's length. He's a complicated sort."

Lindsey didn't elaborate, and Dearing allowed the topic to drop, too reminiscent of why he avoided Adams, although the man had lost when it mattered most. Dearing had taken Charlotte to wife.

"Whenever we meet you're unusually concerned with my marital bliss. Have you become a romantic?" Dearing couldn't resist the jibe, though he'd formed a sound theory why Lindsey meddled.

"Hardly. No woman will ever pin me down." Lindsey flashed a devil-may-care grin. "Considering the favors I called upon and the extenuating circumstances of your arrangement, I'm obligated to keep a close watch on your progress."

"As you do with Mallory?"

"Perhaps." Lindsey's answer was more of a murmur.

"Turned nursemaid then, have you?"

"Enough about that."

Dearing might perpetuate an illusion of calm, but the truth was, he couldn't be unhappier with the situation. His argument with Charlotte remained unresolved and their shared silence had become a constant reminder of yet another failure on his part. He needed to speak to her plainly and explain further. He needed to apologize more fully. He stood, finished the liquor in his glass, and walked away from the club, leaving Lindsey to his own devices.

He returned home to find Hudson in the front hall in discussion with Mrs. Hubbles. The two appeared conspiratorial at first glance, hovered over a collection of invitations on a salver.

"Is Lady Dearing in the music room, Hudson?"

Mrs. Hubbles shot her eyes to the butler and then, with a curt bob of her head, scurried from the hall. Her behavior seemed odd, considering the circumstance, but Dearing assumed she meant to offer them privacy.

"No, milord."

"Abovestairs, then." He indicated the staircase with a nod, noting Hudson's forehead furrowed.

"I'm afraid Lady Dearing is out at the moment, milord."

"Out? What time is it?" He'd purposely left White's and returned before the dinner hour in hope of making amends with Charlotte over their quarrel. Without waiting for a reply, he strode to the doorway of his study and eyed the regulator clock on the wall. Had Charlotte visited her parents? The last thing he desired was for his wife to confess her discontent to her family.

Frustration gripped him, intensely so. He'd only just held her in his arms and established a precious trust. He refused to be shut out once again. Most especially when he considered the matter negligible.

"Hudson." He strode into the foyer and skewered the servant with a direct question. "Where is my wife?"

"She didn't say, milord. She left on foot several hours ago." Hudson's grimace expressed discomfit, and he busied himself with the task of collecting invitations into a neat stack on the silver salver.

"On foot?" His echoed questions labeled him a bloody fool, but he was rescued not an exhalation later when Charlotte whisked through the front door, her face a mixture of concentration and disappointment, a regrettable combination. He took in her cloak, a curious choice considering the clement weather. Hudson had the intelligence to evaporate.

"Where were you? When you leave this house, you need to inform a servant." His words came out in a harsh tone he hardly recognized, immediately aware he'd worsened their upset rather than soothed the situation.

"Because I knew you'd left, I didn't expect you to notice my absence."

Her words were crisp, stated with exceptional cordiality and absent of emotion. He fought a wave of despair at her admittance.

Is that what she believed? Or did she choose her reply to wound him? He watched as she removed her cloak. Sunlight gleamed off her hair, honey-kissed brown and silky, massed in a braided coil at her nape. He missed the seductive decadence of threading his fingers through the length.

And yet she questioned whether he knew of her presence? He couldn't keep himself from the condition. Her existence breathed on the periphery of his awareness.

For the life of him, he couldn't decipher his wife. It was as if she were a map with no key, an unexplored land, both dangerous and paradisiacal. Damn it all to hell, he had no intention of ending his quest.

"I returned early. I wished to speak to you concerning the other evening." There. He had said it. Now to add his apology. "I should never have detained you or kept you from your sister. I can only offer selfishness and my desire to be in your company as explanations, albeit unacceptable excuses." He'd achieved his goal and let out a relieved breath.

"Louisa was troubled." She appeared reluctant to explain further.

"So then, more fault falls upon my shoulders."

"Thank you for saying so."

Had they returned to the stilted conversation and awkward company of only a few weeks prior? Would oppressive quiet replace their recent convivial mood? He wouldn't allow it.

"Dinner will be served soon. We can talk about your sister's worries over the meal." It was an olive branch. An opportunity to see if she would accept his apology and make amends.

"I'd rather not." She averted her eyes and looked toward the stairs. "I should go to my rooms and change."

He wanted to grab her by the shoulders and give her a shake, force her to remember how things had been only a short while ago. Perhaps a kiss would do it. Yes, a kiss would awaken her dulled memory. But his wondering lingered too long and the moment was lost. As he grappled for words and found none of them acceptable, she swished past him in a flurry of skirts to leave him alone in the hall.

Close to weeping, Charlotte hurried down the hall to her bedchambers and rushed inside, blinded by anger, her vision blurred with tears. Why couldn't she sort out her feelings for her husband? Why must every encounter become a trial? The comforting rub of silky fur wrapped around her ankles as she crossed the threshold and, overwrought with emotion, she belatedly closed the door.

She flung herself on the mattress. An immature response to a delicate, *mature* circumstance. Her mind crowded with concerns. An ill-formed awkward marriage at odds. A sister unwed and with child. Distrust. *Secrecy.* The very thing she despised.

Rolling to her back she stared at the white lace canopy, an overflow of tears quick to run paths down her cheeks. Perhaps things weren't as terrible as she believed. It still remained possible her sister wasn't pregnant. That Lord Gordon would behave honorably. Certainly, her family would never reject Louisa's child.

And Dearing . . . Their argument was an excuse for larger issues. Unknown emotions and diffident conflicts. Was her quick anger just another defense to protect herself from further heartache and rejection? She couldn't hold him accountable overlong or he'd ask questions she couldn't answer. She'd promised no secrets, but Louisa's condition and its many complications weren't her problem to share, the matter too private.

Charlotte would never believe Dearing purposely sought to cause Louisa anguish or acted in a mean-spirited manner. More likely he spoke with honesty when he'd apologized and had become too possessed with their intimacy. In that light, she should feel inordinately flattered his desire had wiped all thought from his brain.

A feeble smile replaced her sadness. She exhaled, long and thoroughly, finished with tears. She needed to apologize, to make things right and seek his advice because she did not want to skulk around Mayfair seeking the rogue who took advantage of her sister. In this, she needed her husband's assistance.

Chapter Thirteen

Enough.

Dearing had had enough.

He took the stairs two at a time, his footsteps hard on the treads. Once upstairs, he flung open the door to his bed-chambers, barely aware of the cat who shadowed his heels. He paced before the adjoining door to Charlotte's rooms. Twice, thrice and then not at all.

Hell.

Bloody hell.

He twisted the knob to enter her bedchambers without so much as a knock and booted the door closed behind him. Charlotte startled. The counterpane had been pulled back to reveal crisp white sheets where she'd reclined on the bed before he'd entered. But she shot straight up now, her face a mixture of tearstains and revelation.

A portrait of loveliness.

He wouldn't allow her beauty to detract from his purpose. Enough of this ridiculous argument and pretense, their cat-and-mouse game beyond frustrating. He'd had his fill. Time to finish what he'd begun two nights before.

"Jeremy."

His name on her lips was a gift. He'd half-expected her

to rail at him for invading her bedchambers unannounced. Hope, a useless emotion, stirred with vigor, and he nudged it down. Life had a peculiar way of turning one into a liar, truth more destructive than falsehood.

"Charlotte." He swallowed hard and stepped to the edge of the mattress. "I dislike this silence between us." Her wide eyes searched his face. What did she wish to see? "I'm sorry I behaved thoughtlessly concerning your sister's visit." There. He couldn't state it more plainly. Words came much easier now.

"I know." The corner of her mouth twitched and inched upward the slightest.

"Please extend my apologies to Louisa." He breathed in relief. "I take it everything is resolved?"

"She needed to speak to me, just as you needed to right now."

And then she shifted on the bed, coming up on her knees so she was nearly matched, her petite height not aided enough by the mattress. But surely it was an invitation.

He leaned in, closing the distance between their mouths, his longing on such a tight leash, he feared his heart would give out before he finally tasted his wife and savored her beauty in every aspect.

Words were replaced by actions. His fingers worked buttons and ties without coherent thought, her touch both tentative and bold as she too sought to remove the barriers between them. At last, they existed as one mind and body.

Mostly body on his part. At least at this moment.

In less time that it had taken for him to screw up his courage and enter his wife's rooms, they were undressed to their intimates. His heart thundered in his chest. Her gauzy chemise did little to conceal her full breasts, the satiny skin pinkened from their haste or, with any luck, anticipation. His cock twitched hard and anxious in his smalls. This immediate lust for his wife remained a reflex he hadn't mastered, yet he wouldn't fall upon her like some sex-starved scoundrel.

No matter he yearned to do exactly that.

Repeatedly.

Pined, dreamed, hungered . . .

He watched, mesmerized, as she raised her arms to re-lease her glorious hair. The action brought her breasts to the neckline, the points of her nipples traced in dusky display through the thin fabric. He drummed a concerto against his bare thigh and searched for patience. His wife was delec-table. Did she have any idea how sorely he wanted her?

Her hair fell and so did he, deeper into the abyss he recognized as love but hadn't given a voice. Silence consumed the room instead. This was a long-sought and delicious game, and he *would* savor it.

Then onto the bed, where he caged her beneath him, his arms supporting his weight, his mouth level with hers. He shifted slightly, and the bedframe creaked with such force, the vase of pale blooms on the nightstand jiggled in protest. He wasted but a flick of his eyes on the distraction. His wife was a romantic. He liked that about her. He liked so many things about her.

Most especially the way she felt beneath him.

He sank lower and captured her lush lips in a kiss. Her response was all he could hope for, and their tongues met on a slide of consent. He deepened their embrace and rolled to the side, taking her with him, her surprise expressed in an abrupt gasp that offered him a more luscious taste of her mouth. Each stroke of her tongue reverberated in his groin, yet he held back. He'd waited too long to rush the moment.

Side by side, his fingers gathered the hem of her chemise and raised it in an effortless sweep to reveal smooth, pre-cious skin. Collected in his fist, he removed the garment and cast it aside to the bedlinens. At last, Charlotte in her lacy silk pantalets, was bared to him in pure honesty.

Without warning, a troublesome thought intruded. He should tell her everything. Confess it all before they made love. A piercing ache persisted right below his breastbone, and he held his breath, hoping to shut it away. If only he could cleave the truth and discover the correct words to expose what he'd done. But he knew what naked candor would cost, how his heart would be destroyed. Undoubtedly, she would leave. Yet didn't he owe her that choice?

He pulled free of their kiss, and her eyes fluttered open. And so he watched her, rapt and breathless, though the words wouldn't leave his tongue.

Charlotte stared into Jeremy's lovely brown eyes and envisioned her future. Her husband was straitlaced, duty-bound and terribly traditional, but this epitome of a gentle-man beside her was also a hot-blooded, passionate lover, evidenced by the hard, hot erection pressed against her bare thigh. She laced her fingers through his hair and pushed a too-long lock away from his brow. His throat flexed, as if he wished to speak but had thought better of it and kept the words inside.

She'd come to accept his shyness as endearing, if nothing else. If only she could read his mind. Still, she wasn't fool-ish and would not concentrate on logical thought when at last she was to become one with her husband. She would give him her body. He already consumed her heart. Perhaps, in this act, he would trust her with his, open himself to what their marriage could be. For now, it was little more than words on paper. A trap of secrets, hurtful omissions and polite regard.

He eased over her, deliberately, as if he aimed to make

no mistakes, as if any could be made, this broad-muscled man atop her in bed. Her skin seemed deliriously sensitive and she once again closed her eyes and summoned acute awareness. Her senses awakened to magnify their intimacy. She inhaled, having come to know his scent and covet the masculine spice of shaving soap on his skin.

She'd never lain with a man, but she'd envisioned this moment more times than she could count. Now the cool linen met her back while the heated shelter of her husband's body nestled against her in a glory of sensation and texture. The hair on his chest teased her nipples, alert and tender.

She fluttered her fingertips with featherlight pressure over his shoulder, across his chiseled collarbone and muscular chest, to learn every smooth curve and hard indentation. His muscles jerked beneath her exploration, but she held her eyes closed, lost to feeling, unwilling to relinquish the divine and sensuous pressure of her husband's weight against her body. She settled her palm over his heart and counted the rhythm as succinctly as a metronome marked the notes of her music. She memorized the melody and made it her own.

His hand skimmed her ribs and settled on her waist to grip her hip gently.

"You feel—" He murmured, low and husky in her ear, and a fresh shiver of excitement dotted her skin, regardless he didn't finish the sentence.

Any lingering apprehension unraveled and reformed into intense longing.

He made a soft, pleasured sound deep in his throat, somehow rumbling upward from his chest, and she imagined he would enjoy their joining as much as she. He nuzzled her neck, the prickly growth of new whiskers abrading her jaw, the texture not unlike Shadow's tongue on her fingertips, though her body's reaction proved incredibly different.

It consumed.

He consumed.

And she grew wet and anxious between her thighs, an unfamiliar but welcome response. If sex without a bond of love could be this wondrous, this powerful and completing, her heart soared with the future's potential. If only she could convince Jeremy to love her in return.

He settled his hand against her breast, her nipple taut and aching, the drag of his palm against the tip sweet agony. She arched into his touch, wanting more pleasure/pain. He growled something incoherent against her shoulder, licking, tasting a path downward. He shifted, and the mattress did as well, the vase of flowers nearly upsetting. He paused, aware of the teetering bouquet and, without looking, reached across to set it to rights. He withdrew a bloom and laid the rose upon the pillow, the fragrant scent beside her cheek. Then he returned his attention to her body.

She wasn't prepared for an assault when his mouth covered her nipple, hot and persistent. His tongue lathed across the tender peak, and she writhed beneath him, anchored to the mattress by the weight of his thighs. His hands at her ribs slid lower to rest on her hips, as all the while she surrendered to his attention. With her eyes closed, everything seemed more intense, more alive. The fragrance of the flower beside her, the damp insistence of her sex, the rough burn of his whiskers and the decadent heat of his wicked tongue.

She lost herself to it, offering herself for his worship.

The first stroke of the rose across her skin left a trail of gooseflesh in its wake. Again, she was caught by surprise. Opening her eyes, she watched as he drew a line with the lush-petaled bloom from her collarbone, down between her breasts and below to her navel.

His irises reflected the candlelight, aglitter with mischief and intention. "Relax, darling."

Her body did the opposite, surprised by the brush of his chin against her hip. What was her husband about? She couldn't ask. But she could look. Through lowered lids, she watched the sensual image of her husband, his glossy hair and sharp profile barely visible over her navel. She couldn't manage the myriad emotions and pressed her eyes closed in a surrender to ecstasy.

"So very lovely." The vibration of his voice against her inner thigh was thrilling and terrifying, and she tensed, every muscle locked, though she swallowed any feeble objection.

Was that a brush of flower petals against her skin or did she imagine the velvety, barely there caress? She willed herself to breathe, not to lose herself so much to sensation she couldn't remember each indelible detail.

She eased by degree, the pressure of his fingers as they smoothed over her skin and settled at her waist a steadying force, though she kept her eyes closed. Whatever scandalous, delectable activity he meant to initiate, she would experience it through awareness, not shock.

He traced a fingertip across her core and she tightened her muscles, awed at the vibration that rippled through her body, its beginning and end a divine pleasure. Each repeated touch lured her farther from concern and respectability, but she ceased thinking at that point, too fascinated with her husband's masterful attention.

With precise intent, his fingers played across her sex, stroking and rubbing with exact determination. His touch, gentle yet commanding, seemed to know every secret place to evoke sensation. Back and forth, he slid his fingers with expert skill, and she gave herself over to his mastery, the pleasure unfathomable. Her body hummed from the inside out, lost in a delicate power with a building force she'd never known. What would happen? Was the pleasure unending?

The first stroke of his tongue against her sex bolted her upright, her hands desperate to catch the bedding. He made an abrupt sound of gratification and murmured endearing words before he punished her again with another stroke of divine torture. She clenched her eyes, startled and at the same time drenched in sensual awareness.

Like a penny cast into a wishing well, she floated, dipped, whirled, all the while unmindful of the inevitable landing. An intense tremor of pleasure racked through her and she rocked her hips in what could only be a natural rhythm, inexperienced as she was with the unknown intensity. Had she any control over her emotions, she'd blush darker than the rose petals crushed on the linen sheets.

And then, swift and nimble, in less span than a heartbeat, every frisson of delight gathered into one acute pulse, so overwhelming and encompassing, she succumbed without thought, tight yet free, powerful and at the same time weak.

She lay still until it passed, forever changed and captivated and all the while fully aware her husband had pleasured her with his fingers and tongue. He'd generously offered her precious intimacy while he remained wholly unsatisfied. He came up beside her to lie on his back and stare at the canopy in a similar pose as another moment passed. With unexpected tenderness, he found her hand, limp on the coverlet, and laced their fingers together. The room remained silent, and inside her, a rare bud of hope unfurled.

She had little knowledge of how to offer him gratification, but his jutting sex, thick and hard against her side, seemed an obvious place to begin. Dismayed to break the tender gesture and pull her hand from his, she turned and placed her palm atop his flesh. His erection twitched against her fingers, hot and eager, and she watched his eyes fall closed, perhaps lost in feeling much the way she'd savored his attention.

So much was unresolved between them, but they could have this. He'd offered her pleasure, despite withholding the words she truly yearned to hear. Still, this was a beginning of sorts. They'd done nothing in the traditional order since their first introduction.

Discarding sensibility, she furthered her exploration, noting the way his body tensed and relaxed, how his strong thighs, dusted with light brown hair, flexed whenever she touched his skin. His erection awed her. He seemed most sensitive near the crown, the texture different, softer and pinker. What would he do if she placed a kiss there? He'd brought her immeasurable pleasure in the same fashion. She licked her lips with the suggestion. Could she be so bold? What would Amelia—no. What would *Charlotte* do?

With a faint huff of satisfaction, she adjusted her position on the mattress, her hair trailing along to cause a flickering smile on her husband's lips. Then she shifted her attention lower, and before any more wandering thoughts distracted, leaned in and kissed the tip of his sex.

He jerked, yanked from his languid slumber and thrust into awareness by her daring action.

"Charlotte," he groused.

Had she angered him? Done something wrong? Something shameful? Mayhap touching him there with her mouth was unseemly for a wife. Did it speak of depravity or an act expected of a courtesan, not a spouse? Still, a woman had her own prerogatives.

"Do that again." His husky command warmed her from the inside out. Apparently, her husband was more open-minded than she'd assumed.

With a shy smile, she matched his eyes and obeyed. This time she peeked her tongue out for a teasing lick. He tasted

salty and . . . *male*. No other word described the experience.
She did it again. A little slower this time, with a little more
confidence.

"Charlotte." Again her name rumbled through him. "Do
you have it in mind to punish me?"

His question slayed her newborn confidence. "Did I hurt
you?" She reared up, all at once unsure of herself.

"Come here." He reached for her hand and tugged her
upward until they lay nose to nose on the bed. "There is
only so much torture I can bear." The twinkle in his eyes
confessed he experienced no pain at all.

"Then what would you rather I do?"

This question elicited a chuckle so rich, she couldn't help
but join him.

"And to think I have you to bed for the rest of my life."

She inhaled sharply at his comment, all at once enthralled. His words implied a happy future together. Oh,
how she loved her husband. If only his affection would grow
in kind. Surely their intimate bed play was a step in the
proper direction.

Chapter Fourteen

Dearing stared into Charlotte's cerulean-blue eyes and wondered if she would find it in her heart someday to forgive him. He wasn't foolish enough to believe his concealed secrets, most too ugly to examine, wouldn't worm their way out of hiding. He worked with great effort to remain detached, bury decisions and information that revealed harsh truths, while likewise maintain a modicum of sanity. Yet the more he opened his heart to emotion and the stronger the intimacy shared, likelihood of discovery crowded the issue. No sooner would he let his guard down than disaster would rush in. Or so he believed at times.

Lord help him, he wanted her. Not just as his wife on a document signed under the sight of witnesses. He wanted her beneath him on this bed. His body joined to hers. His cock throbbed with aching want. Damn the consequences, he couldn't pull back now.

But what if a child was conceived due to his selfish, besotted heart? A cheeky son or darling daughter would bind Charlotte to him forever. *Or not.* Were she to uncover the truth and turn her back, she could remove herself and their child from the house as fair punishment. She could insist on living in the countryside where her bitterness would poison his child against him. A more punishing result he did not know.

No, he should wait and allow their bond to grow stronger. He pulled the coverlet across his middle and met Charlotte's expectant gaze.

"Have I angered you?"

Her incredulous tone thrust another knife into an open wound, her confusion at his shift in mood understandable. The air went still. Even the dwindling flames in the hearth did little more than hiss their disgust.

"Not at all." He cleared his throat, aware the moment was nearly lost. "We should—"

His voice snagged as her hand found his erection beneath the coverlet. She canted her head to the side, and he imagined the wheels of logic turning furiously in his wife's capable mind in a desperate attempt to unriddle his behavior.

She stroked him again, smooth and insistent, her fingers around his hard flesh.

And he surrendered.

He dropped to the pillow, where, after a quick examination of the canopy lace, he closed his eyes to all haunting realities and yielded to wondrous sensation.

She worked him into a painful hardness in less than a few breaths. Or mayhap it was his own ramped desire and the interminable wait for this shared intimacy. Every muscle tightened at his mounting climax. He slit his eyes and viewed his beautiful wife, her concentration admirable as she couldn't see a thing below the coverlet across his waist.

Maybe it was better this way. The first time. Not unlike the manner in which they wove their days together, sincerity hidden below the surface, veiled by obstruction and complicated emotion.

No. He thrust the coverlet aside. He'd create no more barriers between them.

He located her hand atop his sex and wrapped his fingers

with hers before he groaned a deep sound of gratification. Another stroke and he found his release, their hands tight as his cock pulsed with pleasure.

Moments later, she slipped free. She scurried to the washstand and returned with a damp towel. Giving him her back, she pulled her chemise over her head, but not before, in an unexpected and erotic discovery, he noticed the dimples on her lower spine just above her derrière. His wife's body was a treasure trove of delight.

Unaware of his avid attention, she climbed atop the mattress, a soft smile curling her lips. With the bedlinens between them, he drew her lithe warmth closer, nestled to his side where his breath eddied across her temple to stir the finest hairs.

A bevy of fresh ideas and hopeful promises teased Charlotte's brain as she slipped from Dearing House the following morning and approached the corner in search of a hackney for hire.

After yesterday, she possessed more determination than ever to settle Louisa's problem to the most advantageous solution, all the while strengthening the tenuous and *intimate* bond made with her husband.

As she walked, she summoned the blissful memory with ease, the time spent in his embrace cherished. They'd talked and cuddled, her heart full, for somehow their awkward relationship had become amiable and playful, as she'd forever hoped.

Later at dinner, their cheerful conversation continued, and afterward she'd played two selections on the pianoforte. They'd ended the evening with a slow, sensual kiss that spoke of more tantalizing embraces on the morrow.

His absence at breakfast hadn't dampened her fledgling optimism in the least, her mind honed to how she must unburden her sister and resolve the problem of Lord Gordon. Louisa read too many gothic novels and lived life with a romantic, and at times infatuated, view of circumstances. It would be fairly easy to lead her astray if a rakehell decided to expend the effort. She knew nothing of Lord Gordon. Was the gentleman a scoundrel? All the more dangerous the situation then, for her to be seen in his company. She laced her fingers tightly determined to protect her identity as well as her fragile hope.

Now, as she arrived in Mayfair and disembarked from the hack, she pulled her cloak closed at the throat, raised the hood and aimed for the gentleman's address. It would be difficult to explain her presence here if she gained notice. Best she scurry up the steps, deliver Louisa's message and be done with the errand.

Prepared for the composed reception from the same phlegmatic butler at the door, she squared her shoulders and raised her chin, startled in midmotion when the door opened although she hadn't knocked. A tall, handsome gentleman in impeccable attire stood within the frame. The voice and shadow of another male loomed behind him.

"Pardon me." Her words stammered out and confidence teetered as she quickly realized the difficulty of the predicament. She'd hoped to speak to Lord Gordon discreetly, but that notion was lost. Lingering on the front steps increased the risk she'd be recognized by any passerby or inhabitant of the house. Gossip proved a reckless, unjust animal, seeking to draw scandalous conclusion from threadbare fact. If she didn't act quickly, the gabble-grinders would label her a harlot and Dearing a cuckold before the Ton sat down for dinner.

"May I assist you?"

The smooth tenor of the refined gentleman pulled her into the present with slapdash speed. But what to do? If she scurried off the stoop she would be forced to return to this place a third time. She swallowed her fear. There was no decision to be made.

"I need to speak to Lord Gordon."

"I am he."

Unease caused the hair on the back of her neck to prickle. Lord Gordon stepped forward and she moved back, while the second gentleman crowded the stoop, his face visible in profile.

Her heart lurched, then seized in mutiny. She matched eyes with Lord Mallory. Indeed things were more complicated than she'd ever imagined.

"Might I have a private moment with the lady?" Gordon canted a sidelong glance in Mallory's direction, while he took in her appearance with patient assessment.

Having received a formal introduction only a few days earlier, she was forced to acknowledge him. "Lord—"

"If you'll excuse me." Mallory stepped beyond Gordon and removed himself from the stoop. "Aren't you a clever fellow to find a lovely stranger at your door this morning?"

The inflection and tone in the latter portion of Mallory's sentence evidenced he knew she was nothing of the kind. He flashed a grin, though his expression held a dangerous edge. Why would he behave as if he didn't know her and cut off her greeting before Gordon realized they were acquainted?

Her eyes trailed after Mallory, who moved to the far pavement with his back turned, well out of earshot.

"I am Lord Gordon. How may I help you?"

Again she realigned her purpose and with a flip of her cloak removed Louisa's message from her pocket.

"My sister, Louisa, asked me to deliver this message in trust you'll read it and agree to call upon her or, at the least, respond somehow. She's confused and distraught." Gordon's face transformed at the sound of Louisa's name, and Charlotte paused to measure his reaction. A spark of alarm lit his eyes, a shadow of deep sorrow followed directly after.

"You shouldn't have come."

He didn't reach out to accept the message, and Charlotte refused to move, though her pulse galloped with a culmination of panic and despair. Her sister would be sorely disappointed and mayhap in the family way with no alternatives. She needed to impress the importance of the situation.

"Please, Lord Gordon, you must understand, Louisa is deserving of at least one conversation. She's explained to me the extent of your relationship." She nudged the message toward his stomach. "Take this." She didn't dare glance to the curb, where Mallory likely watched the interaction. She could only solve one problem at a time.

With a long breath that seemingly brought about a decision, he took the message from her and placed it inside his breast pocket. "Thank you. If the situation warrants my attention, I will find a way to resolve it."

It was Charlotte's turn to dispel a sigh of relief and she turned, chin down and eyes to the pavement as she left in the opposite direction to which Lord Mallory stood.

"Faxman, have you balanced the total revenue from the second quarter?" Dearing rounded his desk and approached the secretary's table. Energetic sunlight warmed the room, but it didn't matter; he still basked in the result of last evening. Holding Charlotte's petal soft skin against his body was glorious, their intimacy cherished as a sign of how well things progressed in their relationship. He glimpsed the cherrywood bookcase on the far wall, where he'd locked away his secrets within a double panel. He'd placed the leather box inside the compartment and closed the wood door, no one the wiser. A few volumes and a miniature framed map of the world graced the shelf to give the appearance of collected whatnot.

"Indeed." The wiry employee met him halfway across

the room, his hands full of papers balanced atop a thick ledger. "If you've a moment, I've come across additional discrepancies that beg for explanation. Your transactions are always fastidious, so the concern this is my oversight and not yours provoked me to investigate. I'd hardly be worth my salt if I committed errors in mathematical calculation, although as my father often reminded, a fair degree of learning comes from failing." Faxman shook his head in dismissal. "Though I'd rather not fail at all."

Faxman's father talked too much, especially from the grave. Dearing swallowed a sudden pulse of concern. Damn him for hiring an intellectual and far-too-conscientious secretary. How much had the man uncovered? "What has caused your concern?"

"There are numerous inconsistent imbursements listed in varying amounts every other week during the last six months. Significant missing funds have been transferred to a singular account, and these totals match equivocally with the profit garnered from the Middleton Railway."

Dearing considered his reply. He'd need to supply something suitable else Faxman believe him dicked in the nob. "It's a complicated matter, having to do with my recent wedding." Perhaps his explanation sounded sufficiently vague and personal enough to ward off the secretary's inquisitiveness. Dearing knew he'd buried the truth adequately if Faxman didn't persist or otherwise surmise.

As an exercise in efficiency, his thoughts sprinted through the negotiations around his wedding vows. It all occurred rather quickly, as was necessary. The proposal was accepted, paperwork drawn and signed, amid a flurry of plans with the goal of securing Charlotte as his wife within a fortnight. One might think his motive centered upon the controlling interest in the railway, but any fool who believed that rot didn't understand love.

All the monies earned from transactions connected to his nuptials were tallied, calculated and summed into reserve, which eventually funneled back into its original source, paid in full to the last penny. If anyone succeeded in unriddling the maze of calculations to question what Dearing had gained by marrying Charlotte, he'd gained *her*.

Still, he could not supply Faxman further elucidation. His marriage remained an unaccountable truth. If Faxman persisted, he would simply dismiss the subject and, if necessary, dismiss the man.

"I see."

And perhaps he did. The secretary snapped the ledger closed and replaced it on his desk.

"I remain unsettled on your behalf, milord." This time, Faxman came forward with a single sheaf. "I received this inquiry yesterday and didn't consider it important until I traced the series of payments through your ledger history."

"What is the content of the letter?" Patience at a minimum, Dearing snatched the paper from Faxman's hand and set his eyes to the words. Bloody hell. It was worse than he'd imagined. Charlotte's father had hired an investigator to look into all failed negotiations and business transactions. The controlling share of the Middleton Railway would certainly fall into that category. Would Lord Notley suspect Dearing of unscrupulous dealings? He folded the foolscap and placed it inside his breast pocket. "Please keep me informed of any other inquiries of this nature." He didn't elaborate.

"Of course." Faxman moved toward his desk, the efficient worker likely anxious to continue with his work. "Your accounts are impeccable. I'm certain there's a plausible explanation." He paused, but only the length of two ticks on the regulator clock. "My father was fond of reminding me that worry gives the slightest concern an unmistakable shadow."

"Indeed." Dearing rolled the words around in his brain. Not an unmistakable shadow but a life-destroying, cataclysmic end. A plausible explanation existed, but he'd be damned if he'd ever offer it a voice. "Let's leave off early today, Faxman. Too much brain work can fatigue later sport." He smiled, his mind already planning a delightful surprise for Charlotte. He enjoyed the playful activities centering around her music and offered a bridge in their relationship.

A smile tempted; he'd almost forgotten, Cricket had somehow taken residence in his rooms. Did his lady wife realize her adorable discretion was literally out of the bag? Best he check on the pet before seeking Charlotte.

Faxman gathered his things and left straightaway. After a fruitless search for the kitten, Dearing returned downstairs and visited the music room, but there too he found no one. He lingered and instigated another pleasant discovery for Charlotte before he sought out Hudson in the front hall.

"I wish to speak to my wife." Said in those words, it sounded as if he spoke to a falling star or rubbed the outside of a magical brass lamp. The fanciful ideas provoked another smile. "Do you know her whereabouts?"

Servants knew everything in a household. *Well, almost everything.* But that was another matter altogether.

"She's not at home at the moment, milord."

"Again? Has she gone to visit a friend?" From recent inquiries at White's, he'd learned the duke and duchess were no longer in London. He regretted not having arranged an invitation of some sort to please Charlotte. This was a small but consistent failing on his part. Although the role of husband was a new business for him. At last he'd found his voice and therefore his way.

"I don't believe so." Hudson didn't offer more.

"Then where is she?" His heart gave an uncomfortable twist, reminding him he beleaguered a servant for information he should know himself.

"I cannot say with surety. Lady Dearing left on foot some three hours ago, milord."

"On foot? Again?" His mind stuttered to a stop. Where could she be off to without the use of the carriage? "Please notify me when she returns. I will be abovestairs." He turned on his heel, brows furrowed as he considered the whereabouts of his wife and the awkward comparison she existed as unaccountable and elusive as the kitten who hid in the shadows.

Chapter Fifteen

Charlotte slipped through the front door and aimed to reach the hall undetected. Anxious to send a note to her sister, she climbed the stairs and hurried to her rooms. She wasn't one made for subterfuge, and her pulse beat triple time. Once inside, she sank against the door and sighed with relief, somewhat amazed she'd made it through the house without crossing paths with anyone.

Though one concern was quickly replaced with another. The lingering worry that Lord Mallory would mention her appearance at Lord Gordon's doorstep pricked her better sense to remain on guard. With any hope, the passage of time would decrease Mallory's opportunity to share and he would eventually discard the notion. The last thing she desired was for Dearing to hear a distortion of the truth. Not now, when things were finally settling into contentment. That considered, she would need to keep Dearing home and not off to his club, where a stronger likelihood presented itself.

A slight smile tugged at her lips. She delighted at the idea of holding her husband captive. Perhaps she should begin straightaway by luring him into the music room for another heated kiss. She could play a favorite arrangement, a passionate sonata or ardent orchestration, and then things would progress with natural ease.

She whispered a sound through her lips meant to call Shadow from hiding, but the kitten didn't appear. When was the last time she'd seen the little darling? With a hasty search beneath the bed skirt and a peek behind the draperies, she made a mental note to speak to her maid. Charlotte couldn't have Shadow slinking around the house until she was sure Dearing wouldn't object. She wondered about his reaction as she glanced in the mirror to pin a few disobedient strands of hair back in place.

Anxious to send word to Louisa, she dashed off a few lines and sealed the paper before she hurried downstairs. Music proved her escape and comfort in times of joy or distress. Today, she was anxious to play Mozart's *Piano Concerto No. 17*, a composition in three movements and a challenge to her current ability. Having practiced the arrangement for weeks, she knew she was close to mastery. One took pride wherever it could be found.

She met Mrs. Hubbles in the front hall and asked for her note to be sent by messenger. Charlotte also learned Dearing recently had returned from Threadneedle Street. Now, as she entered the music room, she found a sudden smile. Mrs. Hubbles had drawn the curtains wide and a sweeping view of the gardens behind the house brought with it ample sun. A few of the black poplar and honey locust trees sprouted to new life after a dormant winter spell. Charlotte welcomed the change of season and the prospect of fresh plantings in the yard. No vase full of flowers graced the corner of the pianoforte, but she stifled that note of disappointment. How silly to believe her husband would continually gift her with roses. She wasn't a starry-eyed debutante but a mature married woman. Of late, Dearing caused her to feel more womanly than even she'd believed possible.

Dismissing the amusing realization, she settled on the

bench and leafed through the sheet music that rested against the rack. Various papers in scattered order were reassembled quickly before she scanned the obedient symbols in patient wait of her attention. When she lifted the pianoforte's wooden lid, her breath caught.

Across the ivory keyboard, in patient wait of *her*, was a single rose, crimson in color and barely unfurled. Its long stem extended more than a dozen keys, while its green leaves and lush petals clashed beautifully with the gleaming white ivory. She knew the language of roses. Dearing must as well. Tears stung her eyes, one sliding free to fall upon her gift. She touched the velvety petals, gently, as if they would disappear, a dream not yet realized if she did so much as whisper upon it. Lifting the flower to her nose, she inhaled the fragrance and set it atop the pianoforte.

Emotion swelled in her chest to restrict her next breath. She sat and stared for several minutes before setting her trembling fingers to the keys. The subtle thoughtfulness of the gesture overwhelmed her, and she channeled the impact into her music, all the while her heart beating rapidly in her chest. Her husband cared for her.

Deeply.

Elusive happiness remained within reach.

She completed the concerto and stepped away from the bench, flower in hand. The door to Dearing's study remained closed so she knocked lightly, hoping whatever business he conducted on the other side could be disturbed, but no one answered. Perhaps he'd gone abovestairs to bathe and change clothes after his meeting. Prompted by the sentiment he'd expressed, she twisted the knob and discovered it unlocked. Without hesitation, she padded farther into the room. She'd never spent time within these walls, his study a personal domain from which she was excluded. But that being so, her curiosity seemed unusually impatient.

A mahogany desk dominated the interior, pristine and organized, whereas the secretary's work area nearby overflowed with documents and sheaves of parchment. A polished spindle-legged table held stacks of vellum and linen, sealing wax and pots of ink. A tall porcelain umbrella stand contained leather tubes tied with string, while the walls were decorated with intricately drawn maps of every color. Her eyes could hardly take it all in, the wonder of the room as lively and vivid as her music, yet so like Dearing: traditional, compelling and orderly.

Heavy draperies, the color of fresh moss, hung on either side of recessed windows with evenly sectioned panes. The windows offered generous light that fractured against the Coromandel wood panels, straight as soldiers along the walls. A multishelved bookcase filled the space in between, its contents a mixture of leather-bound volumes and collected items of interest. She didn't know where to devote her attention first.

This room bespoke her husband in every capacity. Even the air seemed changed, reserved especially for Dearing, a man who evoked intense emotion and respect. Yet he'd shown her a different side of late. A passionate, intriguing, thrilling side. Her heart applauded. She needed to find him and thank him for the hothouse bloom. An insistent flicker of desire accompanied the plan to spur her slippers into action.

Out of the house? Where exactly? Dearing contemplated the question thoroughly, assured if Charlotte were to visit her family, she would have taken the carriage and left word of her whereabouts. In the past weeks, they'd abandoned their habit of skulking about the house and avoiding each other. In fact, it seemed they sought each other out more often than not.

A sharp rap at the door redirected his attention.

"Jeremy?"

Ah, his wife had returned. With a wry grin, he gathered Cricket from the chair near the window and tucked the cat neatly into the crook of his elbow. Then he swung the door wide.

"Jeremy, I . . ."

He enjoyed her surprised stutter before she fought to regain her bearings. An impish smile graced her face. Did she expect to beguile her way out of an explanation? Then again, he didn't mind Cricket at all. The feline was an excellent mouser. When his wife remained silent, he couldn't resist the tease. "Cat got your tongue?"

"Rather, you've got my cat. You found Shadow." Her voice was all humble gratitude now.

"I found Cricket." He stepped backward, released the cat to the floorboards and invited his wife into his bedroom. A delicious decision.

"Are you angry? I know you once spoke of a dog, but we can't very well get rid of her now." Charlotte's words tumbled out in brisk defense. "Most cats have only one name. She'll be a misfit among her peers. Please don't turn her out."

It was a weak and ridiculous argument, but he enjoyed this side of Charlotte, with lowered guard and playful smile about her lips, no matter she had no hope of turning the subject.

"I've made no such plans." He walked to the fireplace and propped one shoulder against the lintel. Then he crossed his arms over his chest and waited. "Were you looking for me?"

Again, her lovely smile appeared. "I found the rose."

It seemed their conversation would be a variety of losts and founds. Lord knew he'd already lost his heart.

"I'm pleased you like it."

"I do." She meandered closer, an alluring gleam in her

eye. Why hadn't he noticed his wife could play the vixen? "I should thank you for finding Shadow."

"Cricket," he corrected. "And how would you do that?"

"A few ideas come to mind."

Her voice composed equal measures temptation and caution, though her beautiful blue eyes were wide with curiosity. She stepped quicker.

"We could begin with a kiss."

The provocative suggestion was threaded with challenge, and he waited no longer. With a lightning-fast maneuver, he captured her to him, her body flush against his. An indignant gasp forced its way from her enticing lips to remind her he hadn't taken her breath away yet.

That would be remedied.

He found her mouth anxiously accommodating and slid his tongue into her hot wetness. She tasted as he knew she would, as he remembered, fresh and sweet, a flavor he craved since their last kiss. What began as wild ravishment soon became something else entirely. They stood heart to heart, his back to the wall, her soft breasts pressed to his hard chest. He shifted slightly, bringing one arm around to support the graceful slope of her spine while the other hand cradled her face. She pressed into his touch, though her eyes remained closed.

"You, my lovely wife, are a mysterious little minx, a secret I must discover." His murmur against her lips had a velvety quality, the vibration appearing to please as the corner of her mouth turned upward.

"Kiss me again, Jeremy."

"Ah, and bossy as well. I hadn't originally thought you possessed that quality." But he wasted no more time on words, crushing his mouth to hers, her lithe heat against his enough to mock the flames in the hearth.

He worked at her hairpins next, dropping them to the floorboards, though this gained him an objection.

"The cat."

It was all she managed, though he paid her concerned warning no heed. "She has nine lives, doesn't she?"

He threaded his fingers through the lengths, all the while kissing and caressing, unable to decide where he wished to touch and taste first. He lingered near her nape, frustrated with the layers of clothing and restrictive ties that kept her raveled up. One palm settled on the curve of her derrière, but the thickness of her skirts again thwarted his efforts. He remembered the delicious dimples waiting for his tongue and frustration mounted.

His wife clearly had other ideas.

Before he could comprehend her intention, she snaked her arm between them, her palm settling on his impatient erection. His heart slammed against his rib cage. What mischief did she mean?

With concentrated intent, she worked the buttons of his falls, each one until she pushed away the impeding fabric and encircled him with her fingers. Glory, it was all he could do not to rock against her, every smooth caress a test of his will, each firm slide a demanding claim. Just as he'd touched her and brought her to climax, his daring wife sought to do the same. He reclined against the wall, his shoulders braced as she worked him to a threatening hardness. His cock ached, though he resisted, enamored as he watched her from beneath lowered lids, his slip of a wife in serious concentration, her full attention focused on his pleasure.

When the last threads of power frayed and tension snapped, he released a loud groan and sensation reverberated through him, flooding every cell as if a reckless storm, each strong peak and resounding echo aiming to overtake him.

At some point he'd closed his eyes, lost to feeling, and now as he opened them and viewed his wife, he cherished her smile of satisfaction. She was a pleaser, and she'd certainly found a way to please him.

* * *

Later, after Charlotte had played several pieces on the pianoforte to her one-person audience, Jeremy revealed he'd planned an outing for the morrow. She was thrilled, still effervescent from the bold and sensual assault she'd seen through to completion in her husband's chambers. Amelia's advice had proven true repeatedly. Charlotte had only to become more assertive, make known her wishes for their marriage to take a turn for the right. She remained in alt at her power as a female, when all along she'd perceived life granted such privilege to men alone.

"Shall we ready ourselves for dinner?"

Jeremy's question brought another smile. She seemed to be doing a lot of that lately.

Hudson appeared at the door of the music room, his silver salver in one hand. "A message has arrived."

"You may enter." Jeremy stood at the ready to accept the note, but Hudson turned in her direction instead.

"It's for Lady Dearing, milord."

She forced a short laugh, the worry that the message came from Louisa and the situation had worsened alive in her brain. "Perhaps it's from my family," she suggested, with no other idea at the moment.

Jeremy approached and then, as if he changed his mind or wished to offer privacy, he turned to the firebox instead. Charlotte thanked Hudson and watched him leave before she broke the seal and scanned the message. Her pulse skipped triple time; the missive was from Lord Gordon. He wished to see Louisa and, if possible, to meet with them the following afternoon. The note didn't elaborate on the circumstances, instead listing a location, a time and little else. Again, worry intruded. Had Lord Gordon shared their discussion with Lord Mallory? The two men had appeared to be on their way somewhere when she interrupted. The possibility they may have discussed her visit presented another layer of difficulty.

She quickly folded the page and slipped it into the pocket of her skirt in hope Jeremy had paid no heed. Yet when she met his gaze, she found the reverse to be true.

The crackle and hiss in the hearth pronounced the silence. She needed to supply some semblance of explanation.

"Nothing more than a note from Amelia." Her palms began to sweat in response to her lie, and a lump of emotion forced its way up from her stomach. She'd chosen her friend and not her sister, too afraid some implication might send Jeremy to her parents' home if things knotted further. If Louisa strove to keep her problem a secret and only confided in Charlotte, a sisters' code bound her to protect that trust.

"Does she wish to see you?" His eyes assessed her intently. Or was it her imagination, already guilt-ridden and conflicted?

"Yes. She wishes to meet tomorrow afternoon." She knew he'd arranged their outing for the morning. With any luck, she would be returned before noon and able to take a carriage to her parents' home, collect Louisa, and they would be on their way to meet Gordon at the time indicated. Another palpitation of dread collected behind the first and she turned her eyes away and back again.

"Here in London, Charlotte?"

His tone acquired a sharp edge indicative of a swift change of mood. Did he doubt she meant to see Amelia? Excuses had been limited. Charlotte couldn't very well explain the note came from her sister and risk the chance he'd accompany her. Yet why would he reject her answer? He knew Amelia to be her dearest friend.

"Yes, of course." She forced a smile and her jaw quivered, aware her attempt was brittle at best. "She'd like to see me one more time before she returns to the Scarsdale country seat."

Refusing to blink, she watched her husband, his eyes dark, their expression blank. Then he turned to the fireplace, lifted the poker and stabbed at the logs. Sparks spiraled into the chimney, fast and furious, as if they anticipated confrontation and chose to flee with haste. When he finished, there was a deadly calm in his voice she'd never heard before.

"If that's what you desire, Charlotte, you should by all means pursue your pleasure."

Chapter Sixteen

Dearing glanced in the cheval mirror above his armoire and straightened his cravat. The sun shone too brightly through his bedchamber windows, and he listed a string of expletives in response. He'd promised a morning outing and esteemed a fair amount of pride in locating the ideal diversion to please Charlotte. Now no amount of sunshine or smiles could blot out the fact that she'd lied to him, openly and without pause.

Since early last evening, when he'd excused himself and come abovestairs, he'd pondered whether he'd misunderstood and Amelia, Duchess of Scarsdale, remained in London, but logic would not allow his anxious excuses. He knew for a fact the duke and duchess had left the city already, the information easily obtained with a few inquiries.

And too, there was Charlotte's blanched complexion and timid response once the note was received and the words read. She'd transformed from bold lover to shrinking violet, and he was certain the contents of the message had provoked the change.

But why? And who had sent the missive?

He'd find no pleasure in their visit to the British Museum, but he would discern the answers. Determined to discover the reason for his wife's odd absences and the contents of the note she'd received, he took the stairs and waited in the foyer while a footman readied the carriage.

"I'm here." Charlotte entered the hall from the direction of the music room, and he turned at the sound of her voice.

"As am I. Let's be off." Short on patience and less on understanding, he escorted her to the steps and up into the carriage. He settled on the banquette on the opposite side with the intention of questioning her, unwilling to accept evasive answers. What he hadn't counted on was the pervasive fragrance of her perfume in the confined interior or the lovely beauty of her profile limned in the early morning light.

"I'm looking forward to the exhibit. How did you hear of its early arrival?"

Like last night, her voice now lacked genuine emotion. Instead, he heard a struggle for pleasantry, a false attempt to persuade him everything was normal.

"It was mentioned at one of my clubs." That wasn't exactly true. He'd enlisted the help of two footmen, sent them about London with specific instructions and promised them additional pay if they returned from their scavenger hunt with advantageous news. Luckily, one of them had succeeded. An exhibit of musical instruments, most especially Italian violins, was being prepared for public display. No one knew of its arrival at the museum, but the curator would allow Charlotte to peruse the collection to her delight in return for a generous donation. Dearing happily paid the sum and anticipated the joyful outing, at the time anxious to please his wife. How quickly things had reversed.

"Thank you."

"You're welcome."

He watched her closely, angry a falsehood had passed her perfectly formed lips. The same lips he'd kissed passionately only yesterday. The same lips she'd used to kiss his—

"I'll be going out this afternoon."

As would he.

"We shouldn't be home too late." He turned toward the window and broke off the conversation, not wishing to continue their dishonest banter. Yet somehow, he couldn't help himself. Mayhap he wished she'd say something to convince him it was all a colossal mistake. He'd willingly admit the error of fault, so he offered with careful hesitancy, "Please extend my kind regards to Amelia."

"Yes." She nodded in the affirmative with the well-chosen word.

At least she didn't smile.

An endless pause enveloped the interior, yet the fraught silence was full of intimate sounds on the periphery of his awareness. Her faint huff of breath when the wheel hit a rut, the slide of her reticule across the silk of her day gown, the restless scuffle of her slippers. It was as though he could hear her blink, the beat of her pulse and rush of life as it swam through her veins, and all the while his chest squeezed tighter. Gone was the ease of conversation and comfortability.

Why, when they'd found contentedness, discovered the decadent emotion of each other's company and begun to build a strong intimate affinity, would she choose to defile that newborn love with dishonesty? A harrowing voice reminded him that he himself was a master of deceit. How dare he judge her? Was this the beginning of the end? When all his past transgressions would cause their complete ruin?

He examined her profile while she avoided his attention. Coruscated light bathed her lashes in amber and gold, the blue of her irises so bright he wondered if they weren't a figment of his imagination. He swallowed and averted his gaze. Better he allow the sounds of life to distract him, an angry barking dog or chiming church bell; much safer ordinary occurrences.

Eventually, he'd stopped thinking altogether, consumed by conflicted emotion, simply waited until the carriage rolled to a stop. He exited and assisted his wife, escorting her to the museum door where, as prearranged, a curator permitted them entry. Public visiting hours weren't until much later in the day. The dim corridor, which led to the private exhibit room, fit his mood, dank and bleak. And then they were alone again, at least in the human sense.

Musical instruments crowded the room from wall to wall, whether shiny brass or high polished wood. Charlotte's face lit with appreciation. He watched as she circled the exhibit, daring a touch to the graceful slope of a harp, its neck carved in relief, gilded gold and hand-painted. She smiled her reflection into the body of a Maplewood violoncello and tapped her fingertip across the silver keys of a polished clarinet. But when she approached the gem of the collection, an original Bartolomeo Cristofori pianoforte from Florence, he noted her sincere awe.

At first, she hardly moved, feasting on the burlwood case and delicate whalebone hammers with her eyes alone. But then, just as she'd coyly convinced him to allow her exploration of his body, the need to touch overtook all other considerations. She ran her fingers in a tender caress across the keys, so delicately not one whispered a sound. She leaned in as if seeing every detail and proportion before she examined the instrument from various angles. Then she returned to the keyboard, set her fingers atop the ivories and played a collection of notes. He assumed she wanted the luxury of having produced music, despite knowing not to expect more from the rare piece.

"It's lovely, isn't it?"

Lindsey's audacious comment, that women enjoyed gifts as large as pianofortes, filtered back, the words brought to life in Charlotte's smile. If only it were that easy to secure her love.

"Rare and beautiful, I agree."

"It's a pity we can't stay longer, although I doubt I'd ever have my fill of viewing this collection." In this, she did sound regretful.

"We can stay as long as you like." He knew it was a barbed statement. She'd already made her decision. For a fleeting moment, her expression pinched as if she'd been stung.

"No. I think it's time to go."

She said this with such calm certainty, he experienced a visceral loss, his next breath a struggle.

They exited the same way they'd come, and after he'd handed Charlotte into the carriage, he spared an additional moment with their driver. Stefan was a dependable servant with trustworthy discretion who would accomplish the task set to him and report directly upon returning to Dearing House. There was no other way to go about surveilling her behavior without evoking suspicion.

Charlotte pressed her back into the banquette and attempted carefree conversation, though her fingers worked the strings on her reticule faster than a rhapsody. Had she imagined the dual meaning of his words in the museum? Was she so ridden with guilt she'd heard notes of sinister distrust when none existed?

Despair swamped her heart. She'd promised Louisa her support and vowed confidentiality, but how she wanted to confess the predicament to Dearing and enlist his help. At the least it would allow him to understand the circumstances. Still, she held her tongue, torn between loyalty to her sister and her husband.

She spared a long look in his direction as they approached Dearing House and wondered if he thought her ungracious for her contrary reception of his thoughtful gesture. "The museum exhibit was wonderful. I've never seen so many rare and finely crafted instruments in one place."

"As you've already mentioned."

She searched his face, his dark brows slashed downward as if he contemplated matters of a serious nature. The carriage halted at the curb before she managed something else to say.

Dearing climbed out, and she willed him to look over his shoulder, to demand to know where she went. If he pressed the issue, she would break her promise to Louisa and salvage a modicum of loyalty. But he didn't turn. He closed the carriage door, and she heard his direction to the driver, punctuated by the crack of the whip.

"Take Lady Dearing wherever she wishes to go."

White's was no place for solitude, but Dearing took himself there anyway, in want of distraction from the turmoil of his thoughts. He'd hardly crossed the threshold when he realized his mistake. Erring on better judgment, he thrust forward into the cajolery of the club. It would appear all London males were of like mind.

Near the front rooms, a smug cluster of select committeemen discussed new applicants to the exclusive salon. The familiar glass bowl, with its white and black balls, rested on a nearby table beside a daunting rectangular box. A secret vote would determine whether the name on the card received membership. Each committee member indicated their preference by a white or a black ball. A single negative vote would result in the applicant being refused admittance. It seemed rather ruthless in the waning light of late afternoon.

Dearing signaled his drink preference to a vigilant footman and, by luck of timing, located a seat near the hearth. He desired company, anything to keep his mind from spinning in repetitive loops, all of which suggested Charlotte possessed ungenuine feelings for him and could very well be involved in something scandalous. It would be fortuitous if Lindsey dropped in a nearby chair or materialized from the woodwork, as he was often apt to do. Dearing smirked at the irony. One day he wished for his friend's company, the next he did not. Yet Lindsey had never done him wrong and often warbled on with enough inanity to set Dearing's mood to right. Alas, today it was not to be. Mayhap Lindsey spent his time with a lovely lady instead of wasting the hours here at White's. He did seem the romantic, didn't he? Always inquiring of Charlotte's welfare and the status of their relationship. For the briefest moment, Dearing's breathing stilled, and an irrational stab of suspicion took hold.

The footman returned with a glass of brandy, and he savored the fine liquor, setting his head to the padding of the wingback chair and closing his eyes.

"Now there is the face of a troubled man." Lord Mallory's sinister comment drifted over the chairback like a caliginous layer of fog. If ever there was a candidate deserving of the single black ball restricting membership, here stood the man.

Forced to acknowledge the remark to some degree, Dearing casually opened his eyes and offered a curt nod. By no means did he want for Mallory's company, and thankfully, not a single chair appeared unoccupied nearby. Still, the interloper intruded with quiet arrogance.

"One would think with a wife as comely as yours, a man would spend his time at home."

"Look around you, Mallory. Most of London's male population is here. I daresay your assumption is skewed." A battle of wits and veiled jibes would prove insufferable, and Dearing refused to perpetuate it. Mallory's pride stung from a variety of missed opportunities, but Dearing knew the man enjoyed causing havoc whenever able, and the tired old rejoinder that a man must spend every waking moment in his wife's presence was wearing Dearing's patience into nonexistence. Not that he wouldn't enjoy the exact circumstance with Charlotte, but that was another matter altogether.

Mallory scrutinized the room with vulture-eyed speculation, his murmur just loud enough to be heard. "As you say."

A lanky upstart with hardly any whiskers vacated an adjacent chair, and Mallory made for it like a shark on the scent of fresh blood.

"I saw your lady in Mayfair recently."

Dearing offered no more than a level stare. He'd be damned before he allowed a show of curious displeasure.

Nonetheless, Mallory continued. "At least I thought it was she. One can never be certain with the wide-brimmed bonnets women favor these days." He glanced to a far-off corner and tapped his index finger to his chin, as if he begged his memory to serve. Most certainly it was all a pretense. "Some say while the cat's away, the mouse will play. One wonders what drives a woman to unfaithfulness."

Dearing clenched his teeth and aborted a foul reply. He would not be lured into a public argument based on Mallory's malevolent speculation, which begged to give strength to his darkest fears. Had Charlotte visited Mayfair? Why would she?

Mayfair was for dandies and those who believed themselves far above most others. Lindsey lived in Mayfair, on Chesterfield Street. His priggishly pretentious terraced town house, with its innocent façade of white-painted render was one of so many that lined the curb and announced the elite.

Hadn't Lindsey remarked on Dearing's marriage? Several times too many, in fact? What would provoke this interest? A sharp prick of ugliness quickly answered, composed of covetous suspicion and edacious mistrust. Too many coincidences began and ended with Lindsey.

"Any interest in selling your shares of Middleton stock?" Mallory's efficient change of subject informed Dearing the man possessed a self-serving agenda, but in this he could comment methodically.

"As I've mentioned during our previous encounters, you've a better chance of propositioning someone in need of funds, or a man interested in an alternative investment. I'm content with my portfolio at the moment." His hand rested atop his thigh, and in a fleeting gesture of impatience, he drummed his fingers twice.

"You're a shrewd one." Mallory shifted his eyes across the room toward the entrance hall, where a Pembroke occasional table held White's prized betting book. "But then again, anyone who would marry to obtain—"

Dearing stood with such speed, Mallory ceased speaking, though his cravat curtsied against his Adam's apple.

"Be careful with your words. A gentleman's code of conduct prevents him from maligning others, but my patience will only stretch so far. Our conversation here is done." Dearing lifted his brandy, swallowed what remained and turned on his heel, confident he'd shut Mallory's chin for at least the next few hours.

Once returned to Dearing House, he didn't enter but followed the winding path to the mews located at the rear. The alleyway stood quiet, the stables lit by a single flickering lantern in a wood-framed window. His boot heels crushed the gravel in a cadence of impending condemnation. But for whom was the sentiment aimed? So many conflicted emotions crowded his chest, he could barely breathe. He pushed the door wide and entered.

"Stefan," he stated in a tone of resignation, uncomfortable with the task of spying on his wife.

The lad stepped forward immediately, his leather cap pushed back too far on his head. "Yes, milord."

"You have information to share?"

"I do, milord. Her ladyship traveled to her familial home, where she remained until she exited with her sister."

Relief, powerful and sweet, sliced through his misgivings. He'd worried for naught. His wife merely wished to see her sister and, for reasons unknown, had kept the event a secret. His heart thudded in reprieve of its earlier ache. Mallory was a son of a bitch for suggesting otherwise.

"You seemed interested in their whereabouts, so I took it upon myself to follow them on foot."

He might have missed the next bit of Stefan's explanation, preoccupied with a cacophony of ideations as he was. "On foot? They went for a stroll?"

He processed the latter news belatedly, distracted by Cricket, who settled beside his boot to remind him secrets took many forms.

"Not exactly." Stefan swiped the cap from his head and pushed a hand through his dark curly hair. "They walked to the corner and hailed a hackney."

"And?" Anger, white hot and immediate, spiked the blood in his veins to eradicate all earlier relief. "Out with it." His harsh command may have riled the cat, who leaped away with a complaint.

"I can't say, milord. They were off and into the flow of traffic before I could attempt to follow." The lad shifted from one boot to the other. "But the ladies weren't gone more than two hours, and I returned Lady Dearing home immediately thereafter. I hope your lordship isn't disappointed in my service."

Dearing took time to coax calm into his voice. "Not at all, Stefan. I appreciate your efforts. It's not you who has earned my disappointment."

Chapter Seventeen

Charlotte paced a hard line beside the foot of the bed, her emotions less straightforward. While she'd accomplished her goal and delivered Louisa to Gordon for a private conversation, Charlotte had left a trail of unavoidable lies in her wake. Lies that if not carefully tended would destroy her marriage.

Her husband was an intelligent businessman, able to read the truth in one's eyes as easily as the ink on paper. And while his own disbelief might interfere, she held no doubt he suspected her of wrongdoing.

And who wouldn't? After the lovely outing to the museum, she'd thanked him with a series of secrets and mistruths. Guilt, as lethal as a razor's path, sliced through her. Only a few weeks ago, she'd believed all time had run out on any chance at marital happiness, but then life had shifted, Dearing had changed and she'd believed they'd both found a promising path forward.

Until Louisa, with her impossible request and personal crisis. Of course she would assist her sister. She loved her dearly. But at what cost to her own future?

Perhaps all would be resolved now that Louisa had spoken face-to-face with Lord Gordon. From what Charlotte could decipher, the gentleman adored her sister, was unable to hide his sincerity. Every nuance of the lord's countenance bespoke a man who was smitten and in exceptional turmoil due to a forced separation. In many ways, the depth of despair in Lord Gordon's eyes mirrored her own.

Charlotte had offered them the required privacy, but regretted not knowing if Louisa and Gordon had planned for the inevitable. She'd promised her sister help without revealing the embarrassment of the predicament, but had she accomplished anything through the meeting? Louisa spoke little during the return hackney ride from Mayfair, and with every minute of her own time under scrutiny, Charlotte hadn't forced conversation. Still, another troubling thought persisted. If Gordon cared for Louisa, why did he insist they leave at once and not return?

There was a riddle Charlotte had yet to solve.

A shuffle near the door drew her attention, the soft knock that followed indicative of her maid, and she bade Jill enter. The maid set about the tasks that waited to be done, the ease of conversation a much-needed balm.

"Shadow has the run of the house after all." Jill grinned in her direction. "You shouldn't have worried. More than once I've seen Lord Dearing with the cat at his heels."

Charlotte couldn't muster a smile, burdened by the desire to confess and seek her husband's support. She gave her head a shake to push her conflicted emotions away until later. "If only all things could amend so easily." Having heard Charlotte's tears many nights past, Jill undoubtedly understood the unspoken reference.

"I'm sorry, milady. Is there anything you need me to do for you?" Jill placed a white night rail on the folded counterpane at the foot of the bed and hung a clean towel on the hook near the mirror. For several breaths, no words were spoken, and only the matter of unlacing and dressing filled the silent void.

"No." Charlotte attempted a word of reassurance. "Thank you." She didn't say more, and her maid left shortly thereafter.

Charlotte settled on the edge of the mattress, too exasperated now to pace the floorboards. She should write to Louisa and inquire as to her sister's plans. One thing remained uppermost and certain: Charlotte would not venture to Mayfair again. Resolute and somewhat mollified, still weary with emotion, she climbed between the sheets and begged for sleep.

Dearing stared at the regulator clock on the wall of his study. He'd not joined Charlotte for dinner the night before or breakfast this morning, and in a cruel twist of circumstance, it seemed they'd landed where they'd begun, in a hollow marriage composed of a vow made with words instead of emotions. He rubbed a hand across his jaw. His teeth ached from clenching, his patience whisper-thin. The only way he knew to overcome his inner turmoil was to work with relentless fervor, much the way his wife chased her distress with musical compositions, though he still found it impossible to concentrate. And of late, her pianoforte had gone quiet.

Across the room, Faxman toiled in absolute consolidation, unaffected by the obnoxious tick of the clock, something that never had bothered him before but now counted the final seconds of Dearing's tolerance. What was he to do?

His mind ran amok with suspicion. Why would Charlotte deceive him repeatedly if not to disguise nefarious deeds? She'd lied about visiting Amelia and instead ventured to Mayfair. Upon her return, she'd scurried to her room to bathe, change clothes and reorder her emotions. That bespoke of a visit to a lover. But could it be true?

His heart thudded, a mockery of this latest fabrication.

He knew the suspicion to be irrational and unsubstantiated far beyond reason, and yet he couldn't keep hold of the reins, his imagination all too quick to suggest the worst and sprint toward unfounded possibilities. Things had taken a turn at the poorest time, when they remained on the cusp of intimacy, a wall of conflicted sentiment between them. Still, similar to business negotiations, the most effective way to resolve concern was to confront it. He needed to measure her reaction. There lay the truth.

Jealousy, an emotion he despised, flooded his veins and drenched his better sense. What if his inquiries yielded an unbearable legitimacy?

He, the master of hypocrisy. A man who kept an unthinkable secret locked in a hidden box. It would be justice served.

"Does something trouble you, milord?"

Faxman's question snapped him from morose contemplation. He gave a terse nod in the negative.

"I only ask because you've stared, motionless, at that same sheaf of foolscap for a solid twenty minutes. Have I miscalculated the sums?" Faxman stood, though he didn't round the desk, his face a mask of genuine concern.

"No. Never mind." Dearing pushed the page across his desktop in disregard, the harsh dismissal intended for his frustration, not the diligent worker.

"Then pardon my interruption." Faxman returned to his seat, though he popped up just as swiftly. "If I may pose a suggestion, perhaps a breath of fresh air would assist with your mental confabulation. I find a brief respite in nature the rightful cure when my thoughts need to be reordered."

Dearing eyed his astute secretary and raised his hand, palm flat, to stop further discussion. His nerves were frayed, his temperament soured, and anything the man might say would result in spark to tinder.

"No need." He dropped his hand and heaved a breath.

"All's well." The tone of the words declared the opposite, mayhap provoking the secretary to persist.

"Quiet the mind and the soul will speak," Faxman mused. "At least that's what my father would say. He was a strong proponent of self-reflection. A religious man too." He cleared his throat, as if unsure whether he'd shared too much.

And in truth, Dearing had had enough. It didn't signify that it was well before their work's completion or that his secretary meant to offer assistance. The last thread of patience snapped. "Yes, quiet would be welcome. I find I'm in no mood for bits of wisdom and tomfoolery." Pity he vented his spleen now of all times. "Even the greenest apprentice knows when to shut his gob and blend into the woodwork. Most especially when I've indicated I require no counsel. Still you continue, and because I cannot bear another word, you're dismissed."

"Pardon, milord." Despite the effect of unadulterated sunlight, Faxman paled considerably. "If I've overstepped . . ." His voice trailed off and he stepped back, as if to reject the supposition.

"For the day, Faxman." Dearing blew out an exhalation in degrees, aware he'd behaved as the biggest cad. "You're dismissed for the day."

"Right." The secretary gathered his bag with alacrity. "Then I'll be off without delay."

Dearing felt no better for having scared his man of business. Yet the same shrewd acumen that enabled him to build substantial wealth from a humble title emboldened his next decision.

He took the treads two at a time and strode down the hall toward Charlotte's bedchambers, all the while his heart thudding in his chest, to kill him or keep him alive he didn't know. What had she done? Not given herself to another. He refused to believe it, though Mallory's insidious suggestions eviscerated better logic. He rapped on her door with insistence, too angry to pause long enough to consider the consequences of his actions.

The door cracked open and Charlotte peered through the narrow space. "Jeremy?"

She appeared startled. *Guilty.* For surely his wife didn't expect him to chase her down and demand answers, but she was caught well and good and he wouldn't allow her to put him off.

"Open the door." He laid his palm against the panel, at the ready to force himself inside if she meant to bar him entrance, but it wasn't necessary. With a slight furrowing of her brow, she stepped back and released the knob. He made quick work of shutting it behind him. "Where were you yesterday afternoon?"

Her face expressed and discarded a series of reactions. "You're angry."

Would she expect otherwise? "I asked a simple question. Where were you?"

"I can't say."

She didn't appear proud of her answer. Nevertheless, it fired jealousy in his blood, searing a path to his brain to obliterate coherent thought. "Ah, but there you're mistaken. You *will not* say. Let me make something perfectly clear. You won't go out without telling me. I will know where you are at all times. You're my wife." Anger equaled by fear caused him to spout the ridiculous commands, although when he'd barked the final sentence he experienced a wash of possessive pride.

She seemed unaffected.

"This is my home, not a prison." Her words rang true, though he rejected their sensibility.

"Where were you?" He clenched his fists at his sides, the words bitter on his tongue, and the wall between them became thicker, not by way of rational discussion, but the other way around.

"I had a visit to make. An errand to run."

She seemed unusually cautious with her answers, or did he imagine it?

"Is that the truth, Charlotte?" He'd offer her every advantage in desperate want for there to be a logical reason she'd abandon propriety and sneak off to another man's home. Yet he couldn't imagine one.

"Louisa asked for my assistance. Nothing more." She backed away, as if she wished to separate herself from the words. Or from him.

"As I recall, you mentioned a visit to Amelia." He drummed his fingers against his thigh in a useless effort to decrease his anger. Just the thought of another man anywhere near his wife caused a strike in temper so strong and wicked, he didn't know what to do with the force. "That's the trouble with lies. They often get tangled with truth and become indecipherable after a time. You should admit all of it, because I know differently."

"What do you mean?" Her brows raised in question, though a flash of challenge lit her face. Then her expression changed altogether.

He stepped closer, wanting to see her eyes when he exposed the mistruths she'd fed him. Needing to witness every emotion, no matter each one would be a shard of glass to pierce his heart. "You went to your home and then took a hired hack to Mayfair." He should assemble the offered facts into a practical conversation, but his mouth seemed disconnected from his brain. "You went to meet someone, didn't you?"

"Yes." Something close to disbelief or injury clouded her expression. "But it's not what you think."

"How would you know what I think? You haven't told me

the truth." His voice rang out, arrogant and demanding against the watered silk walls, and with it his wife's posture transformed.

She squared her shoulders. Her back became ramrod straight. "What difference does it make whether you know the truth? You've created your own version and have already decided I've betrayed you." Anger sharpened her reply. She was no watering pot who would acquiesce easily.

"I've said nothing about betrayal." Every muscle in his body tensed. "Though the word is quick to leave your tongue."

"I've not done so." She looked him in the eye. "You must believe me."

"For what reason? You've offered me no explanation."

"But I have."

"You're the one who asked for no secrets." He spoke with incisive authority, a trap well planned and sprung. "When what you really meant is *do as I say, not as I do*."

She stood determined, and he couldn't help acknowledge much more was at play then her unexpected jaunt. A long minute passed, her eyes filled with sorrow, and his heart clenched. A part of him feared her confession. They'd promised no secrets and he didn't wish to hear one, but she'd left him no choice. He wouldn't be cuckolded, despite that he loved her deeply.

"I've sworn loyalty to my sister Louisa, but you must know it in no way reflects upon our relationship."

Something akin to conflicted amusement danced in her eyes. Was she laughing at him?

"Bloody hell." He strode forward. If he didn't leave immediately, he would say and do things he would never be able to erase. "I'm leaving." He moved toward the door.

"And where will you go? Downstairs to your precious study to fabricate more ridiculous notions concerning my whereabouts?" Emotion forced her voice higher, and he heard her footsteps behind him.

"I owe you the same amount of truth you've granted me." He glanced over his shoulder and turned the knob. Words, even words would betray him if he spoke further. "Why would I tell you when you won't tell me?" He'd reduced himself to a child's argument. With that realization, he slammed the door behind him.

Chapter Eighteen

Charlotte rode toward her parents' house with a bundle of raw emotion eating away at her. She had no right to a feeling of happiness, having argued heatedly with her husband. Her maid, on the banquette beside her, likely wondered at Charlotte's intermittent smile, considering the eager method in which she'd planned this exit and hied to the carriage. Yet Charlotte couldn't help but delight in Dearing's show of bold possessiveness, and dare she believe a more fervent emotion? *Jealousy.* Jealousy implied he cared for her beyond a kiss or an intimate touch, and that he'd developed deep commitment to their marriage.

Unfortunately, an opposing argument could possibly be true. To regard their relationship in more phlegmatic terms, he'd paid for her compliance by rescuing her family from debt and ruin. Therefore, he had the right to judge her and otherwise make the rules of the house, the same by which she was expected to obey.

Either way, before she could sort out her feelings for her husband and convince him he owned her heart, she needed to resolve Louisa's predicament, hence the hasty trip to her familial home.

If only her husband proved easier to unriddle. One minute he kissed her with enough passion to scorch her soul, the next he shut himself away. What did he guard so intensely? And why did he propose in the first place if he desired hardly a marriage at all? She wrapped an arm around her midsection, a silent acknowledgment of her solitary emptiness, the familiar ache for a child abloom once again.

Still, despite her best attempt to calm herself, it seemed the rocking motion of the carriage shook loose the questions she'd painstakingly battled into silence. If only she knew what Jeremy wanted from their union. Companionship? His fickle schedule and unexpected mood shifts seemed to reject that conclusion. Why hadn't he opened the adjoining door of their bedchambers until recently? Insecurity rivaled her feelings of inadequacy to secure a stronghold at the pit of her stomach, only to slink upward to her heart. Was she *that* lacking? And too there was the matter of her family's financial difficulties and Dearing's sudden appearance at their home, all too ready to rescue her father and claim her hand in exchange. Thereafter, he'd disappeared on a business trip for weeks on end. So much seemed unthinkable, clouded by confusion and assumption. When she'd last spoken to her father, he'd shared information she'd never known. Another conversation was due.

The carriage rolled to a stop, effectively forcing her thoughts to reorder themselves. Once inside and installed in the drawing room, she waited for the flurry of attention her visits usually garnered, but none was forthcoming. With impatience, she wandered to the lonely pianoforte, nothing more than a piece of furniture in the room now that she'd left. Lifting the cover, she pressed a few chords before her sister's voice drew quick attention.

"Charlotte, I wasn't expecting you. Have you brought news?"

Louisa came forward, only to pause, then close the doors to safeguard against overheard conversation.

"None other than I've already shared, although I feel you've been stingy in explanation. You've meted the tiniest scraps of information, gained my loyal assistance and put my marriage at risk. Yet while I visit you here today I look worse for the wear." She hadn't meant the words to sound sharp though they held an edge.

"Is that true? Does Dearing doubt your love?" Louisa took a seat and wrapped her arms around her middle, her pose an ironic contradiction considering Charlotte's earlier dismay.

"I can tell you with complete honesty I don't know what Dearing thinks." She swallowed deeply to quell a wave of anxious tension. "But I'm not here to discuss my marriage."

"No. Of course not." Louisa rose and paced across the thick green carpet. "I'm beginning to believe I've caused us all a great deal of worry for nothing."

"What?" A rush of breath held Charlotte captive until she forced herself to exhale. "What are you talking about and why haven't you sent word if circumstances have changed? Do you have any idea the misery I've experienced?"

No, her sister couldn't. She was young, flighty at time and likely consumed with her own distress. Still, Charlotte had no intention of detailing how her sister's predicament had impacted life at Dearing House.

"Last evening, I had the most horrible pains. Sharp ones low in my stomach, but more severe than anything I've experienced with my flux. You know my courses have never been regular." Louisa darted her eyes to the window and back again. "This morning when I awoke, I was bleeding heavily. It appears my body has decided my fate. I don't know if I overreacted or experienced something heart-wrenching and sorrowful, but I can't ask Mother to summon a physician without revealing my relations with Lord Gordon, so your visit this morning is timely." Louisa turned, a morose expression on her face as she settled once again on the settee. "I'm sorry, Charlotte. I've caused so much agony for absolutely nothing, but I was frightened and had no one else to turn to. Until this very morning, I believed my future was sealed and I was with child."

Charlotte sat beside Louisa. "I know you were fright-ened, and I understand why you came to me, although the last week has been difficult for us both. You escaped a har-rowing situation with indelible consequences. I hope you realize the lesson in all this turmoil." She clasped her sister's hand within her own. "Have you spoken to Lord Gordon?"

"No. Not yet." Louisa slid her fingers loose and coasted them over her cheek. "I'm uncertain if he'll court me for-mally. Mother and Father would give permission, but I wonder if he isn't more interested in the clandestine adven-ture of our relationship than the responsibility of a courtship. And too—" Her words stuttered to a reluctant pause. "If I no longer continue our physical relations or sug-gest marriage as the only condition, he may choose to shift his interest elsewhere. I've made so many mistakes. There's no going back, is there?"

"No, I'm afraid not." Charlotte knew that quandary well. For every step forward within her marriage, it seemed she took several in reverse. "But you're lovely in every way, Louisa. You will find a husband who loves and re-spects you for the person you are, regardless of the choices you've made."

"I want to believe that's true. I've sacrificed my virtue for little in return and I must keep this terrible secret locked away or I'll bring shame and scandal to the family. My choices reflect on all of us. I couldn't disappoint Mother and Father any more than Dinah and Bunny. Their futures would be ruined along with mine."

"I'm so sorry, Louisa." Charlotte tried to reconcile her sister's emotional chattering. Too many of the thoughts aligned with worries of her own. "But you will find your own way." It was logical advice, given to her sister and also taken to heart.

"Well, if nothing else, this allows you to repair matters with Lord Dearing. I'm sorry if I caused disharmony in your marriage. You're the dearest sister and friend to put my needs before your own." Louisa rose from the cushions and Charlotte followed. They hugged a long while.

"Promise me you're well. Otherwise I'll continue to worry." Charlotte released her sister. "And I'll resolve my concerns with Dearing, so you needn't worry on my behalf."

"I never meant to create all these problems," Louisa whispered.

"Of course not. People rarely do."

Louisa left the room and Charlotte returned to the pianoforte, her mind busy with relief for her sister and despair for her problems at home.

"Will you play for me?"

Her father's cheerful question near the door caused her to startle. "Father, I didn't know you were here."

Despite what had transpired with Louisa, a genuine smile lit Charlotte's face. Her father's kindness and encouragement provided the ideal tonic for her malaise. She placed a kiss on his warm cheek and they settled near the fireplace.

"And to what do I owe this unexpected visit?" Elias Notley beamed with delight. "Not that I don't welcome a chance to see my eldest daughter at any opportunity."

"I decided rather quickly to come." She forced a wider grin. "I hope you don't mind."

"Not at all. As a matter of fact, I was thinking of you yesterday, when my man of business delivered a bit of information concerning your husband."

Charlotte's pulse leaped. "Concerning Dearing? In what way?"

"You're happy, aren't you?" Her father's face took on a familiar protective expression.

"I'd prefer if our every conversation didn't include that question." She tried to laugh but didn't succeed, unsure how much turmoil to share with her father. "What is it? Is something wrong?"

"No. But while you'll always have a place here, I need to know if you've made Dearing House your home in every sense."

"Yes, I have." Her conscience suffered at the half-truth. Anxious to change the subject, she recalled the last time they'd spoken, and her father's determination to rationalize his investment troubles. "Have you received results from your financial inquiries?"

"The investigator I hired to look into affairs discovered nothing of interest. Yet the three failing businesses that forced me to ruin are thriving now, sound and secure, with considerable profit. I suppose it may be no more than an unexplainable anomaly, although at times I wonder if I should consult Dearing. He's the smartest businessman I know, with an uncanny ability to intuit stocks. With the controlling interest of Middleton Railway in his portfolio, I'm sure his reputation has grown." Her father chuckled. "He certainly gained the most valuable prize I possessed. And I'm not referring to the railway collateral." He patted her hand with gentle affection. "You're far more treasured than a bonded deed."

She rested her head against her father's shoulder and breathed easier. "That's good to know, Father."

"Know it well. As principal shareholder, your husband will provide you a brilliant future once the rails cross England. Your children and grandchildren will want for nothing. Dearing's esteemed reputation and vaunted status will provide innumerable opportunities. Security for your future brings peace to my heart."

"Thank you." She squeezed his arm and lifted her head as she digested the words more carefully. "So, it's important then, this Middleton Railway investment?"

"I should say so, although my one share wasn't worth much until placed in the hands of the holder of a majority. Single shares are hard to come by. Investors hold hope of collecting any available stake to grow their profit once the rails are built. In any case, I was happy to pass my single share to Dearing with your marriage agreement. He rescued our family and I was in no situation to withhold a piece of paper that might benefit my daughter's future, although I did make a prudent precaution."

"All this talk of finance is beyond my interest." She matched eyes with her father's and waited.

"Indeed." Notley smiled once again. "And not suitable conversation either."

"But now you've pricked my curiosity. What do you mean by a prudent precaution?" Charlotte's mind raced with an abundance of questions. Had her father added conditions to the marriage agreement? Dearing was too shrewd to be fooled. What could her father have done? And if discovered, *when discovered*, would Dearing resent her father's interference or, instead, blame her and their hasty marriage for any impact? How had things become twice as complicated in half the time?

"Do you really wish to know, dear?" Notley's brows lowered in discouragement. "I've hesitated in telling you but find myself uncomfortable with the circumstances I've created. You haven't fooled me with your reassurances." He patted her hand again and waited.

Charlotte didn't know how to reply. If her father meant to protect her and the family, she shouldn't pry. It would be best to leave things unknown, and were the day to come when Dearing questioned her involvement, she could reply with honesty. Another few beats of her heart passed. On the other hand, if her marriage continued on a downward slide and she truly believed no hope survived, it would be wise to understand her options, if any existed.

"What did you do, Father? I do wish to know." God help her if she wasn't worsening the conditions of her marriage by carrying knowledge better left unknown.

"I do believe Dearing is an outstanding gentleman. I could never have agreed to your marriage otherwise, but I knew him in a business sense only. His reputation was reported to me as respected and intelligent. There was no time to gain a true impression of his personality. The expected courtship that accompanies a gentleman's suit was pushed aside because of our penurious situation."

"I understand, and you should know Dearing has shown me kindness. He has a thoughtful nature." The unexpected roses, visit to the gallery of instruments and his bone-melting kisses were testament to that. At least of late. She pushed aside the hurt she'd experienced at the beginning of their marriage and focused on recent interactions and how she hoped their relationship would progress. Certainly things had changed for the better.

"That's reassuring. Nevertheless, to relinquish all control was more difficult than I anticipated, and I thereby put into place a small insurance policy of my own."

"Go on." Was the marriage certificate nonbinding? Had

the church never sanctified their vows? A wave of dread and conflicted emotion flooded her every cell. Had she been living a lie this past year?

"I had a duplicate stock certificate created. One that appeared to be legitimate in every way but is nonbinding and counterfeit. If Dearing ever tries to sell or claim the investment represented by the Middleton Railway stock, he will be told it is illegitimate. I have the genuine certificate in my own possession."

This was said so matter-of-factly, the ramifications of her father's action took a long moment to settle.

"Why would you deceive Dearing, Father? I'm confused. What difference could one stock certificate make? And did you believe our marriage would fail?"

"Quite the opposite." He squeezed her hand as he spoke. "I have a sense of surety about your marriage, but as your father, I needed reassurance beyond the immediate situation. You were sacrificing your control, your chance at a courtship, your choice of future. The least I could do was arrange some way to keep you safe if all my instincts proved wrong. I wouldn't be able to salvage your emotions, but as I'd already come to realize my investment choices were not up to snuff, so perhaps I could provide some measure of recovery if the worst prevailed. I'm not proud of my decision, though I believed it necessary. Self-doubt, more than anything else, forced me to take action." Notley sighed and matched her watchful stare. "When the time comes that you assure me you're happily settled and blissfully in love, we will simply switch the certificates, and no one will be the wiser."

"Aside from us."

"Yes, Charlotte. Aside from us. It's a harmless confidence that harms no one." He stood, a flicker of impatience in his gaze.

"You make it all sound remarkably easy."

"And it will be."

"I remain unconvinced."

"See here." Her father moved to his large writing desk near the far wall. He pulled a key from his waistcoat pocket, inserted it into the lock on the topmost drawer and withdrew a long folder. He came back to stand before her while he riffled through the neatly arranged documents. At last he offered one forward.

"Take it now." He gave the document a little shake for emphasis. "You will feel better knowing you have control over how much Dearing knows as you move forward in your marriage."

With a reluctant huff, she accepted the paper and scanned the multiple lines of writing, though they blurred as emotion caught her unaware.

"There's no need for tears, daughter. I never meant to upset you. Quite the opposite." He placed the folder on a nearby table. "It was a necessary precaution on my part."

"So, this certificate is authentic?"

"Absolutely."

Charlotte folded the paper and carefully slipped it into her pocket. She hadn't anticipated yet another layer to her complicated relationship.

"Now, let's find where everyone's hiding." Her father cleared his throat, as if dismissing the subject at last. "I've shared enough this morning and won't monopolize your company any longer."

Despite an enlightening conversation with her father and the relief of knowing Louisa did not face immediate difficulty, Charlotte couldn't dismiss the niggling predicament exposed by the false certificate. He claimed he believed in Dearing as a gentleman and yet created a situation of mistrust by duplicating the stock Jeremy thought valid. What would happen were the information to come to light? Yet another secret she must conceal.

Secrets.

She disliked them. Despised them. She'd asked that there be none within her marriage, and yet when Dearing discovered Shadow hidden in her chambers, he'd done little aside from tease her. Still, secrets came in all sizes and a kitten hardly rivaled a monetary trap as explained by her father. Her mind spun with the effort to unriddle it all.

Her husband possessed too many secrets. Why did he one day seem aloof and detached when only days later he behaved with romance and passion? She wanted a strong relationship, a family and a future, without the tumultuous discord of never knowing what to expect. While her father measured security in pound notes, she'd much rather feel loved and cherished.

As the carriage rolled to a stop, she spared not a word to her maid and hurried inside the house to inquire of her husband's whereabouts. Hudson met her in the foyer.

"Lord Dearing is not here, milady. He requested his horse saddled and then left for the mews." Hudson inclined his head toward the hallway. "A visitor has arrived and awaits in the front drawing room."

"A caller?" Charlotte had no idea who it could be? She hadn't entertained or socialized beyond her family and Amelia in the weeks past.

"Yes, milady. Lord Mallory arrived not twenty minutes ago. I told him there was no one at home, but he insisted on waiting."

"I see." Would this day cause nothing but disquiet in her soul? "I'll go to him now and will ring for refreshments if needed. Thank you, Hudson."

Charlotte took a deep breath and entered the drawing room, unwilling to allow the man's unexpected presence to shake her confidence. Lord Mallory stood near the hearth and turned with the sound of her footfall. He eyed her with an undecipherable expression as she crossed the threshold.

"Lady Dearing." He stepped closer.

"Lord Mallory, this is an unexpected surprise. My husband is not here at the moment." She forced herself into a demeanor of assured confidence.

"I'd hoped to speak to Dearing, although with your arrival I can easily change the course of conversation."

"Forgive me, I don't understand." She moved to a cushioned chair and sat, though she was far from comfortable. She'd like to keep as much distance between Lord Mallory and herself as possible. "I can ring for refreshments if you plan to wait." She certainly had nothing to share with the odious man and would rather he took his leave straightaway.

"Ah, domestic bliss." Mallory settled in the chair across from her. "You give the appearance of having life settled to perfection, but we both know differently."

Did she imagine the threatening edge in his reply? Her imagination was quick to override better judgment, and she voiced the question that should have remained silent. "Why do you wish to speak to my husband?"

Mallory watched her intensely, as if able to peer into her soul, where she held tight to emotion. "You're not feeling uncomfortable, are you? Are you concerned Dearing will discover you visited Lord Gordon's residence? Certainly I understand if you've decided to conceal your actions. It's more than a little scandalous for a newly married woman to be out alone in search of a bachelor's attention."

Charlotte gritted her teeth to quell the instinct to react. The way Lord Mallory stripped the words of their truth and reformed them into an insinuation of reprehensible behavior sent alarm racing through her. She had every intention of explaining her actions to Dearing now that her sister no longer needed her help. Did Lord Mallory seek to malign her? The notion was ridiculous, and she could think of nothing he would gain by making the suggestion. She had no desire to keep Mallory's company a second longer than necessary. "Speak plainly, milord. I have no time for the trifling games you enjoy at my expense."

"Ah, is that a temper I see, or perhaps, a guilty conscience?" Mallory shook his head in mock disapproval. "Either would explain why Dearing spends so much time at his club."

Anger got the better of her. "What do you want with your interest in my marriage? My future bears nothing on yours."

"But it does." Mallory reclined against the chair and stretched his legs forward, as if planting himself for a good long while. "Are you not familiar with the competitive wagers made between comrades? Your unlikely marriage has been on the books at White's for too many months to count and the odds are almost inconceivable; irresistible, in fact. An acquaintance and I have—"

"I have no interest in your poor habits." She stood, forcing Mallory to follow suit. "I believe our visit is concluded."

"Now you're mistaken. You should take a moment to listen. A marriage so closely watched can advance in either direction. Only a fool would ignore the opportunity to pad his pocket."

"You disgust me." The words left her on a hiss. "Rest assured, your wager is secure. Lord Dearing and I are happily settled." She begrudged every word but felt outraged at Mallory's suggestion. She refused to let it go unanswered.

"You misunderstand again. How naïve you truly are." He chuckled, though scant humor lived in the sound. "I need your marriage to fail; otherwise my associate walks away with the spoils."

"Fail?" She shook her head, the notion men would place odds on her broken heart almost too much to comprehend.

"Then you have already lost. Lord Dearing and I are looking forward to many years of contentment and family."

"Were I to drop a few words about the club—words like *betrayal*, *adulteress*, or *cuckold*—I'm not altogether certain Dearing would agree with your view of the future. Secrets have a way of gaining power the longer they are kept. Lies are even more effective. I could conjure a wave of gossip or arrange a little scene that would cast both of you in the worst light."

"You're a despicable man." She turned away, seething with anger as she moved toward the door. "You're not welcome here, Lord Mallory. You've insulted my hospitality. Leave at once or I'll have Hudson show you out."

"Consider this after I've left and my suggestion has had time to ferment. If you'd like me to remain quiet, it will take a little doing on your part."

She didn't wait to hear any more of his venomous slander, her heels hard on the treads as she raced up to her bedchambers. With tears stinging her eyes, she moved to the front window to await the sight of Mallory's departure.

Once, she'd considered her married life staid and boring, with too little emotion and far too much quietude, but how things had changed in the course of a few weeks. Impatient and unsettled by not only the conversation with her father but the confrontation with Lord Mallory, she turned from the window, unwilling now to stare at the empty drive for the satisfaction of the man's departing carriage. Mallory would take his leave in due time. She hadn't the stomach to watch.

Still, as time passed and she'd paced the carpet thin, her impatience won out. Taking the stairs with silent stealth, she made a beeline for her husband's study. If nothing else, she would learn more about the man who owned her heart.

Chapter Nineteen

"Get out of bed, you bloody liar." Dearing grabbed the flannel blanket and stripped it from the mattress with a violent yank. The fingers of his other hand curled, at the ready to clutch Lindsey's nightshirt and force him to stand eye to eye for the fisticuffs he deserved, except the earl was bare-chested, clothed only in his smalls. Dearing stepped back, his punch diverted but his temper in full swing. "I trusted you as a friend. Now get up, you cur, so I can cuff you in the head."

"Milord!" The same elderly servant who'd attempted to stop Dearing at the front stoop appeared within the door-frame, his eyebrows pushed high against his hairline.

With a swift pivot, Dearing slammed the bedchamber door to shut out the servant's appalled expression and return to the subject of his anger.

"Hell, Dearing." Lindsey sat up against the headboard, his arm flung over his eyes as if to shield them from the light of day, though the curtains remained closed. "Are you foxed? Why are you here and what time is it, for that matter?"

"Time for your confession." Dearing reached for the sheet, crumpled at the foot of the bed. He'd drag Lindsey out by a hairy ankle if the man didn't confess. They locked eyes, and Lindsey's voice dropped, low and menacing.

"Is this a result of one of Mallory's ill-advised wagers?" He scowled with the question. "Or have you gone completely mad?"

"Oh, I'm mad and you bloody well know why."

"I see. Give me a moment and we'll discuss your issue."

Lindsey's expression grew razor-sharp, albeit his eyes expressed some shade of understanding Dearing pegged as guilt.

"Otherwise I will put aside our friendship and treat you in a fashion most unbecoming."

The polite threat hung between them for several moments. Lindsey was an avid horseman and outweighed Dearing by at least two stone. Dearing drew a much-needed breath. He squelched the immediate urge to react without thought and forced himself to withdraw. He didn't wish to destroy their friendship, but he was likewise after the truth, whatever the cost. Why would Charlotte come to Mayfair? Was it to visit the very room he stood in now?

Lindsey swung his legs over the side of the mattress, ran a hand through his hair and rubbed his eyes before he strode to the wardrobe, removed a banyan and shouldered into the silky garment. "There had better be a damned good reason for this intrusion."

The memory of Mallory's cutting remarks shot daggers into Dearing's brain.

"While the cat's away, the mouse will play. One wonders what drives a woman to unfaithfulness."

Unwilling to give them voice, Dearing paced to the window and back again. How much of Mallory's unsolicited remarks were irrational jealousy and how much truth? Would Lindsey stoop so low as to betray his loyalty in the very worst way? He drew a second calming breath before he began. "I suspect Charlotte has taken a lover.

She's become unusually secretive and is often away from home without disclosing her whereabouts. It hasn't escaped my notice how often you inquire of my marital harmony. Any dolt can recognize when he's being cuckolded by his closest friend. It's quick work to sum two and two."

"Ah, that's enlightening." These words were spoken plainly. The briefest lopsided grin flashed across Lindsey's face before he schooled his features. "And you're the genius who computed the maths?"

Humor didn't sit well. Dearing formed fists at his sides to suppress his rage. Aware his accusation held scarce credibility, he remained at a loss to understand his wife. Lindsey had a talent with the fairer sex and a debauched history that stretched back all the way to Eton and their wilder days.

"Did you expect to find Charlotte in my bed?" Lindsey canted his head to the left, eyebrows raised. "You can't be serious?"

Dearing jerked his attention to his friend, though he didn't answer. Did the man have a death wish to so much as suggest the idea? His eyes fell to the massive bed at the center of the room, the sheets in disarray. Lindsey was a lot of things, but disloyal? No. Deep in his soul, where he was most truthful with himself, he refused to believe his friend would commit such an act. He'd allowed his emotions to overtake common sense. Clarity returned. Dearing shook his head. It would seem his inability to decipher his wife left him prone to stupidity.

"I'll interpret your recent actions as a lapse in judgment or a rampant case of brain fever." Lindsey knotted the belt of his robe and walked barefooted to the bellpull. A sharp tug on the cord immediately produced a servant, perhaps at wait in the hall for the crash of breaking furniture. "Send up a tray with coffee." Dismissing the man, Lindsey nodded toward the chairs in the adjoining sitting room. "Come along, then. Won't this be cozy?" Sarcasm tinged the question, but Dearing followed nonetheless.

They settled in chairs and not a moment later, a tray appeared with coffee, crusty rolls and a squat jar of orange marmalade. Realization of his foolishness and misplaced conclusions caused Dearing's temper to ease. He reached for a piece of bread but didn't take a bite. "I've committed the gravest error." These words were barely audible and the crux of all his misery. These words were indeed the confession of his heart.

"And that is?" Lindsey raised his coffee with an expression of expectation.

"I've fallen hopelessly in love with my wife." Dearing cleared his throat. "Not the act of being struck with someone's beauty or caught unaware by sudden infatuation. I suppose I could explain my immediate reaction a product of that condition. But now, having shared a modicum of time and happiness with her, I possess love of the most genuine kind."

A strange noise, one of abbreviated mockery or mayhap jocularity, emerged from Lindsey's throat. "Well, that complicates things. Have you informed her of your vile misdeed?" He dared a short chuckle.

Oh, but how that question spoke to another matter altogether.

"I can't." Dearing discarded the mangled piece of bread and shot from the chair, impatient and at odds with Lindsey's waggish attitude. "Everything's in mutability."

"If ever there existed a perfect word . . ." Lindsey muttered before stirring more cream into his cup. "And from this, you believe your wife has taken me as her lover? Good to hear my reputation stands."

Dearing waved away the latter and resettled in his chair. "I don't know how to make things right."

"Of course you do. But you'll need to think on it and act because I have no more counsel for you." Lindsey poured another cup of coffee, silent and seemingly at peace with his final words.

"What do you mean?" Dearing leaned in, impatient for Lindsey to continue.

"Exactly what I've said. It's all in your control from here on. I can no longer continue these conversations. Go home and apologize if that soothes your conscience. It doesn't matter how you've gained Charlotte or what underhanded method secured her vow. She's yours. Stop wasting time. Make love to your wife, passionately and repeatedly. Cease all these ridiculous misunderstandings and preconceptions. Time is wasting. Go. Now. And don't darken my doorstep until you've achieved that goal. The stakes are high."

With Lindsey's sage advice echoing in his ears, Dearing called for his carriage and aimed for Charlotte's familial home. Nothing would be resolved with his wife if he did not first confess all sins to her father. Besides, were he to smooth things with Lord Notley, Charlotte might see reason more readily.

Because he'd like nothing more than to enter his wife's bedchambers and reveal the heartache he'd concealed for far too long. The deceit was destroying him, piece by piece, from the inside out, and he wanted his marriage happy and complete. His despicable secret needed to be told, but only after he first confessed his love for her and how he'd thought of her every moment since he'd first seen her, heard her music and composed his far-reaching wish she would belong to him alone.

So much had transpired between them in a short span of time and he shouldered the fault. Had they built the foundation needed to weather this storm of emotional distress and dishonesty? Doubt threatened. And now, on his way to explain to Lord Notley with painstaking clarity the depth of his manipulation, did any hope exist?

He had no time to chase the answers and once arrived

was shown into the same drawing room where he'd first breached the subject of debt compensation and offered for Charlotte's hand. The irony was not lost on him. In a matter of hours, he might not only see his marriage destroyed but his head handed to him as an extra measure.

Still, Notley was an intelligent man and, with a clear understanding of the facts, could possibly overlook his misdeeds in consideration of the relationship involved. The earl loved his daughter and despite how things would appear upon the telling, Dearing loved Charlotte just as much, if not more so. He would need to assure Notley of the same. Still, he waited and stared into the firebox, aware he'd begun to placate himself with far-fetched wishes and dreams. It would prove his most persuasive argument to convince Notley he loved Charlotte in truth and hadn't concocted the entire plot for the sole purpose of an investment advantage.

"Dearing." Notley entered, his expression more question than greeting. "What brings you here past visiting hours? Is Charlotte well?"

"Yes, of course." Dearing rose and shook his father-in-law's hand. "I hope my unexpected arrival hasn't proven an inconvenience. I need to speak to you concerning an urgent matter. There's a business issue that remains unresolved and I'm here to correct the wrong."

"Wrong? This sounds ominous. Would you care for a brandy?" Notley gestured toward a stout chestnut sideboard where a collection of crystal decanters stood.

"Thank you, no. I'd much rather begin." Dearing watched Notley's expression. The earl looked a bit sheepish, if that could be possible. He certainly wasn't the one in the wrong.

They settled in two leather wing chairs and Dearing quickly began. "First, I'd like to return the share of Middleton Railway stock given to me when I assisted with your financial difficulties."

"Return it? I don't understand. Combined with investment in the company, you hold a fortune in your hands." Notley's expression turned dubious.

"But I don't deserve it."

The earl stared at him overlong, and somehow Dearing maintained eye contact, though the worst was yet to come.

When at last Notley spoke, his voice was an ominous growl. "You don't deserve it? Have you injured my daughter's feelings? Have you hurt her in any way?"

"No." Quick to answer, Dearing rose from the chair and walked to the hearth, the weight of Notley's piercing glare heavy on his shoulders. "At least not yet. The answer to your question is complicated."

"Then by all means explain, and do it without pause."

"Last year I began to purchase Middleton Railway stock with the single goal of gaining a controlling interest. I exhausted every opportunity but still had not amassed enough to hold the majority. Through my secretary's inquiries, I discovered you held a single share. Alone, the certificate held little worth unless leveraged against a larger investment. But that single share was all I needed to hold the majority, so I instructed my secretary to prepare correspondence in that regard. At your instruction, your solicitor declined my offer." Dearing drew a breath. "I assume at that time you had no financial worries and there existed no reason to part with a stock that offered security for the future."

"I understand." The clipped words sounded as if they barely held Notley's impatience at bay. "But what has this to do with my daughter?"

"Please hear me out." Dearing continued, though the telling would only become worse. "Determined to insinuate myself into your company and persuade you to sell, I deliberately attended the same affairs as your family. I made a point to frequent the parties and balls where you'd accepted invitations, and that's where I first discovered Charlotte."

"You explained much of this when you first spoke to me of marrying my daughter. What bearing does this have on the present?"

"It wasn't only Charlotte's music that drew me in. Your daughter enchanted me in every way. The lilt of her voice, the sparkle in her eyes . . ." He cleared his throat briefly. "I became besotted, much more interested in Charlotte than in any share of railway stock."

"And so you mean to return it now? Dearing, you've overlooked an important matter. You saved this family from ruin and asked for nothing in return aside from a woman who you profess stole your heart. It's very generous and kind for you to make this offer and it raises your esteem in my eyes, but it's unnecessary."

The earl's expression again turned sheepish for reasons Dearing could not imagine. He swallowed past his hesitation and pushed on. "It's more involved. Please allow me to continue." He returned to the chair and met eyes with his father-in-law. "Wishing to gain favor with your daughter, I questioned anyone willing to spare a few moments of conversation. In the process I learned several gentlemen held hope of courting Charlotte. Some had already acted on impulse and gained favor in her company. One boasted of an imminent proposal. Their titles were loftier, their fortunes larger, their social standing highly respected. In my assessment, I didn't measure up. I couldn't compete with a pristine pedigree and a bloodline descended from royalty. They were far ahead of me in the game of suitable matches and held all the advantages."

Notley had the polite inclination not to comment, though his jaw was set tight, his interest keen.

"Once my heart was given, my brain worked tirelessly to achieve my goal. I needed to devise an expedient way to win Charlotte's hand and discourage others. I'm a businessman whose greatest offerings are shrewd intellect and cutthroat negotiation, not attributes ladies prefer in gentlemen, but avenues of pursuit to change the rules and outcome."

"So, my fiscal hardship became your advantage. I understand, Dearing, and though it displeases me to hear it spoken aloud, this is not an altogether reprehensible thing. You took advantage of my failing finances, but by the same stroke, you saved my family from destitution." Notley nodded thoughtfully. "One act washes away the other. You salvaged us no matter how you examine the facts."

"You may not see it that way in another moment. I haven't explained everything." Dearing exhaled and steeled himself. Regret knifed him in the gut at the explosive truth he needed to confess. "I manipulated the course of your investments. I purposely targeted the major companies that provided you income and wealth and systematically bankrupted each one."

Notley went incredibly still. It appeared he didn't even breathe. Then he shot from his chair, his complexion reddened and his eyes wide with anger. "What did you say?"

Dearing managed a hard blink, saved from repeating his despicable admission by Notley's thunderous outrage.

"You intentionally bankrupted me. You endangered my family's security and reputation because you wanted Charlotte. My daughter is a treasure, that is true, but you should have courted her like any other gentleman and gained her favor."

"And what if I failed? I calculated the odds. I measured the risk and judged the outcome. Watching Charlotte become another man's wife was an unacceptable proposition. Perhaps too many years of obtaining what I wanted without compromise blinded my better sense, but I have no regrets in making Charlotte my wife, just the manner in which I did it. I never meant to harm anyone and had complete control of the situation at all times, though I find myself at a loss to defend my methods. I only knew how desperately I wanted Charlotte."

"I should call the authorities." Notley strode to the sideboard and poured himself a brandy. He took a long swallow. "I've reassured Charlotte of your feelings and smoothed away her confusion with the explanation that marriage is an adjustment, but I never could have predicted this."

"You should know I reversed all detrimental manipulation of your investments once Charlotte accepted my proposal. Your finances are once again in good standing and all profits you might have earned have been set aside in a separate account for your daughter."

Silence enveloped the room.

"Can you put yourself in my place for a moment?" Dearing waited for what seemed an interminable time.

"No." Notley shook his head emphatically. "What you did was unscrupulous and reprehensible. The reason for your actions doesn't exonerate the method. If it wasn't my precious daughter's happiness at stake, I would show you to the door with the heel of my boot."

"I understand." And he did. Any respectable father would act with equal outrage. "I'm sorry for putting your family through distress. I hope you can come to accept my apology."

"I'm not sure how to react, Dearing. You hurt my family to gain Charlotte because you care for her. Yet if that's true, why would you begin a marriage with lies and deceit? Such an endeavor is sure to fail. And when I think of Charlotte's confusion and yet her total agreement to marriage in light of our penury, my daughter deserves better."

Dearing sighed heavily. "I intend to tell her the whole of it, but I needed to speak to you first."

"Another manipulation?" Notley seemed to adjust to this news.

"No. Charlotte will need reassurance, and if I've any

hope of gaining her forgiveness, she must know you've learned the greater truth."

"Which is what exactly?"

"I love your daughter above all else." He stared directly at Notley so there could be no doubt of his confession. "I went about my business in all the wrong ways, but at the core of every action was my determination to win Charlotte's hand."

"Win her hand?" Notley harrumphed. "You stole her from me." He stood quietly and assessed Dearing with a keen stare. "Have you succeeded?"

"It's my solitary goal and purpose."

Notley nodded. "If you're able to convince Charlotte of your sincere affection and she harbors no anger, then we'll see ourselves to a resolution. Though I daresay I will never repeat this to my wife. She won't behave as graciously. It's best left between the three of us."

Something akin to relief coursed through Dearing. "I'm a lucky man," he assured himself more than Lord Notley.

"Lucky to be leaving with your teeth, Dearing. Keep that it mind when you tell my daughter the truth of it all."

Chapter Twenty

Undiscovered and confident, Charlotte closed the door to Dearing's study behind her with a decisive click. That in itself was an unexpected boon. Had her husband left in a rush and therefore left the lock unsecured? Or had Mrs. Hubbles recently visited to stir the fire and then, called away, left the door open? Charlotte didn't know and didn't care. Answers lie within the room. Of that she was certain. She'd not waste time with unresolved riddles.

She began with his desk, its orderly appearance daunting at first glance. Would he recognize if she left a paper a hair-breadth to the left? With precise accuracy, she sifted through each portfolio atop the blotter. Ledger sheets, contracts and assorted legal documents looked little more than gibberish to her untrained eye. She moved next to the drawers, the two side compartments organized alphabetically and otherwise fruitless, although she did locate the railway certificate to which her father referred. She took a moment to peruse its contents. From the attached letter, it appeared Dearing held controlling interest in an incredibly profitable enterprise. If she ever disbelieved her husband's shrewd financial acumen, this served as proof to eviscerate doubt.

She withdrew the true certificate from her skirt pocket and compared the two. Her father had spoken accurately. It would be difficult, if not impossible, to ascertain which stock document was authentic, which a duplicate.

Had Dearing specifically asked for this share as payment for the debt he'd incurred on her father's behalf? He couldn't have sought her out particularly to gain the Middleton share, could he? Was the investment his main objective or had he truly wished to be her husband?

A rare form of panic seized the breath in her lungs, alarm combined of fear, love and desperation. Her thoughts splintered into too many questions to consider. Could he have acted with malice and calculation? She forced herself to draw air. Dearing's business skill was his pride. To possess the power afforded by the Middleton share set his regard above most others. But was she a way to a means and nothing more than a path to controlling the largest railway enterprise in England? Her heart pounded so loudly the sound reverberated in her ears.

No.

She refused to believe Jeremy would take advantage of her family's unexpected penury for his own gain. As stated by her father, and proved by Jeremy recently, he wanted her, not a share of railway stock. Wasn't that true? She drew in a gasp and considered the idea more closely. Her husband had proved to be many things, but he was not so cold, devious and deceitful as to manipulate people's lives for his profit. She rejected the notion and would not be part of yet another deceptive maneuver.

Careful not to confuse the papers, she took the false document to the firebox and without a second thought thrust it into the flames. The foolscap caught and burned to ash within two beats of her heart. Unwilling to consider her actions further, she returned to Dearing's desk and replaced his folder with care, the genuine certificate folded neatly inside. Then she closed the drawer slowly, so as not to disturb the inkwell or quill atop the blotter, nor the silver letter opener angled across the corner of a thin folder. She drew another breath and stepped backward, as if a separation could calm the frenetic racing of her nerves. Now everything was back the way it should be.

Across the room, she eyed the walnut bookcases, stalwart and looming, at each side of the windows. Dare she continue her investigation? If there was more to uncover, she would know it now. A confrontation like the one brewing would be served best by airing all misdeeds, wouldn't it?

Still she remained motionless, the tick of the regulator clock over the mantelpiece calming her by degree. She should leave now and go upstairs. What if she discovered something truly despicable? How would she continue? Indecision stalled her a moment longer until, on silent slippers, she crossed the rug.

Several tabletops were littered with maps and their necessary wrappings. A satinwood table near the window held a glass pot where a modest Athyrium fern struggled to drink in sunlight. The contrast of green foliage to the piles of lifeless paper proved ironic, the spiny fronds kept alive by Mrs. Hubbles's efforts, most likely.

What was she doing? What did she hope to find and why was her heart poised for disappointment? She swallowed past the emotion in her throat. Was her behavior foolish? An excuse to place blame for the problems in her relationship somewhere else and not with her person? Emotion and intelligence waged war on her actions.

A strong beat of helplessness, *hopelessness*, gripped her, and she sank against the side of a bookcase, all at once defeated. What did she mean to prove? That her marriage was nothing more than a sham? Her emotions unimportant? Her future desolate and unfulfilled?

No. She refused to allow unsubstantiated suspicions to

take hold. So much had come to pass in so little time, her heart squeezed with regret. Had she truly believed she would uncover the source of Dearing's contrary composition, or had she hoped to affirm somehow, through the contents of his sacred study, that he in fact cared for her? One couldn't prove another's devotion by the method she'd chosen. Would she remain in a loveless marriage or find her way to the loving marriage she desired? She remained hopeful.

A wry chuckle itched her throat, but she refused its heartless bid. Leveraging her shoulders against the side of the bookcase, she pushed back on the plank and hoisted herself to stand. A strange shuffling sound, wood upon wood, accompanied the motion, and she turned to repair whatever she'd upset with her actions.

But nothing appeared out of place. Several rows of leather volumes, thick and faded, stood firmly tucked against one another. A decorative crystal globe acted as a bookend on one side, where a brass sculpture shaped into a horse's head secured the other. Each shelf remained intact, untouched and, like so many problems in her life, perplexing.

At a loss, she placed her palm flat against the side of the bookcase and pushed in hope the disturbance would repeat itself, but nothing happened. She was far too slight to cause any significant pressure, and perhaps the shuffle she'd heard was merely the scrape of some shifting whatnot that decorated the shelves.

She dismissed the noise and stepped away, though a voice in her head urged that she take a glance backward. And then she saw it. Behind the largest volumes at the center of the shelf, a panel appeared exposed, the slide of wood against wood apparently the sound she'd heard. Returning to the bookcase, she removed the heavy volumes, five in all, and used them as a stepping stool to gain a better perspective. Her pulse drummed in her ears, louder than her breath, harder than her heartbeat.

As she'd suspected, a moveable panel appeared incorporated into the back of the bookcase. It had shifted when she'd angled her body to stand. Pushed fully to the side, it revealed a hidden compartment, rectangular in shape and as narrow as it was deep. A path of perspiration formed a valley between her breasts. Her chest tightened and her palms became clammy. Why would Jeremy need such a place? What was she to find hidden within?

Most gentlemen kept a safe for important documents and expensive jewels, but a panel and secret compartment screamed of distrust and, worse, misdeed. Did she truly wish to see what was inside? The pulse at her temple hammered an objecting beat, as if to warn *don't do it, don't do it*. Still, insatiable curiosity had long ago become her master.

Piling more books atop those stacked on the carpet, she raised above the compartment far enough to lean in and lower her arm behind the false panel. At first, she believed the space empty and found a moment's respite from fear as her hand swept through the hollowed wood.

But on the third pass, her fingertips brushed against something hard and flat. Despite her best attempt, she couldn't extend her arm deep enough to grasp the object, not even when she rose on tiptoe. Stepping down from the piled books, she pushed her sleeve upward and shook out her arm as if to lengthen it by force. Then she added another volume to the pile, the stack already precariously high.

Nothing would stop her now. Anything worth hiding in darkness must be important, if not dreadful indeed. And if her husband had something so precious it required a secret hiding place, she intended to discover it.

With patience and remarkable agility, she extracted the box from its hiding place, the contortions of her fingers fueled by determination and curiosity, though her hand went numb with the attempt to replace the narrow panel. Then, at last, exhausted from the effort of her exploratory search, she sank against the bookcase with the rectangular black box in her grasp.

She turned it over, the smooth leather cool against her damp fingertips, the box so light it might very well be empty. Surely that was nothing more than a wishful thought. Still, there was only one way to know if it was true.

Her gaze fell to the lock. A burnished bronze escutcheon winked in reflection of the overhead sconces. At its center, a narrow keyhole waited, and her heart lurched with instant recognition.

The key upstairs in her bedchambers.

Heaving a shuddery breath, she clutched the box to her chest and rushed for the stairs, only pausing on the way out to close the study door behind her. A shadow near the hall bid her to hurry. The last thing she desired was for Mrs. Hubbles or Hudson to witness her discovery.

Upstairs, the bracket clock on her wardrobe chimed the hour near midnight as she settled atop her bed, the odd bronze key held tight against her damp palm. She heard the scuff of footsteps and occasional betraying noises that revealed someone's presence in the rooms beside hers. Whether a servant or Dearing, she didn't care. She'd reached her room uninterrupted, pleased Jill had already tended the fire and prepared for the night hours. She'd thrown the latch, placed the box atop her mattress and fumbled through an assortment of hairpins and earbobs in the porcelain jar on her vanity until she'd located the key found weeks ago on her bedroom rug. Then, key in hand, she'd paced, heart and mind at war.

Ultimately, the need to know brought her to a decision.

Yet she still hadn't opened the box.

Now, with the last chime signaling the new day, she waited no longer. The key fit the lock securely and, with a twist to the right, a metallic click confirmed she'd achieved her goal. She released a breath composed of trepidation and relief.

She'd stolen the box from her husband's study with the intention of opening it and revealing something he'd chosen to keep hidden. Did her perpetration equal his? She swallowed past those doubts and slowly lifted the lid.

Inside, a single folded sheet waited. Her heart thudded in her chest, but she didn't hurry her actions. She leaned closer to the bedside lantern and eased the paper out of its hiding place, carefully replacing the box on the mattress.

Her posture stiffened. Her hands trembled. And then she opened the paper and began to read. The neatly printed words had been prepared by her husband's secretary, as indicated in the left-hand corner. The contents composed a listing of negotiations and transactions, but as she continued down the page, Faxman's iteration of the purpose for the series of purchases became clear.

Tears blurred her vision and she wiped them away. Could it be Dearing had never wanted her at all? His actions nothing more than a wicked business maneuver? Each line of writing in front of her seemed to indicate that horrid truth. In a quest for profit and the controlling share of Middleton Railway, *her father's share*, Dearing had stooped to unforgivable tactics. If she interpreted the information correctly, her husband had forced her father into dire circumstances, causing his ruin with deliberate, heartless pursuit. Once Dearing purchased the businesses composing her father's financial investments, he'd forced the same companies into bankruptcy. With the family's security in peril and an isolated share of railway stock left, her father surrendered it, unknowingly granting the controlling interest to Dearing.

Her father's confused frustration at how his investments had deteriorated and then rebounded in the few months after her wedding haunted her. At last she'd solved the puzzle of Dearing's marriage proposal. No wonder he had asked for her hand with rash determination and unexpected resolve. He'd forced her father into crucial insolvency and proposed to her immediately after? Was his goal to avoid discovery and accusation by becoming bound to the daughter of the victim of the crime? Could the same man who'd spoken to her with sentimentality and roses possess a manipulative, cynical heart?

A ragged sob broke loose as the idea gained clarity. It explained Dearing's distance and emotional detachment at the onset of their marriage. Perhaps he sensed her insecurity and now played his role more thoroughly these past weeks by showing implicit interest in her preoccupations. Her hands shook violently as she replaced the paper within the wooden box and gingerly pushed it beneath her bed. She couldn't bear to look at the words any longer. They swam into an inky blur as her tears came fast.

She'd defended her husband to her father. She'd believed Dearing deserved the authentic stock certificate. But now, knowing this, nothing excused the actions he'd taken to destroy her father. She was blinded by affection, convinced she loved her husband and hopeful for their future, but she had been wrong. Wrong in many ways.

Still, one thing remained certain, and her foolish heart ached as she affirmed the decision. She wouldn't continue this pretense of a marriage. She'd tried to become the perfect wife. She offered her heart again and again.

No.

Come morning, she would gain distance from Dearing's conflicted adoration and lies. She would seek the wisdom of the one person who stood by her no matter life's twists and turmoil.

Without a doubt, Amelia would know what to do.

Chapter Twenty-One

Dearing returned home, his emotions spent and his mind clouded with regret and determination. He could very well lose his wife over the mess he'd created, though he hoped somehow Charlotte would forgive him and understand he'd never intended to cause pain and mistrust. Once home, he inquired of Charlotte's welfare, dismissed Hudson and headed for his study. He needed a drink.

Intent on ordering his thoughts before breeching the subject with Charlotte, he went to the door and paused, somewhat puzzled as his hand twisted the lever and found the lock unsecured. He stepped inside, unprepared for the sight revealed by the ample lantern light. Faxman lie face-down on the hardwood flooring, his eyes closed and his body sprawled, as if he'd taken a tumble.

Good Lord, he'd worked the poor man to death.

Dearing rushed to his secretary's side, kneeled at his elbow and pressed two fingers to the man's neck. A rush of relief flooded him as Faxman's pulse, strong and steady, thrummed beneath his fingertips.

With no hesitation, Dearing strode to the bellpull to

summon Hudson and then rushed to the liquor cabinet, where he poured two fingers of brandy and acquired a hand towel to dip into the pitcher of water left there.

He wiped the cloth over Faxman's brow, assured of the man's strength when his secretary squinted his eyes open and groaned.

"What happened?" Faxman moved to sit up, seemingly anxious to regain decorum, though he slowed his actions and raised a hand to rub the back of his neck.

"I hoped you would tell me." Dearing offered the bourbon and, to his surprise, Faxman accepted the glass without comment. "I've only recently returned home and come to the study to think a moment. Instead, I found you sprawled on the floor."

"I was struck." Faxman's expression transformed to one of troubling concern. "I too returned late tonight because the calculations in last year's ledger continued to haunt me. I hoped to review my work and determine why the sums weren't in agreement, but I'd hardly opened the books when I was approached from behind. Someone struck me with something." Faxman's eyes scanned the room. "It could have been anything, I suppose. I didn't have a chance to react." A fair share of remorse accompanied that statement, and he rubbed the back of his head a second time.

"No one would." Dearing rose and walked a small circle, his mind reeling at what the intruder might have sought. Hudson and the full staff remained inside Dearing House. Could Charlotte have allowed someone in? That idea seemed unlikely. He would need to question Hudson further. "Can you stand? Would you like me to summon a physician?" He offered a hand to Faxman and pulled him upright.

"Nothing more than a bump on the head. I apologize for the inconvenience." Faxman's eyes shot to the regulator clock. "The hour is late. My wife must be worried."

"Are you well enough to leave? You're welcome to take a room upstairs. I can have a message sent to your home. Otherwise, my carriage is at your disposal, Faxman. I regret what happened tonight, and the situation is troubling. Whoever struck you must have sought something important." His pulse tripled as he perused the room. Things were out of place, drawers partially open and papers disordered. His desk was in complete disarray. Damnation, what if Charlotte had crossed paths with the intruder? Thankfully, she never entered his study, never searched for the secrets he'd hidden, but if she'd heard a sound she might have entered and been hurt.

"I'm quite all right, thank you." Faxman finished the last of the brandy in his glass. "A good night's sleep will cure this headache, most certainly."

Dearing remained silent in anticipation of his secretary's tendency to quote the wisdom of his father or offer an antidote with some uncanny parallel, but the moment passed.

With little more than a nod, the men parted in the foyer, the hour beyond late. Dearing instructed a footman to summon the carriage and return Faxman home. Then he tried to close off the scene in the study, concern and curiosity gnawing at his better sense. Sleep would not come easily, and he remained anxious to examine the study tomorrow in the light of day.

The house was silent; if only his soul could find the same peace. Once he checked the locks and walked through the ground floor, he climbed the stairs to his chambers with too many thoughts crowding in at once.

He made quick work of removing his coat and waistcoat, his cravat abandoned to a chair in careless preoccupation. He rolled up his shirtsleeves and rubbed his palms over his face. What a complicated mess his life had all become.

He walked to the hearth and poked at the logs in the

firebox, setting a maelstrom of sparks into flight. His mind raced, his blood rushed hot in his veins and he cursed the late hour or else he'd wake Charlotte and lay his soul bare in the hope she would forgive, accept and mayhap attempt to love him. He knew deep emotion existed. They'd come so close. Still, the agonizing truth of his manipulative decisions had ruined every attempt at happiness.

The unexpected situation in his study could be the work of a common thief or mayhap it had been a specific and intentional robbery, yet even that troubling distraction couldn't divert his heart.

In one decision he remained resolute: Come morning, there would be no more misunderstanding of ill-placed sentiment. Come morning, he would finally claim his wife.

Morning brought with it an abundance of sunshine. Ordinarily, Charlotte would delight in the mild travel conditions for her trip to Beckford Hall, the country estate of the Duke and Duchess of Scarsdale, but she experienced no cheer today. Instead, the hour's ride seemed endless.

Before she'd left, she'd dashed off a short note to Amelia, explaining her need to visit, and dispatched a messenger with Hudson's assistance. The butler also arranged for the carriage travel without question, despite the early hour and unusual circumstances.

Now settled against the bolster with Shadow curled in her skirts and Jill at her side, Charlotte exhaled a long sigh of despair. Her maid knew better than to attempt convivial conversation. Much could be explained by the tear tracks and reddened eyes.

The roads were clear and the carriage made good time. As the wheels crushed the gravel of the circular drive before the grand country house, Charlotte managed a slight smile.

At least here at Beckford Hall she knew herself. She was safe and with friends who cared for her well-being. No sooner did the main house come into view than she gained a sense of calm. The expansive estate, built in the Gothic revival style, was faced with Totternhoe stone, and with its low-pitched slate roof and castellated parapet gave the impression one was entering a fairy tale.

Her mood improved further as Amelia fairly skipped down the limestone steps to greet the slowing carriage. Yes, this was her best decision in a long time.

"Darling Charlotte."

Amelia hugged her as soon as she was able, and Shadow skittered from the carriage to slink away and explore before Jill could catch the kitten's tail.

"Thank you, Amelia." Charlotte returned her friend's embrace. "I don't know where I would run if not into your arms."

"Hush. You belong in Dearing's care. We'll have this sorted out in no time." Amelia took a long, assessing glance. "Your note gave me hardly any details. What's happened? I can see the despair in your eyes."

They looped arms and followed a graveled path away from the house toward a garden that bordered the acreage in manicured hedgerows and flower beds of every color and variety.

"I've missed our morning conversations." Charlotte tried for cheerfulness. "We used to walk to St. James's Square and plan our futures as if wishing alone would make them come true."

"Real life has a way of intruding on daydreams, doesn't it?" Amelia answered. "Tell me all of it. I believe Dearing cares for you deeply. He must have behaved horridly to drive you out of the house."

They paused beside a bed of crimson roses, and the memory of the single bloom Dearing had left across the pianoforte caused her heart to squeeze. For a moment, she couldn't catch her breath.

"Do you remember when we went shopping on Bond Street and I mentioned finding a key?"

"I do."

They continued on, unhurried, their stride in tandem. Charlotte sighed. Somehow moving her feet made the explanation come easier, and she let the words flow. "I discovered a locked box in Dearing's study, hidden in a secret compartment behind a bookcase. The key fit perfectly. Inside was a list of several despicable business transactions completed by . . . my husband." She'd once thrilled at that possessive pairing of words. Now she wasn't sure how to feel.

"For what purpose? Dearing has amassed considerable wealth. I imagine profit and investment business are cutthroat endeavors, but how terrible could these dealings be?"

Charlotte matched eyes with her friend. "From my understanding of the document, Dearing's purpose was to secure my hand in marriage."

Amelia's quickly drawn breath expressed her surprise. "That's lovely."

Charlotte shook her head in the negative, leaving Amelia to unriddle her meaning.

"No?" She wrinkled her nose. "I suppose he might have pursued your affection in a more traditional manner."

"Yes." Charlotte dreaded explaining the extent of Dearing's manipulations. She hesitated, even though she knew Amelia would listen with an open mind.

"Still, all things considered, it's quite romantic. Don't you agree? Dearing went to exorbitant lengths to make you his wife. As you remember, Lunden wouldn't allow himself to care for me. I needed to force him to forgive himself and see reason. Otherwise we'd never have found this happiness together. Perhaps you shouldn't discount Dearing's efforts."

Charlotte swallowed hard. "You don't know the rest of it. You haven't heard the worst, and when you do, I doubt you'll be drawing sentimental conclusions."

They walked a few steps farther before Charlotte gathered the courage to reveal her husband's bold misdeeds. Voicing the truth aloud made it more real. And too she didn't wish for Amelia, and thereby Lunden, to think poorly of her husband even though her heart broke further with every breath.

"Dearing purposely forced my father into ruin so he could step in, offer financial salvation, obtain a valuable share of railway stock and gain my hand in marriage." Tears stung the corners of her eyes, but she did her best to resist, pinching her lids closed and wiping away the moisture. "Do you think I was an afterthought, or a means to prevent my father from seeking retribution should Dearing's misdeed be exposed?"

"Oh." It was a rare day when Amelia was speechless.

Charlotte waited, anticipating so much more than her friend's quiet response. "Amelia?"

"Yes?"

"I don't know what to do. I'm married to a deceitful, despicable man. And worse, I love him dearly." She sniffled in a desperate attempt to maintain her composure. "Should I confront him? Tell Father? All the while, I own a part of the guilt. I stole the box from his study. When he discovers what I've done, he'll be livid."

"What *you've* done?" Amelia's eyes flashed with anger. "That should be your last worry. You've done nothing wrong. The larger question lies in the reason for what he's done. With Dearing's wealth and reputation, he had no need to behave so nefariously. Wouldn't you have found him suitable? He's handsome enough. Had he ever approached you before? Called on you to pay suit? Something doesn't make sense here."

"I agree, and I've often wondered. Before all of this, I enjoyed attention from suitors, but I never considered the future in earnest. There didn't seem a need, and I spent all my time with my music. It was my family's unexpected loss of security that brought about the change.

"Jeremy often seems at a loss for words. I assumed at first it was the awkwardness of our new marriage and then perhaps shyness that kept him reserved and locked away in his study. Despite his seeking me out, we were, in essence, married strangers. But then something changed, a shift in mood. It was small steps at first, a few words of conversation and laughter. Then, lately, our relationship has been more like it might have been if he'd courted me. I was encouraged to believe . . . until this." Her voice went soft with sadness.

"There might be a logical reason he would employ extreme methods. I suspect you'll never know until you confront him."

Amelia was a problem solver, although Charlotte doubted her friend could find a way to repair a situation of this magnitude.

"I've tried to reason it out, find an explanation I can live with, but all I've accomplished is headache and heartache. Whenever I think of my parents' distress and how solemn our house grew when they shared the burden of our crippling penury, I despise Dearing. How could he cause such pain for his own selfish reasons? None of it makes sense, yet I saw it with my own eyes, penned out neatly by his secretary." She shook her head in frustration.

She'd lain abed all last night attempting to maintain outrage, but the intrusive memory of Dearing's kiss repeatedly spoiled the effort and the dichotomy of both emotions tore her heart in two. She didn't want to believe the worst.

They'd only just begun to find their way to happiness, and now, through her snooping, she'd brought about a fate that couldn't be ignored and, worse, extinguished any hope for the future.

"All isn't lost." Amelia managed an encouraging smile, though they both knew the seriousness of the situation.

"Was I just a means to an end? Can he truly love me considering his motive for our marriage?" She sighed, her heart heavy in her chest. "And should I love him in return?"

"No one can answer those questions but the two of you, though I suspect you'll both need time and a lengthy conversation to see your way through this." Amelia spoke with such determined intent, Charlotte dared believe it true. "Besides, who couldn't love you? Or wouldn't love you? The very idea is preposterous."

Comforted by her friend's teasing, they held hands and continued their walk, Charlotte's mind busy in an attempt to distract her heart.

It was half past ten when Dearing awoke and, with a few choice curses, dressed quickly without the assistance of his valet. Sleep had proved evasive at first, keeping him awake through the wee hours, and he could only rationalize that condition caused him to oversleep. His heart and mind were definitely not at ease. With purposeful strides he took the stairwell and nearly collided with Hudson. The servant lingered so closely to the newel post, he almost obstructed passage.

"Good morning, Hudson." Dearing inhaled a deep breath. "Is Lady Dearing at breakfast?" He intended to share the meal and then ask to speak to her abovestairs, where they wouldn't be interrupted and the servants wouldn't hear her tears or, worse, her anger.

"No, milord." Hudson's discomfit was palpable, the older servant at a loss to hide his concern.

"Out with it." The day would bring about its own misery without additional household drama.

"Lady Dearing requested the carriage readied and left with her maid at sunrise."

Dearing caught another curse on his tongue. His well-planned confession would have to wait until his lovely wife returned. "A day of shopping, I presume?"

His brain quickly cataloged a series of unlikely departures from Dearing House at odd hours despite his insistence that Charlotte tell him whenever she left the premises. Something was wrong. Hudson still appeared upset, and a chill of foreboding overtook the hall. Had the butler seen something last evening? Was something nefarious afoot? Could the two matters be intertwined?

"Lady Dearing required a footman's assistance, milord."

Hudson's reluctant admittance did nothing to convince Dearing a sense of impending doom was unwarranted. "For what reason?"

"Her traveling valise, milord."

"Her valise?" He skewered Hudson with a glare that had the servant speaking faster.

"Lady Dearing stated she planned to visit the Duke and Duchess of Scarsdale indefinitely." Hudson's eyes flared with the retelling. He finished in a distressed tone, thereby communicating he believed Charlotte's departure was definite after all. "She took her cat."

One didn't pack a trunk and collect the cat if only for a short visit.

Dearing's pulse leaped to a gallop. "This isn't your doing, Hudson." He advanced toward the hall, yet he stalled a pace later. He'd almost forgotten Faxman's injury and the trespasser. "Did you notice anything unusual last evening? Did you see a stranger outside Dearing House or otherwise detect any noises beyond the most mundane?"

"Nothing, milord." Hudson shook his head, his expression curious. "Lady Dearing came home and met with Lord Mallory in the drawing room. She must have kept the visit short and seen the gentleman out, as she did not call for refreshments or my assistance."

"Mallory?" What the devil? "Why was this information kept from me, Hudson?"

"You returned after I'd retired and have only just awoken, milord." Hudson didn't continue, though the natural assumption that his wife would relay the news seemed to hang in the air with a persistent voice of its own.

Mallory was an issue that needed to be solved. The intruder was best left in the hands of a Runner. "Someone accosted Faxman in the study last evening. When I returned, I found him sprawled on the carpet after he'd been struck from behind. I planned to examine my papers this morning with fresh eyes and new light, but finding Lady Dearing away from home requires my immediate attention. I'll need my horse as soon as possible."

"Very well, milord."

Dearing bolted from the hall and into his study, where he took in the interior with exacting detail. Most everything had been displaced, but most notably, the largest drawer on his desk remained open the width of two fingers. He approached, aware without a second glance the certificate of Middleton Railway stock was gone. It made sense. Mallory was the lowest feeder on the social chain of character. Yet Dearing didn't care a bit.

Charlotte was safe. Faxman would be fine. Now to more important things.

He strode to the far wall and stared at the bookcase in a moment of incisive determination and then cleared the third shelf with one sweep of his hand. Hauling his desk chair into position, he snaked his arm into the hidden panel and discovered his worst fear. The reality of the moment struck him hard, a hammer to the heart, leaving him as empty as the concealed compartment.

He removed himself from the bookcase slowly, dropped into the chair and closed his eyes. He'd worked tirelessly to prevent Charlotte from knowing the depth of his dishonesty, but he'd failed, not just in this, but in all things. And at that, he hardly believed they could survive the wreckage of his deceit.

He opened his eyes and waited, as if by doing so the solution would permeate his brain. Faxman chose the inopportune moment to enter, though one glance in his direction had the secretary stalled in midstep.

"Should I return later, milord?"

Dearing could imagine how he appeared, slouched in his desk chair amid the clutter, utter devastation etched into his face. "Why are you here, Faxman?" He collected himself and with a deep breath rose from the chair. "Has the knock on your head rattled your brain?" He didn't offer the chance to reply. "Get yourself home. I won't be available today. I have an important appointment."

The secretary pulled a wary glance.

"You heard me correctly, Faxman. Take the day. Let's make it a paid holiday. Do something worthwhile and unexpected. You have a little one at home, don't you? Spend some time walking in the park while the sun's high." Dearing decided his course as neatly as if he'd swung a sextant across one of his maps. He had no time to waste and too much ground to claim.

"Thank you." Faxman seemed startled by the sudden and unusual suggestion. "She's growing so quickly, and I've already missed some of the finer moments." The secretary picked up his satchel from where he'd only set it a moment before. "In the wise words of my father, one can't go back and make a new beginning, but one can always begin again and make a new ending."

"Indeed." With his own thoughts pressing in, Dearing almost missed Faxman's comment, the message finely tuned to his predicament.

Chapter Twenty-Two

Dearing rode like the devil chased him, the wind in his face, and by the time he'd arrived at Beckford Hall exhausted but determined, he'd considered his argument. He loved Charlotte, and despite the misguided choices he'd made, he couldn't foresee a future without her. Somehow, he would convince her of that truth.

He handed off his mount to a lad at the stables and rounded the gravel path to the front door, where a butler took his card and deposited him inside an intimidating room of dark wooden paneling and navy-blue detail. It was very ducal and reminded any guest left to wait he was of lesser rank than the owner of the premises.

Scarsdale entered swiftly, though he didn't smile in greeting. They shook hands, but by the nature of his expression Scarsdale communicated this was not to be an easy conversation.

"What is this about, Dearing?"

Where to start? How to answer? For all his contemplation, Dearing hesitated. Would the duke appreciate frank honesty or a subtler approach to the subject? He wanted to speak to Charlotte above all else. "You can't keep my wife from me." The words were out before he considered any others.

Scarsdale chuckled, and the sound reverberated in the otherwise quiet room. "I can and I will. Charlotte is a guest in my home and therefore under my protection."

"She doesn't need protection." Dearing took a step closer. They had yet to claim chairs. It would appear the discussion was to be as difficult as he'd anticipated.

"That's debatable." Scarsdale turned and strode behind his desk. He dropped into the leather chair, the position magnifying his authority.

"Come now, Scarsdale, you know me." In truth, their wives were as close as sisters, though Dearing had only spoken to His Grace a handful of times, most recently at his own wedding celebration, but that had been attended by so many people, it offered little privacy for meaningful conversation.

"I don't know you," Scarsdale replied in a matter-of-fact tone. "Not well enough. I know what I've been told by my wife and her dearest friend. And I know what's said about you. Talk at the club paints you as a ruthless businessman who pursues what he wants with relentless fervor without a care for the consequences." A hard beat of silence followed. "Now it seems you've used those same callous tactics with Lady Charlotte and I can't say I approve."

"It isn't that way."

"Are you suggesting my wife distorted the truth?" Scarsdale's voice gained a menacing tone.

Dearing exhaled thoroughly. "Not at all. The ladies don't have the truth in entirety and therefore are only able to judge my actions by a portion of information."

"So enlighten me, Dearing." Scarsdale leaned back in his chair, his stare unyielding. "And then perhaps I'll reconsider."

* * *

"Dearing is here." Amelia burst into Charlotte's room, Pandora and Shadow chasing her skirts in a blur of black fur. "That's a very good sign."

"In what way?" Charlotte stopped her pacing, though her heart launched into a frantic beat. She'd hoped her husband would follow her. Didn't that prove his affection? Or was it ridiculous to cling to every sliver of his actions as evidence he wasn't the villain?

"The only way for the two of you to understand and plan a future is by working together." Amelia stooped and collected Shadow in her arms, much to the objection of Pandora.

"But what he did is appalling, unscrupulous, deceitful—"

"Imagine how much he wanted you, then."

"I don't wish to believe the worst." Charlotte sat on the edge of the mattress and laced her fingers in her lap in an attempt to calm her emotions. It didn't work.

"Scarsdale's with him now." Amelia settled beside Charlotte and handed off the kitten. "If anyone can elucidate the truth, my husband can."

"What if the truth reveals the worst?" She despised herself for admitting her fear, but at least Amelia would comfort her in return.

"Then we're all the better for seeing Dearing for the man he is and not the man we want him to be." Amelia rose and walked to the door. "Though I don't believe he's mean-spirited. I never have. My interactions with him have been limited, colored by what you've told me of your marriage and its difficult beginning, but just as I held fast to my belief that Scarsdale hid a tender heart beneath layers of uncomfortable regret, I believe there's more to Dearing's actions."

"I hope so." Charlotte breathed a little easier. "I love him, Amelia." Her voice broke as tears threatened, but she wouldn't allow them to materialize. "And hold fast to the changes our marriage experienced of late because now he has my heart."

"We won't allow him to break it, then."

Charlotte tried for a smile, the outlandish suggestion and confidence of her friend's comment enough to lighten the mood.

"Why don't you take some air? The flower gardens behind the house served us well when you arrived, and the orchids are in bloom along the eastern path. There's still an hour or two before dinner. I'll join you if you'd like."

"No, thank you. I need to sort my thoughts before talking with Dearing. It's difficult for me to understand his motives, but at the same time, I feel as if I'm betraying my father by loving the man who brought about such hardship and distress." She rose and reached for her pelisse where it rested on a chair. "Scarsdale wouldn't send him away, would he?"

"No," Amelia answered quickly. "But I'll speak to him once he's come from his study, and if there's anything to share, I'll find you among the flowers."

Amelia slipped from the room without Pandora and Shadow, who lazed on the floorboards in a collection of fractured sunbeams. Anxious for a respite from the knowledge Dearing remained in the house, Charlotte went downstairs and out the back door into the gardens. A few ominous, pewter-colored clouds threatened to obliterate the sun, but for now they hadn't succeeded, and she took the winding path deeper into the lawns in search of clarity and resolve.

Eventually, she settled on a limestone bench beside the orchids. Their fragrant beauty offered a peaceful calm. This was what she needed: absolute quiet and the hope her heart and mind would negotiate a truce.

* * *

Dearing found her among the orchids, her complexion as pale and delicate as the blooms near her feet. Scarsdale had dismissed him with a congenial suggestion he peruse the estate's library. Dearing wasn't fooled by the polite invitation to stay out of sight, and he had no intention to abide by it. He'd come to speak to Charlotte, and allowing more time to pass, time that could harden her heart against him, was unthinkable. So, after a brief search within the house, he'd ventured to the gardens. It was late afternoon and the air held a chill, a signal the weather would take a turn, but he followed the slates deeper into the acreage, uncaring of anything besides finding his wife.

And then he did.

He stood motionless in observation, not unlike those first few gatherings where he'd come to appreciate her music and admire her beauty, unsure of how he could ever capture her interest. But that was before he'd machinated the situation that tore them apart now.

He might have exhaled too loudly, or mayhap she'd heard the pounding of his heart, because she glanced over her shoulder and spotted him at several paces. She rose from the bench, her expression stricken and eyes wide, and he put his palm up flat, not knowing if she meant to flee. He didn't wish to startle her and add another sin to a growing list. She looked at him directly. If only she could see inside his heart.

"I know what you did."

Those weren't the first words he'd expected, but it didn't signify. Better to delve straight into the matter than waste precious minutes with meaningless chatter. "But you don't know why."

He stepped closer and she didn't move. If he could draw her into conversation, he could lay bare his soul.

"Does that matter?"

"Very much so," he answered, not knowing where he stood in the conversation.

She huffed, her expression one of hopeless distress, perhaps torn between listening to him or heeding her own objections.

He stepped within a stride. "May I sit with you?"

"I'd rather walk." She notched her chin. How strong she appeared. *And resolute.*

"Then may I walk with you, Charlotte?"

The briefest flicker of emotion showed in her eyes and she nodded consent before she followed the slates. She didn't spare him another glance nor touch him, and he fell into stride.

"I never meant to hurt your family." It was as good as any place to begin.

"But you did." Her tight-lipped answer urged him to continue.

"Yes, that's true. Since that moment, I've rectified every account. Every cent that was ever earned from the transactions has been set aside, separate from personal profit." There was comfort in discussing fact instead of the scalding emotion yet to come.

"Why?" She darted her eyes from his face so swiftly, he felt the loss of her attention like a thorn in his chest. Would she not look at him?

"Because of you, Charlotte." He stopped walking in hope she would do the same, and when she turned, he could see unshed tears in her eyes.

"I don't understand. You went to great lengths to cause my family grief and then come to our rescue. You proposed marriage when I'd never met you and I complied because my family's future hinged on that decision. And yet you stand here and tell me you had no reason for any of it aside from wanting me? Couldn't the same have been achieved through an introduction? A courtship?" Her brow furrowed, and she looked away before she met his eyes again.

"I heard your music first and fell in awe of your remarkable skill. But then I saw *you* and realized whatever I'd experienced previously paled in comparison. All at once I understood why I'd been put on this earth. Why I drew breath and my heart insisted on beating. I was taken with you from that first moment and I've never recovered. But my inquiries met with concern. You were admired by many. Several esteemed gentlemen vied for your favor, and while I attended a few functions and sustained a respectable reputation, I possessed nothing in comparison to centuries of blue blood and societal respect."

Her expression softened, though a hard gleam remained in her eyes, whether from anger or hurt he couldn't know.

"I saw you and I wanted you. At any cost."

"At my family's cost," she answered in a harsh whisper. "At this cost." She waved her hand through the space separating them.

"I admit, I became obsessed. I needed you. Is that an unforgivable sin? To want someone's company so badly you ache from the inside out? To yearn for one touch or smile, the promised glory of a single kiss?" He breathed deep. "I wanted you in entirety."

"Those are pretty words."

"They are the truest truth."

"You expect me to believe that despite our hardly knowing each other, you saw me and became so consumed with the idea of seducing me, you were blind to logic?"

"There's no right answer to that question, Charlotte." He wanted to reach for her. If only he could pull her into his arms. "If I answer yes, you'll accuse me of selfishness and perverse infatuation. If I answer no, you'll be offended and never understand the depth of my sincerest emotions."

"But you didn't tell me what you'd done. Even when—"

She paused and appeared to force herself to calm. "Even when we began our life over again. These past weeks, when you knew I wished to come to your bed, you said nothing."

"No. By then, the risk of losing you was too great, and I feared I would. We'd just begun to discover happiness. Instead one lie led to another."

"That's how lying works."

"I'd already spent the first portion of our marriage racked in guilt, paralyzed by the atrocity of my deeds."

"Rightly so." Her anger was justified. "Omission is the most dangerous lie because it destroys everything without revealing itself."

She glanced to where her fingers gripped her skirts. He watched as she relaxed them against the fabric while her response carved a hollow space in his chest, each word anxious to tear at his heart.

"We promised to have no secrets."

"That promise happened too late." He offered a reminder of a sweeter time. "After a kitten, as well. I'm so sorry, Charlotte. I never wished for this to become what it has. I only wanted you in my life." Emotion clogged his throat and his words came out husky and broken. "For always."

Still she didn't react.

"Did you assume you could confess and be forgiven? That an apology would somehow erase the deed? Was your affection these past weeks a means to guarantee my understanding?"

A tear broke free and slid down her cheek, and it was all he could do not to reach for her. To wipe away her tears and somehow find the words to convince her of his sincerity.

"No." His answer sounded useless and insufficient.

"You didn't just manipulate my family. You manipulated me. You trammeled my future and forced me to make a decision I'd otherwise have time and reason to consider."

She closed her eyes in a long blink and then exhaled soundly. "What about the railway stock?"

"It means nothing, no more than a convenience when society assumed it spurred my interest, but the opposite holds true. As soon as I saw you, I could no longer imagine my life without you. I wanted you at any cost." He would fight for her understanding.

"As you've said." She shook her head in the negative. "I need to think, Jeremy."

He watched her every emotion and steeled himself when she said his name. Would she send him away? Had he destroyed the very thing he'd yearned for from the start?

"I spoke to your father yesterday. I told him all of it." He'd almost forgotten to mention the worth of her family's assurances. "Your father accepted my sincere apology and wants for you to be happy. Nothing more."

"I might have found happiness. I have strong feelings. But this, between us . . ." She shook her head again, and another tear escaped.

A cloud rolled over the sun to cast them in shadow, and though they stood only an arm's length apart, they might have been across an ocean on different continents.

"Can you find it in your heart to forgive me?" He waited, his teeth clenched so hard his jaw ached, but she remained silent. "We're married, and despite my despicable methods in forcing our vows, it was with the intent to love and cherish you for as long as you'll have me."

The unanswered question, of how long that would be, hung in the air between them.

Charlotte looked at her husband and her heart squeezed tighter. He was handsome and heroic, contrite and infinitely saddened, terribly dashing and likewise vulnerable, all at the same time. She believed every word of his surprising truth, his confession a flattering reality. Yet it did little to assuage the storm of emotion within her.

Could she trust a man who manipulated countless people to achieve his goal? Who'd kept a devious secret? Perhaps it was her hand and heart he was after, though the romantic notion was better left aside for later consideration.

"I worried for so many reasons when our marriage began. I doubted myself in every way, unable to understand your unexpected shifts in behavior. You left me to wonder how I'd failed, or if I'd forced you to spend hours in your study without so much as a word passed between us." As the accusations clipped out, her voice and anger grew stronger.

"I've wronged you, Charlotte, and for that I'm infinitely sorry. I can't undo my poor decisions. I don't expect you to excuse them. Even though I achieved my goal and married you, I've never been more ashamed and mortified at the methods I committed to claim you. Still, despite your rightful hostility and anger, if this same course led me to you, I won't regret my choices, only the pain I've caused you and your family."

The tender note in his voice reached beyond her temper and touched her heart. His sincere declaration caused more tears to well. Hope, translucent and ephemeral, pulled her toward forgiveness. The first sob caught her unaware, but then there was no way to stop her emotion. She'd worried he'd found her lacking. That she'd never have an intimate bond with her husband and a loving family of their own. Never that he'd utilized the most extreme method to ensure she would be his wife. Relief rushed in and overtook anger as she wiped at her cheeks, her heart free.

The skies opened in kind.

He didn't move. Neither did she. And the rain fast became an onslaught. It drenched them in a matter of heartbeats, and with belated awareness, he reached for her to provide protection from the downpour, curling her into his body as they moved toward the side of the house.

It might have been laughable if so much hadn't happened before the rain. When at last they reached the shelter of an awning near the rear wall, they were both out of breath, their exhalations a misty cloud of exertion between them. Her clothes were soaked through and the wet silk clung to her skin. Wisps of hair, loosened from the hurried escape, were plastered to her temple and neck. She blinked away a stray raindrop in her lashes, her first thought that she must look a fright. But then she glanced at Jeremy and her heart seized.

Rain dripped from his tawny locks, the droplets lending his skin a glistening sheen, while his velvety brown eyes glittered with unspoken emotion. Behind him, water sluiced off the awning and created a curtain to seclude them from the rest of the world. She didn't know when their breathing evened, when the air changed from cool to warm, when they moved significantly closer, but as they did, pain, loss and unanswered frustration transformed into another ache altogether.

She'd married this man. She'd come to love him and glimpse the future they could share. She wouldn't deny now what she wanted with every fiber of her being.

They fell into a kiss with reckless surrender, aware of the inevitable and the unrelenting desire to feel each other's touch. Their clothes were soaked through, but beneath, their bodies heated. And when he gathered her into his embrace, she knew her heart was given. There was nowhere else she belonged.

Chapter Twenty-Three

Rain splattered against his back, dripped from his hair, ran from his forehead, but he didn't pause to wipe it away. In the shelter of his embrace, her scent wrapped around him and lured him closer. The force of his kiss raised her to tiptoe and sent his senses reeling, much as they had the day he'd first seen her, and his internal compass spun out of control. But this was now, and she knew his grief and still allowed his kiss.

He slanted his mouth hard over hers in a mixture of words and deep, lingering caresses.

"What have you done to me, Charlotte?" He nibbled a path from her lips to her ear, where his whisper induced a shiver. "You've ruined me. Caused me to become besotted and lust-addled, delirious with want."

"Jeremy," she whispered against his mouth.

"What is it, my love?"

She gasped at his question, then drew him closer. Her hands grabbed his shirt and formed fists to hold fast.

"Let me come to you this evening, Charlotte," he murmured the intimate plea. He didn't want to wait. For all the wrong reasons, he'd waited too long already.

"To my rooms? I don't know," she stalled against his mouth, though she didn't break their contact.

"What don't you know?" He withdrew the slightest and wiped raindrops and tears from her cheeks, no more than mist between them now. "So many times I almost told you what tormented my mind and lived in my soul. You've had my heart since the first moment you turned your blue eyes in my direction. I've made many poor choices and I pray you'll forgive me because the one thing I know above all else is that we belong together."

She melted against his chest and he wrapped her tighter. The rain continued, but they stayed blissfully unhurried, captured in the moment. Still, he needed her to know, to believe. His kiss became a declaration of possession, empowered by a cherished memory.

"I remember the moment I saw you. You'd finished playing a masterful selection and a dozen guests gathered near the pianoforte to compliment your skill. A few dashers vied for your attention, and I stood across the ballroom on the fourth step of the marble stairs. A ridiculously thick crush of a hundred people or more celebrated with champagne and laughter, though beat by beat my heart eliminated distraction. First conversation, then melody." He inhaled against her temple, taking in her musky floral scent. "The bidding of servants, the clinking of glassware, and the nearby tapping of heeled slippers. One sound after another vanished, my entire existence reduced to breathing and taking you in. I was changed in that timeless moment, forever altered. I don't know how long I stood there, if anyone noticed, what forced me from that undeniable alteration, but I've fast concluded whenever I see you, the results are the same." He withdrew the slightest. "You're not in my heart, Charlotte. You *are* my heart."

He tilted her chin with his forefinger and lowered his mouth, licking his way into the kiss, finding her hot, sweet and equally anxious. Their tongues tangled, every twist and rub drawing them deeper into an erotic spell, as if they lived in a dream, cut off from the world by the weather and any intrusive emotion. Pressed tight to a blanket of ivy against the house and buffeted from the weather on the other side by a sheet of water, he held her firmly and offered lovely pleasure. His kiss, the slide of his tongue against hers, became a sensual assault meant to convince her they were meant to be.

He cradled her face and somehow reduced all sensation to where their mouths connected. In the past, unspoken words had built walls between them; now, he aimed to topple them all. He nipped at her lips, kissed her possessively, wooed her, worshipped her, all in the span of this moment.

The rain drummed down, the heavens opened and they were soaked to the skin, heated from the inside out. He wouldn't have her catch a chill. He forced himself to break contact, holding her close as their mindless desire abated.

"We should go inside."

"We should."

Neither of them moved.

"I'll get you inside." His voice was rough.

"I'll come to you this evening." She placed a hand upon his chest, over his heart. "It's better that way."

He wondered for the briefest flicker if she wavered but likewise knew she needed to control the decision after having so many taken from her.

They hurried to the kitchen door, located at the rear, and scuttled inside, startling the busy kitchen staff.

With apologies and exclamations about the inclement weather, they maneuvered through the work area and back into the main hall, no longer dripping water on the tiles.

"I'll not be down to dinner." He couldn't sit there and

wait for nightfall while she made polite conversation across her soup.

"I rather wish you would. I want Amelia and Scarsdale to see how truly charming you are."

"So I'm to be charming?" His mouth twitched with amusement.

She returned a grin of mischief. "It's a natural quality if only you'd allow yourself. With our disagreement aside, I would think it's no effort at all." She moved past and took the first few stairs. "I'll see you later."

He raised his eyes to watch her go. "Until then."

Charlotte looked in the cheval glass over the mahogany armoire. Jeremy preferred her hair unbound. She combed her fingers through the lengths and then cinched the sash of her silk wrapper. An eager pulse of anticipation urged her to hurry, but she meant to savor the moment of what would occur tonight, the loss of her virtue and the beginning of her future. She allowed a secret smile. Jeremy waited. They would share a bed, the night and most importantly each other. Effervescent hope tingled through her and she welcomed the feeling as she unhooked the latch and left her room.

"Oh." Amelia stood in the hallway two paces from Charlotte's door. "I was coming to check on you. You seemed unusually quiet at dinner. Was it because Scarsdale spoke to Dearing frankly or because your husband took a tray in his room instead of coming down to the dining room?"

"Neither actually." She folded her lips inward to conceal an anxious grin. "I'm going to his room now." Again, the shimmer of expectation coursed through her. "He's waiting for me."

"I see." Amelia's eyes danced with understanding. "Then I certainly won't detain what's long overdue." Her final words were thrown over her shoulder. "I'll instruct the maids to leave you undisturbed."

Charlotte hurried off in the opposite direction. She breathed deep and knocked, relieved when the door opened without delay.

"You're here." He spoke, his voice soft and serious, though his heart thudded in his chest.

He dropped his arm from the frame and she entered, her hair unbound in a blanket of silk around her shoulders, glistening strands of brown and amber against her white silk wrapper.

She looked at ease, but when she didn't reply immediately, he wondered if she'd changed her mind.

"Of course." She turned to face him. The open draperies on the far wall set her against the night sky and created a masterpiece, Charlotte swathed in moonlight, a familiar midnight dream.

"I wondered if you'd changed your mind."

"You needn't have worried." She smiled then, and he couldn't pull his eyes from her. At last, here she stood, beside his bed, with nothing between them but silk and linen. That thought alone ignited fire in his blood and the randy urgency to get on with it.

"Why?" He threw the latch on the door and locked the past on the other side. He stared a moment at the closed panel, unsure if he wished to read the emotion on her face were she to say something he'd rather not hear.

"Because I love you."

He didn't move at first. Then he turned to find her crystal-blue eyes stricken with honest emotion.

"What did you say?" He'd heard her. His whole body had heard her.

"I love you, Jeremy." She caught his arm, her fingers

trailing down the linen until she captured his hand within hers.

She'd professed her love. The echo of her admittance thrummed in his veins, feeding all pathways to his heart.

He drew her closer, until her head rested on his chest over his heart. "Then I believe we have a bit of unfinished business, wife." He captured her below the knees and lifted her. With three strides, he deposited her atop the mattress. Before she could object, not that he expected she would, he untied the belt of his banyan and shed the garment.

Charlotte watched with avid interest, her color high.

"Are you going to strip down completely?" Her voice was a hushed whisper in the dark shadow of the bed-curtains.

"Yes." He wouldn't mince words. He intended to love his wife thoroughly.

"Should I remove my wrapper?"

"Not yet." He sat beside her on the mattress, pulling her into his lap with one easy swoop, his gaze focused on her mouth.

Charlotte swallowed any further questions, suddenly perched atop her husband's lap, the rigid length of his erection pressed hard against her bottom. It was happening at last. No secrets or misunderstandings. No misplaced feelings. Tonight, they would be together as one.

Her eyes searched his face until they anxiously fell to his mouth, a mouth that tempted and reminded her she was a woman, one who was passionate and eager to explore the man she loved. A trickle of unease skittered up her spine. Would he be disappointed with her lack of experience? Would their joining be pleasurable? There was only one way to discover the answer. Without a word, she skimmed her fingers over his bare shoulder. His muscles twitched, the flesh quivering against her touch. His arm tightened around her waist. His eyes flared with her flirtatious perusal.

"I've waited for this a very long time." Her words were soft-spoken, though she meant them sincerely.

"Have you, now?" There was no mistaking the note of male pride in his husky tenor.

"Yes." She traced her fingertips over the fresh growth of beard along his jaw. The texture enthralled and tickled with the knowledge his body was hers to discover. "I want to be your wife in every sense."

"Charlotte, love." She dropped her hand as he drew her in for a kiss. "You *are* a delightful surprise."

His mouth descended to hers, but he paused when a question tumbled from her lips.

"Would you like me to lie down?" She was inexperienced, and yet she knew enough that intercourse occurred when a man lay atop a woman.

"No." He caught her bottom lip between his teeth and took a nibble.

She moved slightly, the rigid length of his thick erection an insistent reminder they remained in the wrong position.

"Now should I remove my wrapper?" Clearly, she had too much clothing on. Beneath her robe and night rail, a trickle of perspiration traced the curve of her spine.

"No." His voice was a muffled groan against her neck, where he trailed hot kisses.

"But—"

With something that sounded like a chuckle, he shifted her position so she straddled his lap, the motion pulling her silk wrapper tight, though the belt held, her breasts and sex outlined in fine white silk.

"Can we . . ." She struggled to express the idea, her body sensitized and tingling from his every touch. "Like this?"

A grin broke across his face, glorious and devastatingly handsome.

"And so many other ways as well." He inhaled a long breath and his smile dropped away. With a sudden tenderness, he eased her down to the mattress. "Let me teach you the pleasure we'll share for the rest of our lives." He whispered the last words against her lips as he aligned with her body and captured her mouth.

Any thoughts of being ravished, plundered and overcome dissolved in the heat of his kiss. This kiss, his kiss, lingered long, to seep into her bones and settle into the marrow . . . to etch its message upon her heart. This kiss said *I love you.*

And somehow, they both knew they did, at last, and always.

He withdrew slightly, far enough so her vision was clear. When she opened her eyes, his gaze, intense and enigmatic, was filled with unguarded emotion.

She waited for him to say the words she longed to hear.

"I'm sorry, Charlotte."

Her expression must have shown her surprise, these three words not the ones she anticipated, though he continued.

"I'm sorry for interfering and changing the course of your life, for altering the hopes you had for the future."

It wasn't what she'd expected, but it proved equally important. "Don't apologize, Jeremy. I would never have known you had you not interfered. And if I hadn't met you and accepted your proposal, I would never have fallen in love with you."

Everything fell away, leaving only truth.

"I love you, Charlotte." It was the most honest thing he'd ever said. He exhaled and leaned in to savor another openmouthed kiss. "More than the air I breathe. As much as the human heart can hold the emotion."

There wasn't anything left to say after that. In the glow of lanternlight, first her wrapper, then her night rail, met their disposal. He stared at her with such intensity, her skin flushed. He rose and turned to the side while he unbuttoned the placket of his trousers, adding each piece of clothing in an untidy heap on the floor, until he stood in nothing but his smalls. She watched with fascination, his muscles at work with simple domestic movements, though she sat mesmerized in silence.

He returned to the bed and again found her mouth, leaving kisses along her jaw, to her neck and shoulders. "So lovely," he murmured, low and dark, his deep tenor full of forbidden promises. "So very lovely and so very mine."

"Always yours."

"I intend to be gentle and loving and careful, but at the same time, my desire for you has consumed me for so long . . ."

"I am yours, dear husband. I give myself to you with love in my heart."

He climbed atop the mattress and brought her to his side. His eyes swept over her bare body, and her skin flushed from the fervent look on his face. She reached forward and stroked her fingers across his cheek, and from there any remaining words were abandoned.

He angled above her, swept her beneath him and into a deep kiss that caused her senses to reel and her heart to pound harder. Each stroke of his tongue seemed to beckon her further under a passionate spell, and all reservations became lost in the search for pleasure. Everywhere she touched, he was hard, smooth and hot. The muscles at his shoulders bunched and relaxed beneath her fingertips. The solid tenseness of his biceps where he held his arms and braced above her caused her to ache with want, a wish to explore his body as he did hers.

He swept his tongue across her collarbone and down to find her nipples ruched and sensitive. The slight scruff of his chin chafed with a pleasurable burn that hinted at their differences, man and woman, soft and hard. He teased and suckled at her breasts while sensations shot through her like a shower of embers from the hearth; as soon as one extinguished, another burst forth.

The weight of his thighs on either side of hers reminded her of his strength, while every kiss, caress and fondle was tender and reverent. The stiff press of his erection brushed against her and she shivered with anticipation, a coil of desire tight in her belly. Lower, where she grew wet and anxious.

She slanted her hips, encouraging him to cease his fragile treatment. When he didn't immediately respond, she wound one leg around his and opened herself to him, the position of their bodies all at once connected at the core. She heard his groan on a rushed exhalation beside her ear, and then he entered her with a groan of immense satisfaction. She embraced the fleeting spark of pain, the hard fullness of his arousal thrust deep within her sex. Tears threatened from emotion, no other cause, but she blinked them away and watched as he opened his eyes, their gaze locked as tightly as their bodies. They stayed that way a long minute, joined, body to body, heart to heart. And then, with no other goal than to increase their gratification, his movements became a steady rhythm to stoke their passion.

Chapter Twenty-Four

Dearing held tight to the last vestige of control. He'd wanted Charlotte for so long and now, with not a thing between them but body heat, they at last found bliss. Nothing had ever felt so right. Nothing ever would until he bedded her again. His shy, beautiful wife was a passionate, eager lover, and he reveled in the future before them, shimmering with unending happiness.

He buried himself in the lush friction of her warmth, her body soft and accepting, her muscles quick to tighten around him. His heart threatened to burst from its ferocious pounding. His breathing sprinted. Every muscle, every cell of his being, raced toward one outcome. To bring her pleasure. To at last be joined as one. To consummate their marriage as it was always meant to be.

He tempered his thrusts, wanting the first time to be glorious and yet at a loss to control his body's yearning. Her scent permeated the room, floral, light and seductive. Her skin smoother than the finest silk, urged that he savor every moment. He gazed at her face, flushed pink and lost in sensation.

She was close. He could tell from her soft, panting breaths and the tense quivering of her legs beneath him. He angled a little higher and rubbed against her sensitive core until her thighs trembled against his and she hummed out a gasp of utter pleasure. Still he stroked and withdrew, determined to increase her climax. She pressed her hands to his biceps, gripped his arms as the muscles bunched, until she fell silent all of a sudden.

Tempted to close his eyes and lose himself in the tremendous pleasure of each stroke, he forced his eyes to hers, and what he saw urged his release. Charlotte with her lids closed, aflutter to every movement, her satiny bottom lip bitten in a display of withheld passion. He'd never imagined a more sensual vision.

"Let it out, my love." He thrust in deep and she gasped, her eyes wide open now. "Feel me inside you as you've lived in my heart since that first moment." He couldn't last a second longer and braced himself so his weight didn't crush her as his body seized with a burst of immeasurable gratification.

Charlotte snuggled against her husband, wrapped in his arms, the musky scent of his skin a precious reminder of their shared intimacy. No wonder women whispered of such things. Were there any words to truthfully describe the intense joy or steadfast bond formed by their joining? Her body simmered with satisfaction and excitement while her mind imagined all the nights she would spend this way, nestled in her husband's embrace, spent from lovemaking.

As if he read her thoughts, his palm skimmed over her abdomen, up to one of her breasts, where he cupped her and teased the tip.

"We have all night." Her face heated with the blatant suggestion, anxious to bring him pleasure yet shy with their intimacy.

"That's true." He pulled her closer still and his husky reply caused goose bumps to dot her skin. "And at the same time I've wasted weeks, months and have so much to make up for . . ."

His answer transformed into a throaty chuckle as he nipped her bare shoulder, quick to kiss the same spot right after.

"We both do." She shifted so she could match his gaze. "But everything that happened brought us to this place, and now we have forever in each other's arms."

"Forever, yes."

He looked deeply into her eyes and she saw only honesty and devotion.

"You are my today, Charlotte, and all my tomorrows."

He dipped down to steal a kiss, and a lock of hair fell over his brow. She reached up and threaded her fingers through the thick waves, reveling in the gesture as she pushed it back into place.

"I know." She inched closer and leaned into his heat to press a kiss to his jaw. "So much has happened in so short a time and yet we still mourn the loss of what might have been. But I don't wish to dwell on the past. We've come through stronger for our struggle. Nothing else matters now except the future we build with each other."

"Agreed." He caught her mouth in another lingering kiss and they fell back to the sheets.

Nothing would ever feel this right. No matter what crossed their path or attempted to separate them, this was how it was meant to be. She was here, in Jeremy's embrace.

"I can't wait to get you back to Dearing House."

He seemed to hesitate, though he stroked his fingers down the curve of her back in a tender caress. She had trouble comprehending his words. "Mm-hmm." Her answer sounded more like a purr of pleasure.

"We should leave as soon as we've breakfasted and expressed our gratitude to the duke and duchess."

He cupped her bottom with his palm and gracefully swept her beneath him without so much as rustling the sheets.

"Are you trying to distract me with conversation?" She laughed softly against his shoulder, content to feel his weight bear down on her. "You needn't bother. I come to you willing and anxious."

"Thank God for that."

The morning meal proved fast and cheerful, expediated by the unspoken communication between Charlotte and Amelia. Scarsdale seemed equally amused at their hurry to be gone. Not less than two hours later, Charlotte and Dearing were in their carriage and headed toward home, much to her anticipation and pleasure.

"The weather is fair and the roads clear." He took her gloved hand in his and gave it a slight squeeze. "We should be returned within an hour's travel."

"I don't mind sharing conversation with you." She almost giggled, carefree relief and exhilaration lending her words a joyous note.

"We should celebrate this evening. Mrs. Hubbles will prepare us a feast."

This time she allowed her laughter to bubble over. "That's not necessary. I rather like the idea of swift dining. It will have us retired to bed faster."

His chuckle combined with hers. "Indeed. I adore your manner of thinking." He pressed a kiss to her temple, but she could feel the mood change although she could only see his profile.

"What is it?"

"I almost forgot." He reposed against the banquette, though he didn't release her hand. "A troubling situation occurred hours before I left to come find you. Faxman was knocked unconscious—"

Her gasp gave him pause.

"He's all right. There's no need for concern. Although I suspect Lord Mallory caused the injury and then helped himself to something in my study. Something that doesn't belong to him."

"I don't understand." Unbidden, the reminder of Lord Mallory's insinuation that he would spread rumors concerning Dearing and her marriage or worse, arrange for an improper episode, invaded the interior of the carriage and caused her to shiver.

"It shouldn't be your concern." Jeremy gathered her closer to his side. "What did he want when he visited? I've never found the man to be one I'd keep in company, never mind allow to speak to my wife without me present."

A thrilling realization, that Dearing loved her deeply and would protect her without question chased away the unsettled emotion conjured by Mallory's mention.

"I don't care for him either." She huffed a little breath. "He said he wanted to meet with you but would change the course of conversation if I was the only one present. Although I didn't find the conversation to my liking."

It must have been the note in her voice, or perhaps she'd stiffened the tiniest degree, because Jeremy quickly shifted position and clasped her chin to turn her eyes upward. He then dropped his palms to her shoulders in concern. "What did he say to you? I'll call him out if he's insulted you in the least way." A harsh gleam flashed in his eyes. "He didn't touch you, did he?" He punctuated this question with a slight tightening of his hold.

"No." She shook her head, then answered with more certainty. "No. You're becoming angry and there may be a logical explanation for his visit."

"I don't think so. At least not one I'd accept as satisfactory." He loosened his grip and hauled her closer to his side.

"Mallory is orchestrating something. I don't know what it is, though I'm sure it's nothing pleasant."

"He said he would spread unseemly rumors about our marriage, or worse." Her voice held a note of worry.

"And he might, but why? I'm not sure of his goal." Dearing's sigh whisked over her temple. "Lindsey will know. The earl is aware of everything that happens at White's, right down to how frequently the footmen sneeze. As soon as we're home and settled, I'll seek him out." A beat of silence followed before he spoke again. "Was there anything else troubling you?"

"He's a detestable man and I dislike speaking of him, that's all."

She considered the stock certificate she'd discarded in the hearth and her father's trickery but thought better than to complicate the situation further. One had nothing to do with the other, and she could easily read the depth of concern etched in her husband's expression.

Regardless, she bit into her lower lip, uncomfortable with her decision to remain silent. This wasn't a secret. She wasn't purposely harboring the news and would tell Jeremy as soon as he resolved the problem with Lord Mallory. Why add to his distress when the subject of her father's manipulation would require further discussion?

No matter the mental debate, her decision didn't sit well, and she huddled into Jeremy's protection, closer to his warmth for the rest of the ride home.

Dearing strode into White's with a singular focus. Damn anyone who interrupted his passage or attempted inane conversation. He'd deposited Charlotte at home, called for a mount and left before the dust settled in the drive. Whatever

Mallory had instigated, Lindsey would be aware. The earl had an ear to relevant conversation, invited or not.

The club was crowded, the halls humming with conversation, yet as expected, Dearing found his friend surrounded by a small group of neck-or-nothings, none of them Mallory and all easily dispersed with a sharp glare and a jerk of the chin.

"It's about time you've shown your face here." Lindsey motioned toward two chairs in the back corner.

"Make up your mind, Lindsey. You tell me to get on with it and then complain I'm not here often enough."

"This has nothing to do with my personal preferences and more to do with tongue wags and empty pockets."

"Explain yourself and employ brevity. I'm in no mood for your mocking amusement."

"Indeed."

They settled in the corner and Lindsey took too long to begin. Dearing drummed his fingers against the arm of his chair, the polished cherrywood cool beneath his touch, unlike his temper.

"Shall I address the marriage or the cuckold?" Lindsey questioned in a serious tone.

"Who's marriage and what poor bastard's the cuckold?"

Lindsey's half smile escaped despite Dearing's earlier warning.

"Yours and yours."

It took an extra beat for the words to register. Apparently, Mallory hadn't wasted time with his slander. To what end? He'd likely stolen the stock certificate, so if he needed funds he had collateral. At least for the time being. Information like this was why he'd come to White's. He focused on Lindsey. "Explain."

"Your unexpected and suspect proposal to a woman you didn't know, the coincidental acquisition of the majority

stock in Middleton Railway and your lack of attendance
with your lovely wife at society's events has colored your
marriage poorly. Additionally, the gabs are saying your wife
was seen in a place where she shouldn't have been. You
can't expect the Ton to turn a blind eye, Dearing. They are
mostly weak-minded."

"You aren't and you, of all people, know the truth. Why
are we even having this conversation? Are you helping or
hindering?"

"I'm insulted you posed that question." Lindsey gave a
fleeting glance around the room. "Haven't I supported your
plan since the beginning? Haven't I offered generous
advice?"

"The worth of that remains to be seen." Dearing looked
about for a footman, one preferably with a tray full of bourbon. "Besides, I'm not so foolish to disregard that you have
a wager on the betting book to motivate your purpose. I only
wonder if the stakes have changed since you've realized I'm
serious. You had your doubts, though, didn't you? The roads
are filled with flat squirrels, Lindsey. Choose a side."

"Aren't you the clever one?" Lindsey motioned to an ap-
proaching footman. "I remain in your favor, of course, and
to that end I rejected and objected to the rumors bandied about
these walls, but the speculation has benefitted nonetheless,
and there goes the betting book. Neither are concerned with
fact as much as opportunity."

"To hell with the betting book." Dearing accepted a
brandy inclined on a footman's salver and watched Lindsey
do the same as he assessed his friend for the slightest twitch
of telling emotion. "What outrageous sum did you risk on
my success?"

This snagged the earl's attention at last.

"I wouldn't."

"You did." Dearing managed a slight smile after a long
swallow of liquor. The burn was exactly what he needed to

smooth the edges of his temper. "I suppose you'll explain it away as sport, although Mallory is in the thick of it, isn't he?"

"You were always too smart to enjoy a bit of reckless tomfoolery." Lindsey ran his fingertip along the rim of his glass. "Life is more or less a game."

"Go to hell, my friend. This is my marriage." Dearing chuckled wryly. "You know the extent I went to in order to marry Charlotte."

"It wasn't the woman so much as that stock certificate."

"That isn't true." Dearing set down his glass too hard, all humor lost.

"I see that now."

For a long moment, neither spoke, the spill of rowdy conversation an intrusive backdrop to their silence.

"In any case, Mallory's hot to have it. He's against the wall with his pockets to let."

Dearing drained the last swallow from his glass. "And now he does, stolen from my study less than two days ago."

Lindsey muttered a string of black oaths. "I knew the bastard would cheat when backed into a corner."

"What corner?" Dearing grimaced with disapproval. "You make it sound as if Mallory is desperate."

"I suppose he believes he can sell it to the highest bidder."

"Might it be noted that a single stock is worthless without the lion's share."

"You're far too honest to understand Mallory's thinking." Lindsey rested his head against the chair back as if preparing for a long tale. "Let me explain."

Dearing waited.

"Some time last summer, Mallory bottomed out financially. It was right about the time you completed that brilliant merger with the Spode family in Stoke-on-Trent. He'd considered investing in the porcelain factory, but you outbid him, and with coffers lean, he was unable to counter. While I know you for an astute negotiator, he believed himself wronged. There was nothing to his complaint aside from bitterness and unjust accusation, but Mallory vowed retribution nonetheless. So much as to say he kept a close watch on your interests, thinking he could glean a tidbit of overheard conversation to rebuild his flagging accounts."

Lindsey paused, and Dearing did nothing but nod for him to continue.

"When you showed an interest in Lady Charlotte, Mallory saw only manipulation and malice. A bit of digging exposed the fodder he needed and his belief you'd stop at nothing for that share of controlling stock. He assumed your marriage was no more than a charade for you to gain what you wanted. We argued the point, but I also knew I'd ignite his curiosity and he'd pursue his rabid preoccupation with your business acquisitions if I took too firm a stand. We entered into a wager I never thought would cause harm. The opposite, in fact. I hoped it would extinguish his misplaced anger.

"But things didn't proceed as either of us anticipated. His goal was financial recovery, while I sought nothing more than to best him and mayhap teach him a lesson. Anyway, if he does have the Middleton share, he likely plans to sell it back to you or the highest bidder, our wager be damned. He has a more profitable opportunity now."

"The bloody bastard." Dearing shook his head with disbelief. "He's a fool. My secretary has detailed records of every transaction, investment and deposit ever made through my accounts. The stock certificates are signed, numbered and registered. What could Mallory seek to achieve?"

"Blackmail."

The word sat between them.

"Then we'll turn the tables. I know what you want. I have what I want. I say we give Mallory what he deserves." Dearing stood, his mind spinning and his heart anxious to return to Charlotte in his bed. "It will take some arranging to devise exactly what type of retribution serves my purpose, but I'm up to the task."

"Excellent plan." Lindsey also stood and collected his cane. "Might I add that you hurry. I have a large sum riding on your success."

Chapter Twenty-Five

Dearing moved quietly up the stairs. He was exhausted, yet at the same time his heart sped within his chest. He'd asked Charlotte to wait for him, not knowing how long he'd be at White's or whether she was fatigued from their broken sleep the night before and their travel through the day. Understandable on both counts, and yet he couldn't help but hope she was waiting within the sheets in nothing but her lacy pantalets.

He turned the knob to his rooms and eased the door just wide enough to pass through. If she slept, he had no wish to awaken her, though a shadow of contrary disappointment muddied that consideration.

He'd dismissed the servants and now, alone by the fireplace, he removed his boots, coat and waistcoat, untied his cravat and pulled his shirt from his breeches. In this state of disheveled comfort, he moved across the floorboards, his footsteps silent, until he nearly jumped out of his skin when Cricket crossed his path. The unrepentant feline slinked below a camelback chair, no more than a whisper in the darkness.

With only fractured candlelight from a lantern left burning on the mantel, he walked to his bedchambers. His eyes adjusted to the dim interior and then his breath caught, the thud of his heart a resounding reminder he lived in the moment and not within a dream.

Charlotte lay nestled in his bed, the soft linen sheets at her waist like unfurled rose petals. He dared not move, unwilling to disturb her slumber and destroy the scene before him. He'd come to believe he would never see her like this. His wife. In his bed. A vision of everything he'd imagined and so much more yet to come.

Emotion gripped his heart and squeezed so tightly he stuttered for breath. Yes, they'd repaired the damage that had driven them apart. Yes, they'd at last consummated their vows and found pleasure in each other's embrace, but this . . . this was much more. This was an image of his future. Charlotte in his bed, in his life, in his heart.

Perhaps she heard the thunderous force of his pulse thrumming with exhilaration or sensed the heat of his desire despite the silent room, because she stirred, her creamy skin against the white linen pillow a tempting proposition to his senses.

She wore a lacy gown, something made of silk and fantasies; still, he couldn't see very well from where he stood and took another step.

This was all he'd ever wanted.

This was his now, his future, his forever.

They would share the rest of their days. Grow a family. Laugh together. Cry together. Celebrate their love.

He cherished the precious moment as a delightful suspension between lucidity and reality, when everything exists in the realm of possibility. He sighed with the peaceful completeness of that thought.

And then her eyes fluttered open.

"You're here."

"As I always will be." He moved closer to the bed, a stronger awareness taking hold now.

"Is everything all right?"

"No." He paused to remove his shirt.

"No?" She pushed up against the pillows, her brows lowered in concern.

"I'm not beside you where I belong."

She smiled, a slow curve of her lips that caused his blood to heat. And then she folded down the covers, an invitation for him to waste no more time with conversation.

He shed his trousers and smalls, quick to climb beneath the sheets and counterpane to pull closer the silky warmth of his wife. She laughed against his chest, a light, bashful sound, and he pressed a kiss to the top of her hair, anxious to taste her, inhale her fragrance, coast his fingertips over every inch of her skin.

"Jeremy, I—"

"Look at me, Charlotte." His voice came out in a husky command.

She met his eyes without pause. "I tried to stay awake, but I suppose I fell asleep. I hope you don't mind that I waited in your bed."

"Mind?" He almost chuckled. "I'm not a foolish man. In fact, I'm the luckiest man to draw breath."

She smiled, her expression one of disbelief.

How could this be? How could her torment and heartache have led her to this place? Wrapped in warm sheets and strong arms, safe in Jeremy's bed. His velvety voice said her name as if every sound was meant to be savored like a kiss from his lips. He looked at her as if he saw beyond her pounding heart and deep into her soul. She would remember the deliciously wonderful moment always. Not just for the intimacy but for the complete union of their hearts. No longer did hers beat to its own metronome, one strike at a time, but now with his in absolute symmetry.

She brushed her fingers through the hair on his chest, delighting in the texture, the skin beneath heated, the bands of muscle across his stomach smooth and hard. His gaze turned dark, his eyes as well, and she continued her exploration, coasting her palms over the broad expanse of his shoulders, the flex of his biceps under her touch. His hands tightened at her waist and she wrapped her arms around his neck and lowered his mouth to her own. They fell to the pillows, his kiss, hot with desire, delved deeper with every stroke of his velvet-rough tongue.

Sometime long ago she'd offered him her heart only to discover he wouldn't accept her gift, but now their entire world had altered and shifted into the perfect arrangement.

A sense of contentment and unexpected relief drenched her, and she allowed all logic and reason to slip away with her next breath.

Jeremy deepened their kiss as his tongue rubbed against hers with erotic invitation. They both knew what lie ahead. They chased the same pleasure. Without effort, he removed her night rail, the cool silk discarded to the floorboards. He skimmed his fingertips down her spine, tracing the arch and settling near her hips, where his thumb stroked the curve of her bottom. It must have pleased him as much as she because he growled, low and intimate, unlike anything she'd heard from him before. Her body responded, her nipples ruched tight, and below, between her thighs, she grew wet and sensitive. In a bold response, she copied his caress and found the firm muscles of his buttocks. He adjusted their position and aligned their bodies, hers beneath his, their kiss unbroken, their bodies pressed together with heat and desire.

He pulled away and whispered her name on a broken sigh. When he shifted the slightest his erection pressed against her core, hot and insistent. She trembled with anticipation, wanting to give more than receive, yet at odds, anxious to surrender to the pleasure promised by his kisses.

"Jeremy."

"Hush." He kissed her again. This time he trailed nips across her mouth and jaw, down the slope of her neck and shoulder to find his way to her breasts, the brush of his whiskers a sensual enticement.

She clenched her thighs, a ripple of urgent tension settling in her sex as he took her nipple into his mouth and suckled, the determined press of his tongue against the tip almost too much to bear. Inside, sensation swirled and built, each tremor and vibration more powerful than the last. It was as though she no longer had control of feeling and emotion. Like pinpricks of sensation, instinct and desire coursed through her with delicious force. Her thighs went slack, her legs boneless, and with that she parted beneath him, the tip of his erection against her wet heat divine. Still, he didn't enter her.

With unexpected grace, he rolled to the side and took her with him, bringing her leg high on his hip as his fingers found her sex parted and wet. She shuddered, undone by sensation, her head bowed against the muscles of his chest, her eyes closed to every nuance of their lovemaking. He smelled musky and strong. She felt cherished and loved. And when he at last stroked over her core, she called out from the sheer relief his touch offered. Yet how she ached for him and wanted more. Time ceased to exist. Sensation claimed every part of her being. He slid his fingers against her flesh in a rhythm both strong and nimble. Ripples of pleasure claimed her, beckoned her toward climax, yet he worked her still, and the tension within built toward release, as flawless as the musical pieces she practiced, as beautiful as the melodies she produced. Every caress against her folds, every touch to that bud of sensitivity, provoked another tremor of pleasure so powerful she could think of nothing else.

He slid a finger inside her, her muscles quick to tighten and quake, desperate to keep him there, but he tortured her instead. She moved closer and then back, restless with ache, and pressed her face against his heart, wanting him to somehow relieve the impatient pressure alive within her. He stroked and fondled, rubbing her, pressing in and out each perfect stroke until she could no longer bear it. She gasped, the indrawn breath fast and hard as she shuddered with release, filled with the vibrant power of climax, unable to think, only to feel.

He held her and captured her mouth for a long, lingering kiss that amplified the tremors of subsiding passion while her body remained lost in sensation, every cell alive and alert. At last, they parted on a sigh. She withdrew the slightest and found he watched her carefully.

"Jeremy." He would let her speak now. She'd have it no other way.

"Yes, sweet Charlotte."

She smiled at the endearment. "I've dreamed of your bed . . . of lying with you like this."

"As have I." The right corner of his mouth curled.

"I've imagined so many things, all of them pleasurable, some extravagant and some as commonplace as—"

"Finishing each other's sentences?"

He chuckled soft and quiet, and the sound reverberated in her chest.

"Yes." She smiled. "But I never realized how they would all feel. How you would feel . . ." She swept her palm over his chest and rested it against his heartbeat. His muscles twitched below her hand.

"How we would feel together."

He lifted her by the waist and deposited her atop him, straddled around his waist where she sat in protest, only to realize his hardness rested against the curve of her bottom. What outrageous idea did her husband have in mind now?

This was what he'd always wanted and damn anyone who thought to take it from him. He refused to think about anything beyond this moment.

Good Lord, she felt glorious.

He'd happily enlighten her chaste sensibilities with a bit of sexual knowledge. A sense of possessive pride followed that conclusion, and he gripped her hips and raised her above him before he settled her atop his aching erection.

She gasped and her eyes flared, though she didn't object. In fact, he admired her eagerness to please. Instead, she quickly adjusted her posture, flipped a length of long silky hair over her shoulder and pressed her hands against his chest in the position of someone who meant to ride.

"I didn't know this was possible."

Her quiet admission floated down to where he rested against the pillow, a man content in all ways. "We've only just begun to explore."

She rocked slightly, and he moaned.

"Have I hurt you?"

She leaned closer to his face and he groaned again, his cock hard and throbbing within her heat, every movement an excruciating stroke of pleasure/pain.

"Not at all," he gritted out before she sat up once again.

"Do you like this?"

She moved back and forth, a subtle rhythm that could only please her as much as him.

"I do."

Who was this adventuresome seductress? It would seem he still had many things to learn about his wife.

He allowed her to find her own way from there, words

no longer necessary, and threw an arm above his head on the pillow before closing his eyes. How a fetching little slip of a woman could spin him out of control he had no way of explaining, but with every back-and-forth motion, he believed his world exploded and began again, all due to Charlotte's tight grip and sweet caresses.

His endurance ran the race along with her as he lifted his hips to match her thrusts forward. He buried himself deep inside her wet softness and forced himself to withhold climax until the torment became unbearable, his own body betraying his command.

With one last joining, he slit his eyes, gripped her hips and held firm, buried to the hilt inside his wife as his entire body throbbed in release. She rocked forward, her muscles tight. Lengths of hair fell to skim his chest and heighten every sensation. Her breathy sighs whispered past his face. And then her mouth fell to his. She pressed her breasts to his heart and they lay spent in each other's embrace.

Chapter Twenty-Six

The fire was reduced to embers, but Dearing dreaded leaving the bed to add a log to the box. Charlotte lie snuggled beside him, awake despite the late hour.

"What is it?" Charlotte shifted to one elbow, her head turned to his as if she could read his mind, aware something troubled him.

"Mallory." It wasn't right to allow the distasteful name a voice in his bedchambers. The lingering delight of their intimacy still laced the room and he didn't wish to dismiss it.

"Has he spread harmful rumors? Has he wronged us?"

Clever. His wife was as intelligent as he. He wrapped an arm around her shoulders and tucked her into his side.

"Lindsey believes he has and will continue to do so. Mallory wishes to paint our marriage as a failure to win an indulgent, albeit reckless wager. He's desperate, no doubt, and likely with pockets to let. I suspect he's after the money to be gained by sale of a specific stock certificate as well." Dearing took a long breath. "Mallory stole the document from my study while you were at Amelia's."

"The Middleton Railway investment."

She stated it so matter-of-factly, he was immediately taken aback.

"How did you know?" He leaned in and kissed her hair, though his mind raced with answers to his question. "Did he speak of it to you?"

"No." She waited a beat too long. "He hinted at blackmail, so I assumed there was something he wanted."

A stretch of silence followed.

"Jeremy?"

The note of uncertainty in her voice snagged his attention. "Yes."

"I visited my father the morning before I riffled through the papers in your study." She paused, reluctance tinging her words. "Before I found the box."

"And?"

"He told me he never gave you the railway certificate."

"But that's untrue, darling. I had it in my office in my desk drawer." He wondered if she worried about their solvency. "It's of no consequence to our future and you shouldn't concern yourself. We're more than financially secure."

"No. I don't mean that. Please listen. Father had a copy made. An imitation certificate that you never questioned. He did this to protect me. I suppose he felt obliged to have some control, some tool to thwart you if you behaved dishonorably within our marriage. At least, that's what he believed and explained to me when I visited." She squirmed a little to twist out of his hold.

Dearing released her shoulder and pushed back against the pillows. Did he understand his wife correctly? "So the stock certificate in my possession all these months was a reproduction?" A bark of ironic laughter escaped. "Mallory, the fool, has stolen a fake."

"Yes . . . well, no." She shook her head. "Not exactly."

He sobered, unsure of what Charlotte tried to explain.

"You had the false copy." She clarified and hemmed her bottom lip in a moment of hesitant indecision. "You *had* it." She nibbled harder.

He thought the action endearing.

She blew another breath and continued. "I was unhappy my father had so little faith in you and so I insisted on taking the genuine document from him. I threw the counterfeit stock into the fire and put the real certificate in your desk the day I searched. That was before I found the box hidden in the bookcase and ran off to Amelia's house. Had I left things alone, Mallory would have stolen the worthless stock and not the one that holds value."

"You've no need to worry, love, despite the story being remarkable." He pulled her back to his side and stroked the pad of his thumb over her lower lip in the spot where she'd worried it. "Faxman has all my accounts in order. Real or not, Mallory can't lay claim to our funds or blackmail us. If he attempts anything nefarious or tries to sell the certificate, I will contact a Runner. He's a fool who will get what he deserves. And regardless, even if he somehow proved himself the owner, you're the only part of the marriage contract I truly wanted. I needed no stock certificate, incentive or dowry."

Her eyes crinkled at the corners, as if she were sorting through a mental argument. "You're not angry with my father?"

"No. Not one bit. I commend the earl for his clever thinking. I'm impressed, in fact." He leaned closer, their noses neatly aligned.

"Or me?"

"Never you." The words heated the air between them.

"But what will Mallory do?"

"That's another matter altogether."

Charlotte approached the staircase at Dearing House, her steps tentative in her new heeled slippers. She imagined Dearing at the foot of the stairs, gazing up at her as she descended, her lacy ballgown the exact color of her eyes, her hair done up in an elaborate style. This was the first time they would attend a ball together, and her heart quickened at the thought of dancing with her handsome husband, whirling about the parquet floor in a graceful rhythm of a waltz. It was the last celebration of the Season and she smiled to herself, glad they would have this one night to mingle among society.

Things had progressed swimmingly. Each day they became closer, more comfortable with each other, and while their nights were filled with passionate lovemaking, their days were often busy with cheerful conversation and jaunts about town. How everything had transformed so quickly was beyond belief. She held not one complaint about her dashing husband and knew Dearing House now as her home, the place she'd longed for at last a reality.

Yet when she reached the newel post on the last step, Jeremy was nowhere to be found. Hudson was absent as well, and she wondered if Jill had misinformed her when the maid stated the carriage was ready and it was time to depart.

Shadow scuttled past her hems in a swish of blue silk and ribbons. The cat had full run of the house, and Charlotte delighted in how she and Jeremy quibbled over their pet's name. Jeremy insisted Shadow have nine names to match her nine lives. Charlotte stood firm: two was more than enough.

A tenor and distinct throat clearing drew her attention to the left hall. Hudson entered and placed a vase full of crimson roses on the entryway chiffonier. Mrs. Hubbles and two housemaids followed with additional vases, each with roses of extraordinary color and fragrance. Charlotte watched with eyes wide as the maids snuffed out several candles, all save one, left flickering in a brass lantern near the foyer, before they hurried away with Hudson and Mrs. Hubbles.

The large windows above allowed ample moonlight,

which lit the marble tiles with the shimmer of golden beams. Candlelight created an enchanting softness that seemed at odds with the manner in which her heart pounded in her chest.

Then Jeremy entered in his formal attire, and she wondered if she wouldn't swoon from the sight of him. Dressed in his finest velvet tail coat with ornate brass buttons, he looked every part the dashing gentleman. His Hessians were polished to a high gleam, his snug trousers fitted to exactitude and with his hair combed back, she was quick to note the wicked gleam in his eyes.

"What is all this?" She was breathless and excited and a multitude of other wonderful emotions she couldn't take time to label.

"Tonight, at the ball, our first dance as husband and wife will occur in a room with more than one hundred people." He came to stand before her and tilted up her chin with the press of his fingertip. "I found that unacceptable."

He didn't say more but stepped back and extended his gloved hand.

"May I have this dance, Lady Dearing?"

He hadn't used the formality in so long, and yet with it came none of the reminders of where their relationship had started and how far it had progressed. Instead, her heart applauded, her body filled with happiness down to her soul. She was his lady in every sense of the word.

"It is my honor and pleasure, Lord Dearing." She placed her fingertips within his and he swept her into his arms. His scent, masculine and spicy, filled her lungs, and she breathed deeply, longing to remember every detail.

A single violin's sweet melody filled the air. Her eyes shot over her husband's shoulder, where in the shadowy corner a musician stood, stroking the bow across the strings to produce the loveliest serenade. Tears stung her eyes, the romantic gesture almost too much to bear.

Jeremy had arranged this for her. Like the roses and the trip to the museum. Her husband was romantic and thoughtful, sensual and intelligent. She was the luckiest lady in London. In all the world.

She gazed into his eyes, touched to see equal emotion in their depths, and naturally fell into step, the moment too precious to squander. His hand clasped her at the waist and she settled hers on his shoulder, the wool warm beneath her touch, her senses acutely aware of his every nuance.

He inclined his head the slightest.

"Forgive me if I have no clever conversation. Your beauty silences me. Even the smallest word seems out of place."

Her throat went thick with sentiment. "You needn't say anything, my darling."

They danced across the tiles in absolute symmetry, their steps perfectly timed; yet, as they turned circle upon circle, it was as though her emotions wound tighter and her heartbeat raced faster. He watched too, his eyes never leaving hers. She noticed the flecks of gold in his eyes, the length of his lashes, the strong woodsy scent of his shaving soap. What did he see? Did he too imagine the future ahead, filled with enjoyable days and passionate evenings?

The music ended too soon. She'd looked forward to the ball with eager anticipation, but now all she wished to do was stay home. To kiss her husband and feel his strength above her in their bed. To bring him pleasure in every way imaginable. Her mouth ached to taste him, touch him, love him as he loved her.

"We should be off." Dearing stopped dancing and traced a line down her jaw, the soft glide of his glove a sensual invitation.

"We can stay home." From the corner of her eye, she watched the violinist take his leave and Hudson return. Her husband had orchestrated a perfectly timed plan.

"You don't wish to allow me the privilege of showing

London I have the most beautiful wife?" Dearing accepted her wrap from Hudson and tucked it neatly around her shoulders. "That is equally unacceptable."

She let out a squeak of protest, too awed by the activity around her to offer a rebuttal. Jeremy donned his top hat and Hudson opened the front door. A footman appeared to follow them out, and as Charlotte climbed into the carriage she wondered at the time. How soon could they return?

"You're wearing a frown. Has my surprise upset you?"

The question was ridiculous of course, but how could she confess to her husband she'd rather they go upstairs to the bedchambers instead of greet society? Even now, under several layers of silk and linen, her body yearned with fraught sensitivity for his touch.

"Not at all." She gave him a smile.

"Then you're pleased." He sat beside her and placed her hand within his.

"Without a doubt." She leaned her head against his shoulder, unable to look in his eyes as she continued speaking. "Although I'm already anticipating our return."

He chuckled, a deep, lovely sound that hummed within the interior of the carriage. "Ah, my shy wife has a secret of her own."

A startling revelation, that. The worst, their missteps and reconciliations, and best, falling in love, seemed perfectly in place now. The future was theirs to embrace. A lifetime of contentment and love.

And when the carriage finally rolled to a stop before Compton House, Charlotte knew their arrival home would be all the more satisfying for the keen anticipation of what would transpire later that night.

Dearing exited the carriage and escorted Charlotte inside for formal introductions. The weather was fine, the evening entrancing and, in regard to his wife's pleasure, the single dance they'd already shared worth every bit of effort.

As expected, the ballroom was a crush. The end of the Season was near, and anyone wishing to be seen made haste to attend the last functions as their social calendars thinned and families vacated the city for their country estates.

A quick scan of the room confirmed his prediction. Decadently dressed ladies conversed with men in their finest attire. Wallflowers hovered near the perimeter and waggish lads strutted past, testing their confidence. The Comptons' elaborate decorations created an undeniably festive atmosphere, with an expanded orchestra ensemble to the left and a variety of refreshments near the right corner. Brightly uniformed livery served champagne and spirits from shiny trays and chaperones and dowagers clustered near the syllabub bowl, where they had a clear view of the dance floor.

"Shall I pencil your name on my card?" Charlotte's whisper grabbed his attention.

"Write my name on every line." His tease produced a delightful giggle.

"You know that's hardly acceptable."

She looked up, and the candlelight reflected in her irises, brilliant blue and sparkling, as lively as their banter.

"Perhaps you shouldn't carry that silly card at all. I'm not sure I like the idea of other gentlemen vying for your attention, unless you welcome a dance with a rake in fine clothing." He couldn't help but return her smile.

"I believe my escort fits that description best of all."

They might have continued their flirtation if Lindsey hadn't sidled up, brandy in hand, droll smile in place.

"Dearing."

"Lindsey."

"Lady Charlotte." Lindsey took her gloved hand and placed a lingering kiss on her palm. "You're even lovelier than I remember. It would appear marriage suits you. Why would Dearing bring you to this ridiculous crush when he could have you at home, all to himself?"

Lindsey's scandalous murmurings caused Charlotte's face to pinken, although she wasn't one to shy away. Among the many gifts of their newfound happiness, confidence seemingly bloomed within her.

"I've wondered the same several times this evening." Charlotte eyed Dearing with an impish grin. "Although my husband mentioned wanting society to see us happily about."

Lindsey inclined his head closer to Charlotte, and Dearing watched with restrained patience. "I thought his boastful nature was contained to business dealings and shrewd negotiations." Lindsey surveyed the crowd expectantly. "Though I can't blame him in this instance."

"Are you through maligning my character? I consider you a friend, but that's subject to change." Forcing the earl's attention to their conversation, Dearing followed Lindsey's line of sight and discovered Mallory across the room, engrossed in conversation with Adams. More than once, the men turned in their direction, a look of malevolence holding Mallory's features tight as he stared toward the three of them. Dearing curled his hands into fists and struggled to maintain a look of amusement. Adams existed as nothing more than a nuisance and a reminder of foolish decisions made in the past, but Mallory presented a more difficult situation. With certainty, Mallory had an agenda to cause harm, and Dearing didn't want anything to mar this evening for Charlotte.

Unfortunately, his intuitive wife noticed the shift in his demeanor. "What is it?"

"Nothing, love." Dearing shot Lindsey a knowing glance. "The earl brings out the worst in me. An abrasive commentary and devil-may-care disposition will do that to anyone."

"As you say." Undeterred and not insulted in the least,

Lindsey drained his glass and set it on a passing footman's salver. "Allow me a dance, Lady Charlotte. Mayhap I can redeem my reputation by escorting you through a feisty quadrille or Scottish reel. It's said I'm quite the charmer on the dance floor."

Chapter Twenty-Seven

As much as Dearing despaired at seeing his beautiful wife depart on Lindsey's arm, it allowed him the opportunity to warn off Mallory. He wanted no part of an altercation and hoped whatever the instigation, it would be settled privately. Charlotte didn't deserve a shred of humiliation, and no doubt Mallory already had fed the gossip mill with a tawdry dose of maligning fodder and fabrication in regard to their sudden marriage. With the music begun and Charlotte in Lindsey's care, Dearing arrowed across the room, intent on resolving the issue before it became a bigger problem.

"What do you want?" Dearing pierced the man with a glare meant to indicate his lack of patience.

"Now there's an interesting question. Especially when I've several options." Mallory appeared in no hurry to pursue a conversation.

"Accosting my secretary, riffling through my papers and absconding with the Middleton Railway certificate should be enough to keep you content." Dearing's voice lowered to a snarl, though he kept his gaze riveted on Charlotte as she twirled through the dance. "You're as transparent as crystal."

"You can't prove any of it."

"Half of society knows you're shot through the pocket

and the other half suspects it." Dearing shook his head with frustration. "But I've no desire to seek the authorities and am willing to look the other way if possession of that certificate keeps you out of our lives. I'll not have my wife upset or our relationship maligned." He turned again to the dance floor, where Lindsey led Charlotte through a promenade. His gaze fell to where they'd clasped hands, their smiles rich with laughter, and his heart clenched. Damn the situation that would cause him to miss one moment of Charlotte's pleasure. "Keep the damn stock. I never sought it in the first place."

"It's hardly worth anything alone."

Mallory leaned to the left, as if to locate Charlotte as she danced, and Dearing forced his attention away.

"So you've made a fool's wager to accompany your theft?"

"The betting book at White's is open to the public. My wager is square, though a smart man arranges for insurance. I'll have the stock and win the wager too."

"You can't possibly believe that will work in your favor." Dearing suppressed the desire to laugh outright. "You've always proven dangerously careless, without a thought for anyone but yourself, as evidenced by the company you keep."

"I'm willing to settle this in a manner that leaves all those involved as they should be. Meet me in Compton's library in thirty minutes." Mallory turned to step away. "Don't be late."

By the time Dearing glanced toward Charlotte and back again, Mallory had melted into the crowd. The man had robbed the night of enjoyment and it would be hell trying to deceive Charlotte. Not only did his wife understand his body language, intuitive as she was to every emotion in his eyes, but she could tell by the tone of his voice or slant of his jaw whenever the slightest dispute held him ill at ease, and Mallory had his blood close to boiling.

As soon as the music ended, he claimed the next dance with hope that another spin around the ballroom would distract Charlotte's perspicuity and borrow time until he made an excuse and found his way to Lord Compton's library. Damn it all, he wouldn't lie to Charlotte, no matter if he had to take her with him while confronting Mallory.

No.

Poor idea.

He'd rely on Lindsey. It was the only way to keep Charlotte's reputation pristine in case Mallory planned something truly despicable.

Bankruptcy drove people to make rash decisions and enter into foolish ventures. The irony of the situation wasn't lost on him, even though by salvaging Charlotte's family and restoring their solvency, he'd won the most precious prize and now cherished the love they'd found together.

The same couldn't be said for Mallory. Who knew what the man deemed necessary in his desperate attempts to pad his pockets? A sensible assumption indicated blackmail or another equally harmful ploy. Still, nothing about Mallory bespoke a sensible inclination.

"You seem preoccupied." Charlotte's slender brows furrowed. "Are you angry?"

He led her through another turn. How he wished they still danced in the foyer of Dearing House. "Yes. At myself. I regret not accepting your tempting offer to stay at home and warm the sheets in our bed."

She answered with a knowing smile and blushed so prettily, his heart thudded in response. "Jeremy . . ."

Forced to change partners due to the arrangement of the dance, their conversation ended abruptly, though he found himself aside Lindsey with the next exchange, their positioning fortuitous.

"I'll need you to keep Charlotte busy in fifteen minutes. I'm to meet Mallory in the library. Emboldened by his thievery and aimed for blackmail, he must believe my priorities are skewed. I assume he plans to inform me of his terms."

"Alone, the certificate holds little value, and while Mallory is in dire need of money, he may have concluded you'll do anything to see the share returned. But I suspect you aren't of like mind." Lindsey swept a glance toward Charlotte, at the end of the line. "In the meantime, I will gladly entertain your wife. A trip to the refreshment table and an inability to find you afterward should suffice to keep us occupied."

The exchange advanced them to different ends of the floor, but not before Lindsey added a friendly word of caution.

Dearing nodded as he rejoined Charlotte. "There you are, my beautiful minx." He grasped her hand and twirled her in a circle. "I missed you sorely."

"As I missed you," she replied, a mischievous gleam in her eye. "I can't stop thinking about your suggestion."

"*My* suggestion?"

She sent him a secretive grin. "Well, yes and no. It was mine, I suppose."

The lines broke apart and they were forced to opposite sides of the floor, but this time their eyes never left each other. He was a lucky man. He'd not have Mallory or anyone else interfere with his happiness.

The music ended, and before Dearing could excuse himself, Lindsey appeared, looped arms with Charlotte and led her toward the refreshment table with an exaggerated desire to quench his thirst.

An unwelcome shadow of discontent ran through Dearing as he watched them depart, but then he turned on his heel and made for the door. The sooner he dealt with Mallory, the sooner he could have Charlotte in his arms again.

Careful to avoid guests who lingered in the halls or invite a situation that would stop his progress, Dearing moved through the dimly lit corridors and farther toward the back of the town house. He found the library at the end of a corridor and entered discreetly, shutting the double oak doors behind him. The room was also dim, only two sconces near the mantel beside the fire in the hearth. At first glance, he believed the room empty. He must have arrived before Mallory. But then, he noticed a person silhouetted near the far window, a tall, statuesque woman in a seductive gown, the plunging neckline and tight fit scandalous by its design.

"Pardon me." Damn it to hell. Mallory should have chosen a better meeting place, the library most likely popular for illicit liaisons.

"I've been waiting all evening to see you," the woman drawled as she moved forward, her face and voice vaguely familiar. She took a sip from a champagne glass, and with what could only be described as a seductive smile, pushed her hair over her shoulders to reveal even more skin. "Don't leave when you've only just arrived."

"I'm sorry, but I'd planned to meet someone here. A business associate," he corrected, not willing to be the subject of speculation. "I must have been mistaken." He stepped back, uncomfortable with the situation and anxious to leave. "Excuse me."

"It's been too many years, Jeremy, and our time together so short, but you've hardly changed at all."

Her use of his Christian name gave him pause, though his mind worked swiftly. He should have known better than to presume Mallory wouldn't sink to the lowest tactics. In another moment, recognition gripped him, and he ascertained the identity of the woman before him. Nora Woodson was the actress he'd known all those years ago at Eton, though she was hardly discriminating with her affection. Their days together had been brief and nothing more than a lad's meaningless exploration of manhood. The likelihood of their paths ever crossing again was slim and, in a test of one of Faxman's adages about time and wounds, Dearing realized he felt nothing except surprise at her presence.

He shook his head in disbelief at the length of Mallory's efforts and the depth of his desperation. He'd enlisted the help of Adams, apparently. Such dedication to his task would be commendable if not employed totally in malice.

"Mallory must have promised you a handsome sum for this ridiculous charade. Although anything falls into practice for an actress's skills, I suppose, no matter who is hurt as consequence." Dearing pivoted and made for the door, despite hearing Nora's slippers tap the floor in pursuit.

"Wait. I need to speak to you about exactly that."

He slowed, unsure if she would share information useful in disentangling Mallory's ploy. At her silence, he turned.

"Sit with me." She settled on the damask sofa and patted the seat beside her.

"No." Apparently, she believed him as gullible as herself. He shouldn't have hoped for a better outcome. "I'm leaving."

"Stop, Jeremy!"

Her voice raised with an insistent plea at the same moment the doors opened, and he paused in the act of turning. Behind him stood a woman from his past while before him, framed in the polished mahogany doorframe, was his future. Charlotte's smile dropped away, a question in her eyes before they quickly filled with dismay. Mallory and several other onlookers crowded the entrance behind her. In less than a minute, a dozen or more guests had surged into the room, while Dearing stood motionless, ten paces from the door, the situation laughable in its context if not so easily misconstrued.

Until he glanced behind him.

Nora lie across the cushions, her bodice lowered to display the swells of her breasts as she shuddered within a distraught performance, tears on her cheeks and anguish in her eyes. A sob broke free as she continued her portrayal of scorned lover. "Why, Jeremy? Why now? You'd discard me after I've allowed you—" Her sobs prevented an end to the sentence, though none was necessary. Each word uttered painted him in a scandalous light.

A collective gasp chased by fervent murmurs moved about the room, inciting what was meant to be irrevocable damage.

Gossip.

A simple weapon, yet accurate and unerringly lethal in its effectiveness. The Ton thrived on every word and assumption. Within hours, the razor-sharp tongue wags would be revealing he was involved in a torrid affair and Charlotte would be humiliated, pitied, despite not a word of it was true. Mallory had machinated the scheme and it took little to plant the seed of mistruth, though Dearing hadn't anticipated a scene of this magnitude.

In any event, he didn't give a damn what society believed, except there was Charlotte's reputation to uphold and, more importantly, his wife's view of the outcome. He'd feared their love would never withstand the revelation of his past misdeeds, but now to have her question his sincerity by way of a ruse seemed ironic and unjust.

"Charlotte." Dearing reached out his hand as if to touch her would anchor her to his side and erase any ridiculous conclusions drawn in the room.

"Jeremy?" Her expression was more confusion than anything else. "What are you doing here? Do you know this woman?"

"I do. Although this scene has been carefully arranged to appear as something it isn't." He kept his voice calm, unwilling to upset Charlotte or allow Mallory the advantage.

Nora reassembled herself, remarkedly composed as she sauntered up to the gathering, her audience in place. "Never mind reputation now. Tell your wife about us and we'll end your pretense of a marriage at last. It's what you said you wanted not five minutes ago."

"Caught with your mistress, Dearing?" Mallory's question cut across the room.

"Mistress. Lover." Nora's low, earthy reply oozed sensuality. "Whatever he wants me to be."

Dearing speared her with a glare before he returned his attention to Charlotte. "Know that none of this is true."

"Pity; we all thought it was Lady Dearing who had stepped outside her vows. But the reverse is here before us, or mayhap neither lady nor lord is faithful to the other. Interesting, Dearing. Your mistress is disappointed. Your wife is ashamed." Mallory continued, his voice louder as he turned toward Nora. "Are you all right? What exactly happened here?"

"Nothing happened," Dearing snapped, his anger on a short leash. Mallory was too desperate, too obvious, to achieve his plan, but would that play in his favor? Society had a habit of only seeing what it wished to see. "Whatever you've concocted here to imply a scandal isn't working. Cut your losses, Mallory. This pathetic attempt to interfere in my life won't succeed."

Undeterred, Nora came forward, her confidence unshaken. "I met you here as you asked me to, Jeremy. I've done everything you've asked." She produced a tremulous pout. "Don't pretend it isn't what we'd planned. You promised we would finally be together."

"He did no such thing." Like a slap to the cheek, Charlotte's voice rang out, and Dearing's admiration for his wife's bravery multiplied tenfold. A wave of commentary followed, all eyes trained on Charlotte as she stepped away from the onlookers and further into the conversation.

"So, you're the docile wife. No wonder he prefers my bed." Nora notched her chin, a grin twitching at the corners of her mouth.

Silence fell. The very air in the room stilled, so much so, Dearing could hear his own breathing, the thunderous beat of his heart, impatient and at odds with the guests who watched, unwilling to miss a single word.

"Who do you think he ran to after your wedding? Where did you think he went for weeks and weeks on end? He came to me. He promised we would be together if I had patience, but I'm tired of waiting." Nora set down her glass and advanced toward Charlotte.

Dearing watched his wife's face pale. He felt her tremble, though he still stood several paces away. "Don't believe a word of it, Charlotte. Mallory concocted this entire scheme in order to win some wager."

"Wait!" Lindsey appeared at the door. He pushed through the men who blocked the frame and passed over the threshold. "You can't stoop to cheating, Mallory. What exactly are you about?"

"There were no conditions. All's fair play," Mallory shot back, though his eyes never left Dearing. "And it hasn't reached midnight. Our bet remains valid. A bet I'm about to win." He nodded with misplaced confidence. "By the lady's admission, you keep her as your mistress. Caught in your despicable affair, any denial made is to save face, nothing more, Dearing. In a war of words, one must always defer to the lady in question. And too, you were caught here, in a dim room, with the lady's clothing in disarray. No one believes your cry of innocence."

A hushed flow of conversation began as the onlookers gathered more information. Jeremy watched Charlotte as she surveyed the crowd, until at last her attention came to rest in his direction. Did she believe this tripe?

"What wager?" Charlotte's question brought everything in focus again.

"A bet made against the success of your marriage." Lindsey cleared his throat, seemingly uncomfortable with his role. "Mallory placed a wager Dearing would never make you happy, Charlotte. And that your marriage was destined to fail because he could only have an ulterior motive for his unexpected proposal. All this to the tune of ten thousand pounds."

Charlotte gasped, her expression a mixture of sadness and outrage, yet she pressed for more details. "Go on."

"The whispers are true. Mallory hasn't a penny to spare. He's squandered all his money and opportunity and saw your recent nuptials as a chance to recoup his losses. I accepted his wager knowing once he lost he would be ruined, and perhaps humiliated enough to flee London. I've known Dearing a long time and never believed Mallory could win. Not even when things didn't proceed smoothly. While society chose to draw its own conclusions from your unexpected wedding, I knew Dearing as a man of integrity who would never stoop to manipulative malice." Lindsey shifted his attention to Dearing. "As a friend, I attempted to influence you, but eventually, you proved you never needed my help in any way, other than for me to insist you get on with it. Your feelings were always indisputable in regard to your lovely wife, and they still are."

A long quiet moment passed as Dearing eyed the crowd. His gaze came to rest on Mallory, who still remained with his back to the French doors. Did he think to make a hasty escape?

"If you're trying to provoke me or prove me unhappy in my marriage, you've wasted your time. It's as Lindsey states. My marriage to Lady Charlotte is based on affection and esteem." Dearing aimed his words at Mallory, though now he'd shifted his attention to Charlotte. "Genuine adoration and commitment."

Charlotte answered, as if no one stood in the room other than the two of them. "I don't understand what's happening or why you've come to this room, Jeremy, but I know you would never intentionally hurt me."

"No, I wouldn't."

"Lord, this is all so touching." Nora sauntered across the room, to the delight of the gawking males who watched her every step. "When only a few minutes ago *we* were on the sofa and you were showing *me* your esteem. Why don't you tell your wife about our private arrangement? Or does keeping it secret add to the allure?"

Dearing couldn't believe the extent of Nora's acting or how far Mallory would go to achieve his goal. "Don't believe a word, Charlotte. There are no secrets here. Only lies."

"That's what you'd like her to believe, isn't it?" Mallory quickly replied. "When it's obvious you met Nora here clandestinely and now, having been discovered, hope to salvage your marriage and reputation. Lady Dearing isn't so easily fooled, nor is anyone else."

"Jeremy, I—"

"And why wouldn't she believe it?" Mallory sneered, fast to interrupt Charlotte. "Your marriage has been the gossip of the Ton for months. The chances of its success have raised the odds in White's books to incredible stakes. Anyone here can see you've an impatient mistress and an unhappy wife." He jerked his head toward Lindsey. "That settles it. I've won."

"You haven't won a penny." Lindsey's mouth curled in a mocking grin. "And this little performance proves nothing. You've taken things too far. I demand you forfeit."

"Never." Mallory's voice rose with anger. "Not when I'm this close. Not when I have the win. You'll not steal it from me."

"Charlotte." Dearing's eyes hadn't left his wife and he noticed, despite her effort to conceal all emotion, the evening had taken its toll. Yet he wouldn't believe she could so easily be swayed. Not after all they'd shared and how far they'd come. Where once he'd been insecure and awkward in expressing his deepest feelings, now he experienced a surge of pride and held back nothing as he bared his heart. "I've told you before, when you're lying in my arms at night, and I'm proud to repeat it here before any who will listen. You are my today and all my tomorrows. I love you. Only you."

A hush effectively silenced any conversation in the background. No one moved, scarcely murmured, waiting to see what would transpire next.

As did Dearing.

His breath stopped in his chest, every muscle seized tight.

Until Charlotte rushed across the carpet, her padded steps in tune to his heartbeat, and when he captured her in his arms and pressed his mouth down upon hers, he didn't care if the whole bloody ballroom watched him kiss his wife, long and thoroughly.

Chapter Twenty-Eight

Three months later

"It's not my birthday." Charlotte turned a shy smile on her husband where he sat beside her, a pile of gifts on the satinwood table in front of them. "You do know when my birthday is, don't you?"

"That's a ridiculous question." He tapped the tip of her nose with his finger before gesturing to the tabletop. "One of the pleasures of being your husband is buying you presents for no reason. Our entire courtship was hurried. I missed too many opportunities to make you happy."

"You've done a very good job of making up for lost time." She laid her head against his shoulder in one of her favorite positions. Jeremy proved incredibly thoughtful, all through the day and most especially at night. Now that all the nasty business with Lord Mallory was behind them, she couldn't wait for the days ahead. It was equally just and satisfying that the one man who wished to destroy their marriage had become fodder for the rumor mill himself, his character and reputation maligned. But she didn't wish to discuss unpleasantness and instead reflected on her husband's generosity. "You've already redesigned the gardens at the back of the house. The Juliet roses and boxwood hedges are delightful to view while I play my pianoforte. That was a wonderful surprise." She sighed. "Why don't we wait until later? It will take me all morning to unwrap these gifts. How many are there anyway?"

"Not enough." He moved to the side and forced her to sit up again. "Open a few at least. Most women enjoy baubles. At least that's what I've been told."

"By Lindsey, no doubt." Charlotte shook her head. "It would be pleasant if the earl found someone with whom to share his life and make a home. He's not a bad sort."

"Ha! I doubt that will happen anytime soon." Jeremy's brows shot high. "I'd like to meet a woman who could put up with his inflated sense of self-worth and devil-may-care attitude. He thrives on recklessness."

"Seriously, Jeremy." She couldn't help but giggle, though she'd given the subject considerable thought. "I believe deep down that's exactly what Lindsey wants, and all his philandering is only a display to disguise his unhappiness."

"I hadn't considered that." Jeremy's eyes narrowed, seemingly surprised. "Of late he has seemed preoccupied. I wonder if something else is the cause. Although no one can truly know. He runs with a fast set and always has. I'm more than a little shocked our friendship has endured all these years."

"Exactly my point. You're the man he wishes to become." She warmed to the subject. "It's as you've shown me on one of your maps. He needs the meander line or some boundary to help guide him. And that's you and your friendship."

"You're a quick study in so many ways." Jeremy flashed a wicked grin. "And while an interesting suggestion, I've never known him to make an effort in that direction." He clasped her hand and gave it a squeeze. "Now, open one of these gifts. Here." He selected a flat, rectangular box wrapped with a red satin ribbon. "Unwrap this one first."

Knowing it was useless to object, she carefully untied the bow and lifted the lid. Inside, beneath layers of thin paper, was a silver hand mirror, its handle carved from mother-of-pearl and detailed along the back with scrollwork of florals and vines.

"This is absolutely lovely. Thank you. My old mirror is chipped. How perfect that you would notice I needed a new one." She ran her fingertips over the etchings and then angled the mirror so both their reflections shone on the glass. "We do make a charming couple."

She gently placed it back in the box and shifted her position on the settee. Leaning in, she pressed a kiss to her husband's cheek.

"If I'm to receive a kiss for each gift, I'm especially pleased I've purchased so many." He chuckled and nudged another box forward on the table. "Let's get on with it."

"If you insist." She opened several more in succession. A porcelain jar fashioned in the shape of a miniature piano, along with several sets of bejeweled hairpins, each gift more thoughtful and delightful than the last until only one small box remained. She hadn't noticed it before. Perhaps it had been buried beneath the huge pile Jeremy had arranged on the table.

"I'll save that one for later." Feeling cozy and very well loved, she snuggled closer and again pressed her head to his shoulder, nearer his warmth and easily accessible to the scent of his shaving soap. How she loved her husband. Despite their domestic bliss and genuinely cheery approach to each day, she had a sudden need for more rest. It was as if all their happiness tired her. Of late, she felt a bit hungrier too.

"No." His reply was firm. "The other gifts weren't as important. I purposely put this one on the bottom of the pile so you would open it last."

"But I'd rather sit here with you right now." She exhaled,

comfortable and spent from the busy day. "This is my favorite place to be."

Jeremy slid his arm around her and tucked her closer. "And my favorite place for you to be as well. Right where you belong."

They stayed that way for several minutes, and Charlotte closed her eyes in surrender to the glorious feeling of contentment. With all the excitement over unexpected presents and the past few weeks, it was no wonder she felt drowsy. Her heart was full. Her life was full. Who knew happiness could be so fatiguing?

"Now." Jeremy shifted quickly and picked up the remaining square box. "Open this last one and then I promise not to bother you with gifts for at least a week. Maybe two."

She laughed softly and forced herself upright to accept the package. There would be no peace or quiet until she finished the task.

Slipping the silk ribbon free, she removed the wrapping to find a tiny black box inside. She looked at him, but he didn't give anything away in his expression.

"What is this?"

"Lift the top and see."

She touched the lid and as she did so, Jeremy slid from the cushions and went down on one knee in front of her, his eyes filled with adoration.

"Charlotte, my love, my wife. I never had the opportunity to ask you the most important question any man can ask a woman. I never had the chance to see the reaction on your face or the light in your beautiful eyes when I asked for your hand in marriage. All I have to offer is my heart in return, but it overflows with love for you. Charlotte, will you marry me?"

Stunned, she swallowed past the sudden emotion in her throat and fought to find her voice. "Yes." The word whispered from her lips, as strong as the song in her heart.

Her fingers shook as she opened the box. Inside, nestled on a velvet blanket was the most beautiful betrothal ring she'd ever seen. The center diamond caught the candlelight in every direction and the smaller stones, set in a circle around the larger, twinkled as if full of myriad wishes and dreams.

Jeremy gently removed the gold band she'd worn without complaint and slipped the glittering diamond on her finger instead.

"Now . . ." He stood and pulled her flush against him. "Now everything is as it should be, my wonderful wife."

He dipped his mouth down for a tender kiss that repeated all his confessed emotions, and tears welled in her eyes. She blinked them away quickly. What had begun as an ordinary morning was fast becoming the most romantic and meaningful day of her life. She'd married this man to rescue her family, no matter she found him pleasing to the eye, but she'd never anticipated the profound love and precious treasure they'd find together as husband and wife.

"Jeremy."

"Yes, my love."

She wriggled free from his embrace, just far enough so she could look up into his warm brown eyes.

"I have a gift for you as well." She tried desperately to control her elation, though the words she held inside bubbled like a magnum of champagne in her chest.

"I thought that's what you gave me last evening."

He winked before he captured her mouth in another lingering kiss, one that reminded them both of all the passion they'd shared the night before, but she pulled away, his power to send her good sense careening a dangerous threat.

"Not that." Her face heated. "Something much better. A special secret I've been keeping." She grasped his hand and tugged him back to the settee, where they resettled on the cushions.

As if on cue, Shadow, sometimes Cricket, leaped up and nestled between them. They reached out to remove the animal at the same time, their fingers lost in the feline's fur and intertwined with each other's. Impatient with their lingering affection, the cat leaped away, entranced by a long blue ribbon once wrapped around one of the gift boxes.

"Are you breaking your own rule? We promised no secrets." Her husband tried for an admonishing tone, but the attempt proved laughable.

"I wanted to be sure. To have no doubt." Her answer was a reverent whisper.

"And?"

She saw the twinkle in his eye, aware he already suspected the secret in her heart, her husband far too clever for his own good. Still, she wouldn't miss this moment for all the world.

Without another word she took his hand and laid it flat on her stomach. Her fingers trembled as she did so. His eyes grew wide with awe.

"Is it true?"

"As true as my love for you."

"Charlotte."

"Yes, Jeremy."

"I—" He stared at their hands laced together across her middle. "There are moments every day, random moments, meaningless in some ways but there nevertheless, and in those infinitesimal spans of daily living, I often wonder how I can love you more than I do. We have our whole lives ahead of us and my heart is already full, so I question if I've somehow reached capacity. It's possible because I love you, body and soul. Still, here we are on an ordinary morning, this day like so many others before and ahead, and yet I find my heart at the ready to expand and offer you more with every breath, every blink, to you, to our family and this gift that we'll share."

Tears blurred her vision. His declaration of love and devotion matched her most precious dreams, and as he enfolded her in his arms and they whispered plans full of hope and wonder, the future promised a lifetime of unmatched joy and happiness.

Can't wait for more secrets?

Keep reading for a sneak peek at

LONDON'S LATE NIGHT SCANDAL,

the next in the
Midnight Secrets series.

Coming soon from

Anabelle Bryant
and
Zebra Books!

London, 1817

Lord Matthew Strathmore, Earl of Whittingham, slapped the leather reins and urged the four dappled greys into a faster gallop.

"You're concerned about the weather."

"Astute observation, Coggs." Whittingham heaved a breath of impatience. "Not only are you an excellent man-of-all-things, but a master of insight and circumstance." He flicked his eyes from the unending roadway to the servant seated beside him. Coggs was more friend than valet; still, the man possessed the ability to irritate at times, and this was one of them.

The weather grew increasingly threatening the farther they journeyed from London, and during the last few miles, the air had transformed from chilly to the sharp edge of frigid until each puff of breath that evaporated before their faces was a stark warning that too long spent outdoors would bring a brittle end.

Worse, they were far from any familiar thoroughfare where another stubborn, albeit foolish traveler might discover their frozen corpses once the cold claimed its victory.

Thus, the only hope of reaching their destination before nightfall relied on Whittingham pushing his well-bred stallions to full speed.

"You would be warmer inside the carriage. You haven't a hat or a muffler, and the wind has a nasty bite this late in the afternoon."

"If your only purpose upon this seat is to act the nursemaid, I suggest you climb back inside and keep George company." At the last coaching inn, Whittingham had insisted on taking the straps from his young driver. Not only would the lad hesitate in pushing the horses as hard as necessary, but there was no reason to have George suffer the brunt of the fierce weather and ill-advised, impromptu travel when Whittingham was the one who had insisted they take to the road with haste.

Besides, one more minute trapped inside with his legs folded at an uncomfortable angle would provoke a fouler mood than he already possessed. His left leg throbbed like the devil, and no matter the gunshot wound that caused his difficulty occurred a decade before, the injury needed no provocation to cause pain. The cramped confines of the coach, poor roadway conditions and brutal, uncompromising temperature, guaranteed he'd pay for his decision in spades. Hopefully, not the kind that dug graves.

"I'd rather sit beside you in case I'm needed."

Abandoning his grim thoughts, Whittingham resumed the conversation, offering Coggs a nod of appreciation. His mood was blacker than the storm clouds riding the horizon, but snarling at his valet when the man endured the cold to offer support wasn't common to Whittingham's congenial nature. "Are you certain? No doubt George has a wool blanket across his lap and a heated brick at his feet."

Saying the words drew an enticing image he'd rather not think about. He flexed the muscles in his bad leg and glanced at the sky. If the snow held off, they would make it to Leighton

House before dark. Being cold was an inconvenience. Being cold and wet was an invitation to illness. "You should ride inside. I'll rap on the roof to signal you if the situation warrants it."

The valet looked upward and shook his head. "How much farther can it be?"

In a ruse Whittingham knew well, Coggs deflected the uncomfortable subject of limitations, unforgiving injuries and common sense. His valet deserved a better employer. "At least another hour if the roads remain clear. Leighton House is situated on a sprawling plot of land near the western border of Oxfordshire."

"It was hospitable of the master of the house to invite you on such short notice."

"Agreed." Whittingham tossed a too-long lock of hair from his forehead. He'd neglected a haircut much as he'd ignored other ordinary tasks, his time spent within the pages of a book. "My studies are of the utmost importance."

"I know that well."

"Do I detect a note of censure in your reply?" Whittingham slowed the team to a lively trot as the road dipped, marred with stony ruts and misshapen holes the perfect size to catch a horse's hoof and damage his leg for a lifetime. The similarity wasn't lost on him, and once free of deterrent, he jerked his wrist and jolted the carriage forward to resume their breakneck travel.

"Nothing of the sort." Coggs pulled his woolen collar more tightly around his neck to combat the wind that whipped between them. "I hardly wonder why you need to address the issue. You're an impatient scholar. No sooner do you form a hypothesis than you seek the solution with relentless fervor. Why would this endeavor follow a different path?"

"It's reassuring the last eight years of your service haven't gone wasted," Whittingham replied. "You do know me well."

Nothing was said for a time after that. Whittingham

owned the fact that his work habits were intrusive, if not obsessive at times. He pursued a course of academia once he realized the debilitating wound to his knee would never allow him the gallant luxuries other gentlemen managed with ease. Riding a horse was bearable but hardly enjoyable. Dancing was out of the question. On most days, the pain remained a whisper, no more than an aching memory of a poorly made decision from his past.

Other days—this being one—the muscles of his left leg cramped and twisted, a relentless reminder of his limitations, all too quick to persuade him to go home, sit quietly in an overstuffed chair near the fireplace fender and politely die of boredom.

He would have no part of surrender and therefore endured the sharpest spike of pain without complaint. He wouldn't be compromised by circumstances he couldn't change.

No sooner had he repeated this silent vow than a gust of wind hurried past with a burst of icy air that could only be God's laughter at the earl's ignorance.

True enough, tomorrow he would pay a deep price for his travels today.

"I sincerely hope you acquire the answers to your questions. As your loyal servant, I do as I am told, but as a simple man on this driver's seat, near frozen and somewhat hungry, I pray this trip into nowhere proves worth the effort."

"I have no doubt it will, Coggs." Whittingham smiled, though his mouth was tight from the harsh temperature. "One cannot publish a journal article in the *Philosophical Transactions of the Royal Society* without the correct proof of knowledge, and I intend to investigate and repudiate the claims made, if for no other reason than to defend the truth. While Lord Talbot may know his way around scientific theory, his lack of detail leaves me curious and more than a little suspicious. The hypothesis presented in the article failed to contain the precise proof expected from someone of Talbot's notable reputation. The earl hadn't the decency to answer my inquiries through post but has now unexpectedly agreed to meet. That's an adequate start that I intend to see to a satisfactory conclusion. I couldn't wait around in London at risk Talbot might change his mind. His invitation was surprising but fortuitous. And so there you have it. Despite the ill weather and spontaneity of our travel, I had little choice but to act immediately once I received his response."

"Indeed."

"It could be my own perspicuity that raised false suspicions, though Talbot hasn't lectured in London or sought attention for any of the evidences proposed in his series of articles, and it's been several years since his breakthrough experiments have warranted news. Most leaders of academia strive to share knowledge, not hoard it. No one at the Society for the Intellectually Advanced can understand his reclusive behavior. A commitment to speak to the most elite intellectual organization in all of England would be a rare and gratifying opportunity, most especially if I brought it forward as chief officer." He flicked his eyes toward the sky and then to the roadway just as quickly. "And as the members of the Society continue to question the validity of the claims made, verifying the article and engaging the earl to speak in London—or exposing him for fraud—will accredit my newly gained position."

"So, with this jaunt into nowhere, you have a multipurpose agenda." Coggs turned toward him, his brows lowered in question.

"Don't I always?" Whittingham answered. "Science is truth. Thanks to my sister's interference, my succession into the position of chief officer was less than smooth. Ferreting out faulty, half-baked experimental reporting will prove I'm qualified for the position, knowledgeable and otherwise worthy."

"I see." Coggs nodded.

"That said, putting past publication aside, Talbot might

be nothing more than a charlatan. A dreamer. A man who knows nothing about scientific philosophy other than how to manipulate syntax to thread together a credible suggestion and bamboozle trusting souls. Wouldn't that be an interesting turn?" He looked toward Coggs with a knowing stare. "Either way, I intend to find out."

Theodosia Leighton, granddaughter of the earl of Talbot, stood before her work table and stared intently at a glass beaker filled halfway with a mixture of agitative liquids. She checked her grandfather's notations scribbled on the page of the open journal in reference to the measurements. Something should have happened by now, but the clear liquid inside the glass remained unchanged. She blew a breath of exasperation and stepped away.

"I don't know what went wrong, Nicolaus." She didn't expect an answer; he was accustomed to her thinking aloud. She paced to the hearth and back again as a way to expend energy while she waited. Curious now, Nicolaus approached the beaker, leaned in, sniffed the liquid inside and withdrew right after.

"I know." She understood his displeasure. "The formula smells horrible and Grandfather hasn't a notation anywhere to explain the chemical change. With the remaining pages of his journal missing and only half an accounting, I'm at a loss to reproduce the outcome."

Disinterested in disappointment or any recitation of complaint, Nicolaus silently left the room. Theodosia watched him go, hardly blaming his reaction. She'd recreated the experiment several times without success, and yet her grandfather was the most knowledgeable and meticulous scientist Oxfordshire had ever produced.

At least, she believed so.

What had she missed in his documentation? She'd honed

her skills of observation and detail to an exacting degree. Through practice, sampling and sketching every specimen available to her, she'd created a catalog of scientific knowledge in her brain. With an excellent memory and concise methods of deductive reasoning, the idea that she had failed to reason out the problem with the experiment irked her.

At a loss for the time being, she strode to the window and glanced at the foreboding clouds. *Snow*. Everything about the view outside predicted an imminent snowfall. A strong wind bent the tree limbs of the sole remaining chestnut tree spared by the fire years ago and not a creature could be seen. Most likely they burrowed beneath the hedgerows or sheltered by the dense Scotch firs that lined the perimeter of the property, farther from the house. Even the air seemed raw and crisp, no matter that she remained inside and viewed the world through glass. These conditions were a precursor to significant precipitation. She would record her observations in her weather journal later that evening, when she was too tired to do more than move a pencil across a page.

Snow complicated even the simplest tasks. Before dinner she would check with the housekeeper, Mrs. Mavis, and ensure they had provisions in case this sudden unsettling cold spell hampered them for a few days. They were too far from town to be caught unaware in bad weather. Food items, candles, firewood and the necessary supplies for daily living, would all need to be secured. A few of the stable hands would see to the work of bedding down the horses. Eggs would have to be collected, and then there were all her animals to tend.

These tasks would have been accomplished with a smile if she'd mastered her research this afternoon. Instead, she could only review her grandfather's notes and attempt to understand his reasoning. It had taken her the better part of half a year to learn his notation system and decipher many of his complicated trials. But omitted text . . . that created a difficult hurdle, far beyond her until she fully understood the theory behind his work. When questioned, Grandfather waved away her inquiries, as if his notebooks were no longer a language he understood.

Returning to the table, she stared down at the open book. She needed the missing pages. Nearly a third of the entries were gone and the current passage was incomplete. She touched the paper and smoothed a fingertip over the scrawled notes, careful not to smudge the graphite. If only she had someone other than Grandfather to ask for assistance. When she closed her eyes and wished hard enough, she could still hear her parents' voices, though so many years had passed, she wondered if it wasn't an imagined attempt to soothe the bottomless ache in her heart.

Her parents had perished in the fire nearly twenty years ago. Theodosia was carried to safety in her grandfather's arms. At five years old, she mourned the loss of her parents, but she never anticipated the loneliness that was to follow despite the loving attention of her grandfather and the extensive kindness of the household staff.

She shook her head and forced her eyes open wide, quick to blink away the threat of tears. She wouldn't conjure memories now. She couldn't. Seeking distraction, she flipped the journal closed and moved away from the table. She had animals to attend to and other important tasks before dinner. Where was Nicolaus anyway? Only a fool would go out in the unforgiving winter cold.

She needed to check on Grandfather before it grew much later, but first she would find Mrs. Mavis. If the weather was to rack havoc on Leighton House, the least she could do was prepare for the worst.